NORA WOLFENBARGER

THE DEFIANT

The Blackbird Series – Book Two

D1738920

This book was professionally typeset on Reedsy.
Find out more at reedsy.com

Contents

Acknowledgement	v
CHAPTER ONE	1
CHAPTER TWO	3
CHAPTER THREE	5
CHAPTER FOUR	10
CHAPTER FIVE	18
CHAPTER SIX	21
CHAPTER SEVEN	27
CHAPTER EIGHT	34
CHAPTER NINE	37
CHAPTER TEN	45
CHAPTER ELEVEN	48
CHAPTER TWELVE	54
CHAPTER THIRTEEN	61
CHAPTER FOURTEEN	63
CHAPTER FIFTEEN	70
CHAPTER SIXTEEN	73
CHAPTER SEVENTEEN	80
CHAPTER EIGHTEEN	87
CHAPTER NINETEEN	94
CHAPTER TWENTY	99
CHAPTER TWENTY-ONE	105
CHAPTER TWENTY-TWO	115
CHAPTER TWENTY-THREE	118
CHAPTER TWENTY-FOUR	123

CHAPTER TWENTY-FIVE 125

CHAPTER TWENTY-SIX 132

CHAPTER TWENTY-SEVEN 139

CHAPTER TWENTY-EIGHT 147

CHAPTER TWENTY-NINE 154

CHAPTER THIRTY 168

CHAPTER THIRTY-ONE 173

CHAPTER THIRTY-TWO 180

CHAPTER THIRTY-THREE 187

CHAPTER THIRTY-FOUR 191

CHAPTER THIRTY-FIVE 198

CHAPTER THIRTY-SIX 203

CHAPTER THIRTY-SEVEN 207

CHAPTER THIRTY-EIGHT 215

CHAPTER THIRTY-NINE 219

CHAPTER FORTY 228

CHAPTER FORTY-ONE 232

CHAPTER FORTY-TWO 237

CHAPTER FORTY-THREE 241

CHAPTER FORTY-FOUR 249

CHAPTER FORTY-FIVE 254

CHAPTER FORTY-SIX 260

CHAPTER FORTY-SEVEN 263

CHAPTER FORTY-EIGHT 266

CHAPTER FORTY-NINE 268

CHAPTER FIFTY 272

CHAPTER FIFTY-ONE 276

Acknowledgement

There are not enough words to express my appreciation to those who supported me in the creation and development of The Defiant. Thank you Goldie Edwards for never losing patience with me as I fought my way through the process. And, Stan Smith, your computer savvy kept me from losing my mind.

I am so blessed to be a part of the best writer's group a person could ask for. Love you guys.

Once again, my family has been there for me through thick and thin. Proud to share this experience with you.

CHAPTER ONE

A breeze stirs the pungent odor of damp ashes and charred wood. I ease deeper into the gloom of the burned-out storefront. Leah waits for me in the Mazda. Minutes pass, and then comes the click of heels against the sidewalk. My mouth goes dry.

The girl is young, fourteen at the most. Still the age of innocence. But like the others, she is not. At the edge of the building's shadow she hesitates, glancing at the Mazda as though a sixth sense tells her something is off. Lightening plays across the sky in the distance. She is desperate. We both are. My chest heaves. I ache to tell her I'm sorry.

Thunder rolls. She glances to the heavens. A whiff of fear, maybe mine, maybe hers, stings my nerves. The air between us ripples as she sucks in a breath. I slide one arm around her neck and execute the sleeper hold.

"No screaming," I whisper.

There is a youthful softness to her skin, the kind buyers in the business appreciate. Her feet tap the concrete in a mysterious dance as the flow of oxygen to the brain is cut off, and then she eases into my shoulder.

Lights from an approaching car touch the Mazda. Blood roars in my ears. I drag the girl to the ground and camouflage her with my own darkly-clothed body.

1

Twin beams pass over us then swing to the left. I dare to breathe. Rain pelts my face, cooling the heat of the moment. Practice will never make this perfect.

I gather the girl under the arms and drag her to the car. She stirs. The jab of the needle elicits a mouse-like squeak and fills me with silent triumph. The next payment to Sunny Hills Care Center is the same as in the bank.

CHAPTER TWO

A ir brakes hissed. A solitary passenger struggled from her seat on the bus and lumbered to the front. She exchanged a good night with the driver and stepped down to the sidewalk. Streetlights picked up the silver in the woman's hair.

"Hi, Josie," she said, scanning the area. "Your girl a no-show?"

Josie rose from the bench and joined a fellow Blackbird. "Thought I had her convinced to get off the street." Her shoulders slumped. "Failed again."

"There's no pass or fail in this work."

"I know," Josie sighed. "It's just, Asian girls are disappearing from the streets without a trace. This one thought her pimp had someone following her, but I wonder." The Blackbird checked her cell. "I'll Give her five more minutes. Surely, she'll show up."

The woman patted Josie's arm. "We can't save them all. Let's sit. My legs are killing me."

The two women settled on the bench beneath the canopy. A breeze scented with rain brushed at the thick July humidity. Josie broke the silence. "Think you'll ever stop working as a Blackbird?"

"Not while I'm walking upright. Silas Albert taught me how to spit in the devil's eye. I like the feeling. You?"

Josie warmed at the older Blackbird's candor. Years after joining the sisterhood of abuse survivors, Josie still craved the respect of the group

3

and the homicide detective Silas Albert, who had orchestrated their rescue and pulled them together one by one.

Fat rain drops plopped against the awning. "I'll never quit," Josie said. "There are too many women who need..."

The slap of shoe soles against dampening concrete brought Josie to her feet. She scanned the sidewalk, hoping. A man entered the sphere of light, shielding his head with a pizza box. He jogged past.

"Might as well go." Josie pulled a signal torch from her pocket and flashed it three times. The rescue van's headlamps flicked on then went from low to high. "It's too dangerous for her to come now. A pimp would know something was off if a hooker from his stable went out in the rain."

For the first time, Josie wanted the pimp to be the reason the girl hadn't shown.

CHAPTER THREE

Rebecca Haze drew Silas Albert's attention as soon as she entered the coffee shop. Shoulders back, neck perfectly aligned, and purpose in her step, she crossed the distance to his table. Heads turned, following the redhead who dominated the TV news reporting scene in Kansas City.

Despite himself, Silas straightened in his chair. He and the reporter's goals couldn't be more different. He sought the truth. She twisted it.

Her exaggerated reporting in the past had led the city commissioners, and even, the mayor to question Silas's integrity.

He stood, a little uneasy of his own intentions.

The scent of summer accompanied Rebecca's outstretched hand as she shook the only real one the detective still had.

"Thanks for meeting me, Silas."

A dry palm returned his grip. "No problem, Rebecca. I learned a long time ago to keep my friends close and my enemies closer." He dipped his head. "Have a seat."

She slid into the booth. "And in which category do you place me?" Her teeth flashed white.

"I think you know." He gave her a tight-lipped smile. "I'm having a coffee. If I remember right, you prefer hot tea, plain. Can I get you one?"

"Thanks. That would be nice."

Silas guided his six-foot frame between a conglomeration of mismatched tables and chairs to reach the coffee bar. He liked this little shop. The bare brick walls spattered with patches of colorful plaster appealed to his nostalgic side. The detective placed the order, hoping there wouldn't be a hidden price to pay for sharing a carafe of coffee and pot of tea with the calculating Rebecca Haze.

The male server set the order on the counter. "Need a hand with that tray?" His face flushed. "Sorry. I didn't mean—I mean—can I carry the tray for you?"

"Thanks, but I can manage." Silas paid the bill, adding a ten-dollar tip for the young man's efforts. Once, he would have been bothered by the attention to his prosthetic arm, but his hide was thicker now. He stepped away from the counter, feeling the doubt of the onlookers as he wound his way back to the booth, settled the tray on the table, and took his seat.

Rebecca raised an eyebrow. "You never accept much help, do you?"

"No. Not much." Silas filled his cup, raised the mug to his lips, and met her blue eyes over the brim.

She poured her tea and took her time blowing it cool. "Still holding a grudge, even after I ate my words?" Rebecca cocked her head. "I did convince the station to do a special report, showing the public what really happened."

Silas sipped his coffee. "Don't expect a merit badge from me for cleaning up after yourself. I see you're focused on Clarence Rochester now. That's ironic. Have you set out to ruin a city commissioner this time?"

"I don't ruin people," Rebecca argued. "They quite naturally do it to themselves. You think I was the one who fed Clarence bad information about the serial killings, but it was the other way around." She slapped the table with the palm of her hand. "You're not the only one who nearly lost their job because of him. I'm showing Clarence for what he is. You should be happy."

"I'm never happy when someone is hurt."

The reporter's chest rose and fell. Then her demeanor changed. She gripped her tea cup and sipped, eyes far away, seeming to savor the beverage's flavor. "I know that about you, Silas." Her focus returned. A calm tone replaced the agitated one. "The way you help abused women is proof. The House of Audrey hides a softer side of Silas Albert the tough homicide detective. What's happening inside the shelter is the reason I wanted to talk to you."

Silas tensed. *What did she think she knew?* "How could a women's shelter possibly interest you?"

"It's not the shelter so much as the man behind the scenes who intrigues me." Rebecca's lashes fluttered. "My manager is pushing for a human-interest story. The idea appeals to me. You are the most well-known homicide detective in Kansas City, possibly all of Missouri, but there is a side of you few are allowed to see. I want to bring a more complete image of you to the public."

A ball of nervousness spun in the pit of Silas's stomach. A reporter's scrutiny of the shelter posed danger for the Blackbirds. He hesitated. An automatic rejection would pique Rebecca's reporter instincts. Showing a keen interest in the story would too.

"The words of a campaign manager. I don't need one of those."

Rebecca leaned in, showing a hint of cleavage. "Maybe before long you will." She offered a conspiring smile. "Another subject for another day. Today, my intent is to give the public a new topic of conversation."

"Or open another door for criticism?"

"Hear me out. The House of Audrey is unique. The women sheltered behind those walls get more than a place to heal their wounds. A survivor talked. I listened. Your program cries out to be shared."

Silas's anxiety spiked. What had the reporter learned about his *program?* The House of Audrey was private and discrete. Had one of the

7

Blackbirds given the reporter reason to snoop? Silas ran through the roster. Josie came to mind. Each Blackbird bore the scars of a wounded warrior. Josie more than most.

Silas drank his coffee black, but he added cream to give himself a second to think. Josie needed redemption. Silas understood the challenge all too well. He fought his own burdens of guilt. But Josie, in her urgency to reclaim her self-worth, could have slipped, been too obvious. He sucked up a swallow of coffee. No, even if Josie made a mistake, she would never have talked to a reporter.

"Your audience wants a homicide detective to spend every waking moment investigating murders. The public will see the shelter as a distraction from my duty to serve and protect."

"Or as an enhancement." Rebecca's eyes narrowed. "How many women have you helped? How many have helped the police in return? What is the ripple effect?" She spread her hands in appeal. "See, Silas, there are many threads to this story."

"Showing cops in a positive light isn't exactly popular these days."

"The documentary I plan to produce would be. The public will applaud the shelter's success and want to mirror your methods. Your battle scars give your image authenticity. You might get more funding."

"I don't need funding."

Rebecca's ivory skin flushed. "No. You don't. I forgot for a moment—you're a millionaire." Her lips flattened. "Does it make you feel good, pretending to be one of the peasants?"

"Will that question be the opening line to your documentary?"

A layer of frost, colder than Antarctica, shimmered in the reporter's blue eyes. "Silas, you're an ass. I don't have to have your blessing. I'm doing you a courtesy."

The detective swallowed back his anger. "Let's be clear, Rebecca." He met her gaze, sending his own icy message. "You know the law. Use of my name or any person associated with The House of Audrey without approval is a legal nightmare you don't want to encounter."

"You can't..."

"I can—do a lot of things, Rebecca. Remember, I'm a millionaire." Rebecca sputtered, but Silas held up his hand. "I'll review a synopsis of your idea, but only if you promise it won't be a comedy. Then we'll talk further."

The reporter's jaw dropped. "I never really thought you'd agree."

"You don't have any skeletons in your closet do you?"

Rebecca shook her head. "I'm estranged from my mother. That's my burden of shame." Surprise registered on her face. "Amazing how you did that. I've not spoken to another person about my mother in over a year."

Silas studied the reporter for a moment. "Here's the first lesson for a battered woman at The House of Audrey. Every person has the power to be defiant, choose a smile over tears, self-defense skills over battery, or just plain honesty. If I agree to let you do the documentary, you'll learn more about how that works."

"I don't need your lessons, Silas. I'm not a battered woman."

"Are you an honest journalist?"

She blinked.

"Rebecca, you have the skill. Can you move beyond sensationalism?"

She swirled the tea in her cup then met his eyes. "I'm not sure I want to."

Silas stood. "I've enjoyed our discussion. Remember, bad reporting has a ripple effect too." He turned his back and walked out into the July heat.

CHAPTER FOUR

Darkness cloaked the Sentinel Park trail. For Josie, it didn't matter. The path was as familiar as the grooves in her teeth, and night vision goggles made up for the absent sun. Nature's secrets whispered through the leaves, and the scent of the wild honeysuckle sweetened the earthy aroma of the woods. These sounds and smells usually eased Josie's stress, but not tonight.

The image of Amber's face haunted Josie's thoughts. She had returned to the street every night for a week, asking questions of the other working girls. No one admitted seeing Amber. "Girls disappear all the time and never come back," one said. Even Amber's pimp claimed he hadn't seen her since the night it rained. Josie feared the worst.

Kansas City's Sentinel Park closed at sunset, but Sam, the park ranger, was Josie's friend. Their grim connection had earned the Blackbird after-hours access to the trail when she needed it, like tonight.

"Be sure to carry pepper spray, and your cell." The ranger had warned her a month earlier. "You can't be too careful." Concern had dug lines deep enough to plant sunflower seeds between the ranger's bushy brows. Josie was sure he had been thinking about his own daughter.

The Blackbird had no argument then or now. Pounding down this trail at midnight wasn't about breaking rules or tempting fate. Josie had faced Evil, life's cruelest headmaster, long before she became a Blackbird. Back then she had no idea how to fight, let alone win. She would pay back for those lessons every day for the rest of her life.

She curled the fingers of her left hand. The specially designed glove tightened across her knuckles. She'd ordered the self-defense tool two months earlier and now it felt natural. Funny how a tiny free-range-of-motion weapon, loaded with enough pepper spray to bring a big man to his knees at sixteen feet, gave a woman a healthy level of comfort.

Josie had Silas Albert to thank for teaching her about self-defense. Eight years ago, he saved her life, kept her out of prison, and gave her a reason to live. Tonight, was her opportunity to do him another small favor in return.

Asked by Special Agent Archie Hamilton to find the right Blackbird to test a new piece of equipment, Silas had approached Josie. A request from Archie wasn't unusual. Blackbirds worked occasional undercover operations for the FBI and Homeland Security. Josie was a bit surprised when Lila Girard, Silas's niece, had suggested Josie was the right choice for the assignment. Lila was second only to Silas in the training and guidance of the Blackbirds.

Josie and Lila didn't always agree, and Silas's niece probably wasn't aware she was Josie's inspiration. Lila hadn't become a Blackbird as a result of abuse like the other members of the sisterhood. But she'd been through plenty.

After Lila's mother died, Silas became Lila's guardian. She grew up in The House of Audrey, learning every nuance of living the life of a Blackbird.

Lila had survived a heart transplant at ten only to discover at seventeen the donor had been a convicted murderer. Another blow had come when Lila found she'd been conceived as the result of rape. Through the years, Silas had taught Lila to weather her storms the same way he did the other Blackbirds.

Josie knew Lila was aware of Josie's preference to run in the isolation of darkness and therefore the perfect fit for the test. She had accepted, considering the invitation an honor. Evaluating the top secret, fifth generation night vision goggles was the least she could do. Her payment had been the smile that graced Silas's face.

At one time she'd thought she was in love with Silas, but that was when he was involved with Elizabeth Cartwright. Now he had Sydney, and Josie simply admired the man for what he stood for.

Three miles into her run, the Blackbird found the Gen-5 goggles amazingly comfortable. A full pound lighter than the Gen-4, they didn't require a helmet mount. Improved access to air flow and the reduced strain on her neck set this version apart. She didn't need to perform a bobble-head routine for balance. All valuable. But the digitally enhanced combination of thermal imaging and infrared illumination was *wowza*—a scientific breakthrough.

The sound of a car disturbed the quiet. Close. Inside the park. Josie's wits snapped to attention. No headlights. The vehicle noise came from the general area of the playground. Her own Jeep Rubicon was parked nearby.

Josie passed the tree scarred and splintered by the force of lightening. The path ended a hundred yards ahead at the picnic area. A savvy car thief would electronically disarm her Rubicon and be gone. Her stomach tightened. *Not if she could help it.* She loved that Jeep.

How had the driver unlocked the gate? As well as Josie knew Sam, there was no way he would spread the electronic code around willy-nilly. The Jeep wasn't visible from the road. Unless she'd been followed, her vehicle wasn't at risk. Logic said there was a different motive at play here.

Josie stopped, touched the screen of her cell, and punched the ranger's icon. She tapped a short text. *Car inside park. Okay?*

Seconds passed. *No! Where?*

Playground.

Don't approach. Be there in a minute.

Josie sent Sam a thumbs up but raced toward the sound of the idling engine. Sam wouldn't be surprised by Josie's decision to act on her own. Ignoring similar orders had saved his daughter's life. The madness of violence waited for no one. In this case, there might not even be a crime, but Josie's history made her keenly aware of the critical element of time.

Energy quick-stepped through her veins. Fifty yards through the grassy area with no cover would get her to the playground. To skirt the perimeter was safer but twice the distance. Darkness was her friend, and the element of surprise on her side.

Never slowing her pace, Josie drew a six-inch baton from her vest and slipped her right hand through the rawhide loop. A snap of her wrist would extend the steel shaft two feet. Best scenario, she would find a couple of kids smart enough to short circuit the lock and open the gate. But if Evil attempted to flex its muscle tonight, the Blackbird was prepared.

Through the night vision goggles, Josie spotted the trail's exit. She slowed to a cautious walk and edged into the playground. An owl hooted. The Blackbird flinched. Infrared imaging showed one car parked alongside a bench shrouded by a metal canopy. The driver's door hung open. No loud music. No laughter. No voices.

Grass cushioned the sound of her feet as the Blackbird traveled in a straight line toward the target. The Gen-5 goggles highlighted two people. One lay prone on the bench. Bare, slender legs dangled off the edge. *A girl.* The other person wore dark clothing, face shadowed by a hoodie. An unwelcome memory sprang from Josie's past. She thrust it aside. Unlike then, the goggles registered heat—the measurement of life.

Twenty-five yards to go.

The hooded figure arranged the too-still body along the length of the metal seat.

Ten yards.

A gloved hand smoothed long strands of hair away from the girl's face, lingered on the child's cheek, and dropped to her shoulder. The scene jolted Josie to her core.

"Stop," Josie screamed.

The person whirled. The silhouette of a gun slid into Josie's line of vision. She flicked her wrist, extended the baton to its full length, and closed the distance. Contact with flesh and bone made a satisfying thump, but the thud of the gun hitting the ground was better.

Josie spun and threw her weight into a kick. The solid connection vibrated the roots of her hair. Landing on the contact foot, a rock rolled beneath the sole of her boot. The ankle turned in a way it wasn't meant to go, and Josie slammed into the dirt. Air emptied from her chest. Her frozen lungs refused to cooperate.

She steeled herself for a bullet, but instead the hooded figured stumbled toward the car. A moment passed then the engine sputtered alive. A hulk in the dim light, the vehicle careened from one side of the road to the other. One door swung free as the driver accelerated through the open gate.

The Blackbird gulped air, rolled to her knees, and crawled to the bench. She touched a button on the glasses. A beam of light exposed the victim's face. A wave of cold swept over Josie. Could it be? The child would have to be fourteen now.

"Rose?"

Josie checked for a pulse. Steady. At the same time, she scanned the girl's body. No sign of wounds or torn clothing. She sniffed. No smell of alcohol either. The Blackbird patted the girl's cheek. "Rose. Can you hear me?"

Rose moaned.

"Open your eyes, it's Josie. Remember me? I lived across the street from you."

The girl's eyelids twitched, fluttered, and blinked open. "Josie?" Pinpoint sized pupils, shallow breathing, clammy skin. Junkie signs. But that didn't make sense. A dealer would leave the user where she fell. Why bring her here?

Rose's head lolled left then right. "Sick." Her hand clutched her belly.

Josie rose to her feet, grinding her teeth against the pain. She grabbed the girl and swung her to a sitting position. Vomit spewed across the ground. Josie held the girl and smoothed the black hair away from Rose's face. "Better?"

"A little." Rose glanced around the playground. "Where—where—am I?"

"Sentinel Park." Josie's throat tightened around the next question. "Are you hurt?"

"I—uh—don't think so."

"Thank God." Josie heaved a sigh of relief. "How did you get in that car?"

"I uh—don't know." A sob burst from Rose's throat. "I had a fight with Mom. I crawled out my bedroom window and left."

"At midnight?"

"I know. Stupid, right?" Tears trickled down her cheeks. "I was upset. Thought I'd walk to my friend Mark's house. I must've got mixed up on where I was. Someone grabbed me. I don't remember anything after that." Another sob. "Mom is going to kill me."

Josie pulled Rose into her arms. "Maybe not quite. She'll be upset but glad you're safe." Mosquitoes circled the Blackbird, whining for blood. She held Rose tight. "The park ranger is my friend. He'll be here in a minute. Then we'll decide what to do."

A moment later, a four-wheeler motored down the sidewalk. "Josie?" Sam called.

"Over here?"

15

Sam shut off the Arctic Cat and climbed to the ground. "Where's the car?" The beam of his flashlight found Josie's face. "You alright?"

"Car's gone. I sprained my ankle."

The torch first illuminated the ground around her feet, and then climbed to the bench. "Whoa." Shock rode Sam's words as he caught sight of the girl. "What's going on here?"

"Meet Rose Pham. She was drugged and dumped here."

"Rose, are you hurt?" Sam asked. "We need to call the police and get you to the hospital?"

"No." Rose was emphatic. "Josie, can you take me home? I could sneak back in through the window. Mom doesn't need to know."

Sam stepped in a little closer. "Your mom does need to know, and we are calling the police. We can't let someone get away with this."

"You're right, Sam." Josie placed a hand on the ranger's arm. "But let's keep this low key. I'll take her to the House of Audrey first like we did your daughter. Silas can take it from there."

"Please don't send a bunch of cops to my house," Rose pleaded. "My parents would die of embarrassment."

Sam hesitated and then nodded. "I'll keep the area secure until the investigators arrive."

"Silas will appreciate that." Josie tapped a code into her wrist phone and sent it to the supercomputer. Big Bertha would notify the Blackbird team to prepare for a guest.

"Give me your keys." Sam held out his hand. "You can't walk. I'll get your jeep."

"Thanks, Sam." The ranger jogged into the darkness, and Josie called Silas at the women's shelter. "I'm bringing in a rescue," she said, when he answered. "I know this girl."

"I saw the alert." Silas hesitated. "Is this related to the kidnappings?"

"Maybe. We'll be there in fifteen. Tell you more then." Josie disconnected.

CHAPTER FIVE

Blood soaks my sleeve, and my shoulder throbs with a heartbeat of its own. On a scale of ten, the pain registers seven. If an artery is nicked, I could die in a matter of minutes. I try to calm my jiggling legs, but they refuse to cooperate.

The secluded parking area of a darkened restaurant offers temporary protection. I pull in. The lot is empty and silent, except for the scurry of three fat raccoons racing for cover in a row of shrubs. The vehicle weathers the concrete's dips and cracks, its suspension bumping. As the car rolls to a stop, the southern sky cradles its July moon. I find no comfort in its glow.

"Leah, I need help."

No answer.

The wet sleeve makes a sticky sound when I peel it away from the wound. I grit my teeth. Blood streams from the gash. I can't get stitches. That requires an explanation. Leah should have stayed in the car the way we agreed. Then she could help me.

There is a rag in the glove box. Using one hand and my teeth, I tie the wound in a sloppy bandage.

I cradle my wrist and rest my head against the steering wheel. Our plan had been flawless until now. How did this happen?

The catastrophe replayed in my mind. The abduction hadn't seemed right from the first moment.

* * *

I loaded the girl into the front seat of the car. "She seems smaller than the others," I worried aloud to Leah. "What if the tranquilizer is too strong? I'm stopping to check."

"What if someone sees you?" Leah argued.

"What if she dies?" I was so scared my chest vibrated. "I'm not a killer."

I stopped the car under a streetlight, keeping one eye on the surroundings. I leaned over, grabbed the girl's wrist. Her pulse was normal. Her breaths puffed soft and regular against my cheek. She might have been sleeping.

That's when I recognized her. The details of hair color, the olive skin and the shape of the eyes were right, but this was not the average Asian streetwalker that no one would miss. This Vietnamese girl was an innocent with a family who cared about her. An only child, they had named Rose.

"I can't sell this one. I know her."

"You need the money to pay Sunny Hills," Leah preached.

"I've got enough to make the next payment."

"Do what you want. You will anyway."

"I'm taking her to Sentinel Park like the others, but I won't call the buyer. I'll let the park ranger find her."

"Count me out." Leah's tone had turned petulant, and then she was gone.

My plan was moving along with the girl placed on the bench, until the crazy ninja woman had appeared from nowhere. Her attack was vicious, and yet, when I flung myself into the car to escape, my hood had remained in place. Never was my face exposed.

* * *

A barking dog jars me back to the present. One of those raccoons and a scraggly German shepherd are in a standoff near the shrubs. The other coons are long gone, and I better move along too. There is nothing to fear from the ninja woman. She is a mystery, but she can't identify me. The strange glasses and cartoonish clothing make her a curiosity, not a threat.

But Rose—she's a different story. What did she expect walking the street in the middle of the night? How dare she shame her family.

"You may have recognized me, Rose, but when I'm done, you'll be too scared to ever say a word."

CHAPTER SIX

Silas leaned in as the security cameras captured Josie, guiding a teenage girl into The House of Audrey. She was a tiny thing, Asian, and fourteen or fifteen at best. He tensed. She fit the description of other girls reported missing, except she wasn't dressed like a prostitute. No skimpy clothes or heavy makeup.

Silas paced the floor. Waiting was not his strength. In fact, lately, if a person asked what his strengths were, he wouldn't know how to answer.

He went back to the pleasant surprise he'd received from Rebecca Haze. It had been a week since their meeting in the coffee shop. Fresh and original, the ideas in her synopsis showed potential. It was too soon to tell, but on the surface, Rebecca appeared to have taken his advice. Silas would set up a second meeting, but not until he discussed the idea of a documentary with key players within The House of Audrey. The project intrigued him. But the possibility of this particular reporter finding an honest motivation fascinated him.

Thirty minutes passed before Josie joined Silas in his office. He rested a hip against the corner of his desk as she limped toward him. No longer dressed in Blackbird gear, she wore a casual tee-shirt, jeans, and sneakers. One ankle was heavily taped. The test goggles and evidence bags dangled from her hands.

Josie plunked one bag on Silas's desk. "Glock G42. Dropped by the perp during the struggle. Not fired. Serial number removed." Her voice came off robotic. Silas didn't like the signs of an emotional backslide.

"The victim's name is Rose Pham. Age fourteen." The Blackbird dropped two more bags next to the gun. "Rose's clothes. No rips or tears. No visible signs of body fluids."

"She wasn't assaulted?"

Josie shook her head. "Not sexually."

The last bag held a self-defense baton. Silas recognized the beaded loop on the grip. After Josie completed the advanced level of Blackbird training, he'd tied it there himself.

"My baton." Josie motioned toward the evidence. "I used the weapon in self-defense when the perp made a threatening motion with that." Josie pointed to the Glock. "The assailant knocked me to the ground and escaped in an older model car. A dark color. Make unknown. The perp wore a hoody. At no time could I see his face."

Silas stepped in close and rested a hand on the Blackbird's shoulder. "Relax, Josie. This is not an interrogation. You saved Rose."

The skin bunched around Josie's eyes. "If I hadn't been in the park..."

Under the weight of his palm, Silas felt the shudder. "You were there, and you acted."

"Yeah. I acted like an amateur. I'm sure you and Lila are proud of the Blackbird who let a kidnapper escape." Josie massaged between her brows. "I wouldn't blame Lila for kicking me off her team."

"She won't do that. Who would she have to argue with?"

The corners of her mouth softened. "Nothing gets by you."

Silas shrugged. "So this thing you interrupted was not a random act. The perp had the code to the gate. We don't know what made Rose get in the car, but she ended up on a bench, unbound, and not gagged. As soon as the drug wore off, she could have gone for help. Why would a kidnapper do that?"

"Who can explain crazy? Could be he's taunting the police, or he wants to get caught."

"I called a team to work the crime scene. That could turn up more evidence, and if we get lucky the DNA on your baton will get us an arrest." Silas stood. "Is Rose stable enough to talk to me?"

"I sat with her through the worst of the examination. Without parental consent, we could only do a visual. The doctor found nothing to warrant a transport to a hospital. She's upset, but not hysterical. She might respond to you."

"You take the lead." Silas followed Josie to the shelter's small clinic, nodding to the doctor as they entered. He couldn't help but compare his niece to the girl staring at the floor. Through the years, Lila had defied him too. He and Lila's mother had done the same to their parents. Growing up was never easy.

Rose sat in a chair along the wall, elbows on knobby knees, chin in her hands. Tangled strands of dark hair dripped across her cheeks. She was dressed in clothes borrowed from the shelter, and one big toe bore a fresh bandage.

"How is my little friend?" Josie's warm smile showed she'd allowed her mind to open another compartment. One that operated with emotion.

"Okay—I guess." Rose studied the floor.

"Rose, this is Silas Albert. He is my friend and a police detective." Josie took the chair next to Rose.

"Hello Rose," Silas said. "I'm sorry to meet you this way." The girl flicked her hair away from her face but didn't speak.

Josie rested a hand on the girl's arm. "Silas wants to ask you a few questions. Is that all right?"

"I guess." Rose gave him a hang-dog look.

The detective angled a chair into a position where he could observe Rose's face but not be intimidating. When he sat, he kept his expression relaxed.

The doctor broke the silence. "I found an injection site on her neck."

Silas leaned in a fraction. "Are you okay?"

Rose bit her lip and remained quiet.

The doctor spoke. "I've drawn a blood sample. Her slow reflexes suggest the administration of a tranquilizer. We'll know the specific drug in few hours. Other than mental trauma, I've found no physical injuries. Well, I did bandage your toe, didn't I?" The doctor smiled at Rose.

Tears welled in the child's dark eyes. "I'm so dumb. I guess I'm lucky I'm not dead—or worse."

"Tell me." Silas offered Rose a simple invitation, an opportunity to share a burden. Rose accepted.

"I'm sorry," she said, at the end her story. "I just can't remember much."

"Don't worry, Rose." Frustration nipped at Silas's throat. "Bits and pieces may come to you later. Write everything down. Even smells. Or something you heard, like a unique accent. Minute details are important."

"Wait." Rose sat straighter. "The voice. It was weird. You know—fake. He must have used one of those things that changes what you sound like. I think it's called a voice modulator. I saw one used in a movie once."

Silas's nerves crackled. "What did he say?"

"It's all so confusing." Rose's hands twisted in her lap. "This must have been when I was on the bench. Kind of like all woozy. I think he said something about making a mistake. The next thing I remember, Josie was yelling at me to wake up."

Silas gathered his thoughts. Josie had been concerned the kidnapper was about to molest the child. But according to Rose, the abductor had acted remorseful. Was it sorrow for what he'd done, or what he was about to do? The perp's behavior indicated confusion, instability, or even mental illness. "Any idea what he meant by—mistake?"

Rose shook her head.

"Has anyone shown unusual interest in you, lately?" Josie spoke in a soft, non-threatening way. "Somebody you wouldn't normally talk too. From the neighborhood, maybe? Or online?"

"You think he knows me?" Rose shrilled.

"Probably not, but we can't rule out the possibility." Silas hastened to minimize her alarm. "Let's go back to the beginning. I'm not clear on how he tricked you into getting in the car."

"Umm." Rose frowned. "I know, right. I wouldn't go with a stranger." One foot slid on top of the other. She winced and brought them parallel. "The street was empty. Two or three parked cars, but no people. Not much light. There was a tall fence and bushes. I had to walk in the shadow." Her face brightened. "I tripped." She lifted her bandaged foot. "I had on sandals. Like these but different. Felt like I tore part of the nail off. Then, his arm was around my neck. He must have been hiding in those bushes."

"You're amazing, Rose," Silas said. "What about his face, jewelry, tattoos, or anything unique?"

"I'm sorry Mr. Albert. I'm trying. I'm really trying." Tears leaked from the corners of Rose's eyes and trickled down her cheeks.

Josie laid her hand on Silas's arm. The touch sent a message. *Back off.*

Silas relaxed his posture. "Rose, you've been a big help. Now young lady, the best place for you is home. Josie will take you, and she'll stay long enough to keep your parents from killing you. The Crimes Against Persons unit will take over from here."

"Will I have to, like, tell everything all over again?"

Josie put her arm around Rose. "Silas will fill them in, but they're better at this than he is, so yes, they'll need your help. You did great, tonight. Don't worry."

Silas handed a card to Rose. "Give this to your mom in case she has questions."

"Let's go, Rose," Josie said. "Time to face Momma and Poppa."

CHAPTER SEVEN

La ila Girard stood ankle-deep in dusty strips of old wallpaper. Three weeks had passed since Josie rescued Rose in the park, and the list of missing girls was growing. Big Bertha's artificial intelligence programs banged together theories, but there was no evidence to single out one over another.

Despite Lila's concern she continued to work on the new children's shelter. This was the last room on the second floor to renovate. Conversation filtered through the walls, where Josie and Janelle were applying the finishing touches on the other bedrooms. The Elle was about to open. A first day of school eagerness danced beneath Lila's skin. She couldn't wait to show Silas the latest progress.

This building didn't carry the sentimental history of The House of Audrey, where Lila lived with her uncle and never could. That story went all the way back to when Silas was twelve-years old, when he and Lila's mother inherited ten million dollars and an old warehouse.

Lila's mother was gone now, lost to cancer years earlier. The warehouse had been converted to a high-tech sanctuary. The brick walls still housed a shelter for abused women but had grown to be the secret epicenter for the Blackbirds, a sisterhood of survivors.

"Lila. Aren't you going to answer the phone?" Josie broke into her thoughts.

"I got it." She bolted for the stairs. *Please. Please. Please, keep ringing.* Her feet pounded down the curved stairway. She skated to a stop in front of the new kitchen counter and snatched the phone from its holder.

"Hello. This is The Elle," Lila said.

"We need help."

Lila's attention sharpened. "What kind of help?"

"My brother's hungry. Uh, he needs a safe place to sleep, too."

"That's what we're here for. I'll bet you love hamburgers and French fries." Lila stayed calm. "Are you hurt?"

"No. I'm doing this for my brother."

In the background, Lila detected cars, loud music, sniffling, and then a shushing sound. "Is your brother hurt?"

"No. Just scared." The girl's tone was low, guarded.

"I'll do everything I can to help. I'd like to know your name."

"Maybe after we check out your place."

Lila pictured her nervous. Careful. Say too much and you pay. Lila had witnessed the same thing in abused women at The House of Audrey. "My name is Lila," she said. "It really helps if I know who I'm talking to."

"Okay. I'm Elsa. My brother's Gordy." The words whispered into Lila's ear.

"Can you tell me how old you both are?"

"I—I'm twelve. My brother's eight."

Babies.

"Do you need me to come and get you?"

"Will you put us in the system? Been there, don't want to go back."

Lila stiffened. The Elle wasn't isolated from the system, but Silas had connections with excellent social workers—and caring families. "We can keep you safe. Where are your parents?"

There was a long pause. Lila sensed a lie coming.

"I don't know. Haven't seen them in a while. Tell me what the catch is. We don't want no dirty slave stuff."

The hair on Lila's arms stiffened. Children this age shouldn't even know about the *dirty slave stuff.* Had someone threatened to sell them? *Please let her trust me.*

"Elsa, I promise this house is a safe place." Lila wasn't sure how she'd come up with beds. She had to get the two children to the shelter first. "When was the last time you ate?"

"This morning. There's this nice old guy named Walter. He takes us to the soup kitchen. They think he's our grandpa and nobody asks questions."

Nice old men on the street often had hidden motives. "Where are you now?" For a moment, Lila thought the girl had hung up. She tried a softer tactic. "How did you know to call?"

"There was this paper at the Quick Stop. I read about your place."

Lila had placed brochures at Quick Stops all over the city. "I'm the one who put it there."

"Oh yeah?" Elsa whispered. The other child sniffled in the background. "Guess you better come get us," Elsa said.

"Where? Give me the address."

"We can't stay here, but there's an empty house with a treehouse in the back at the corner of..."

"Hey you?" An angry shout overrode Elsa. "What are you doin' back here? Put that phone down."

"Run. Gordy. Run."

"Wait," Lila cried out. "Tell me where you are."

"Who is this?" A deep voice burst through the phone."

Lila prayed to stay connected long enough for Bertha to capture the location. "That little girl and her brother are hungry. Give me your address. I need to find them."

"Don't need no trouble." The connection broke.

Lila needed the location to search for the kids. She tapped Big

Bertha's icon.

"Good afternoon, Lila. How can I help today?"

"Please identify the address for the last incoming call."

"One moment please." Seconds passed. "Lila, information is unavailable. Incoming call number four's origination is blocked. Bertha discerns from Lila's tone the importance of this data. Bertha is sorry."

The computer's attempt at emotion sent a lump to Lila's throat. She swallowed. "Thank you, Bertha."

Lila stood in the middle of the big kitchen. The evening sun poured through the freshly washed windows. A new paint smell permeated every angle of the room. She returned the phone to the holder. The first authentic call for help and she'd failed. She couldn't bear to tell the other Blackbirds.

"Lila, come see. We've got two bedrooms finished." The olive-skinned woman, fifteen years older than Lila's twenty, peered down from the second story landing. There was no mistaking Josie's happiness. This Blackbird didn't smile often, but now a gigantic grin swept across her face. The emotionally scarred woman had found purpose through the future of the children's shelter.

Lila studied the phone. Surely if Elsa had called once for help, she would call again. Lila hid her disappointment and bounded up the curved staircase marked by years of tromping feet and a bullet hole in the walnut banister. For her, the character of the house was important to retain. She imagined pointing the blemish out to the children and listening to the stories they conjured up about its origin.

Duplicating the success of The House of Audrey was Lila's plan. She wanted to give children a safe place, a new beginning. The rescue of one child would help to ease her grief for Elizabeth Cartwright. The woman who had it all. But even with beauty, intelligence, and a successful career, Lila's friend had never found her true safe place.

Lila followed Josie into a large airy bedroom straight out of a home decorating magazine. The palest of blue covered three walls. On the fourth wall, eight-inch stripes in dark blue highlighted the same light background. The bright white woodwork gleamed in testimony to the efforts of the sisterhood on a mission.

The psychiatrist, Janelle, a gentle woman in her sixties, glanced up from where she was tapping a paint lid back into place. Salt and pepper curls framed her plump face. "What do you think?"

Lila spun in a slow circle. "It's perfect." Janelle beamed, while Josie grinned. "Can I see the other room?"

The ladies led Lila into the next bedroom. A silhouette painted in a muted rose dissected the wall horizontally. She took in the reproduced skylines of Paris, Istanbul, Budapest, and finally Kansas City. Inside a cloud drawn above each vista, a sweeping calligraphy named the city. "This is gorgeous."

Josie pointed up.

Lila craned her neck. A painted rendition of a dozen diverse types of aircraft flew across the ceiling. "Oh my gosh! Josie, did you do this?"

Josie raised a paintbrush handle to her brow in salute. "We're almost ready."

"We could take one or two now," Janelle boasted. "When will the helpline go live?"

"It's been active for a week," Lila said.

"A week. And not one single call." Josie's face fell.

"Hang-ups and pranksters. I thought there was one possibility, but nothing came of it."

"Did you try to identify the hang-ups? Sometimes a person loses their nerve. Did you check the caller I.D? Can't Bertha get us an address?" Josie was almost shouting. "Not taking action is what gets people killed."

Lila locked on to the desperation in Josie's eyes. "Whoa. Hold on. We have limitations." This Blackbird wanted the shelter to be a success, even more than Lila. If that was possible. But a need for redemption could be a friend or it could be an enemy. "I can't force a person to ask for help. The lack of calls means we're not needed yet."

Josie's expression flattened. Her olive skin flushed a deeper tone. "Lila. You know better than that." The Blackbird stalked from the room, her black ponytail swinging.

"Not the best response for a person who wants to be a team leader," Lila muttered. "I can't check a blocked number. Believe me, I tried."

"Josie will be alright," Janelle said. "Your words could have used a little restructuring, but you know that fear is the root of Josie's anger. She's afraid of failing again. She blames herself for the death of her daughter at the hands Celia's father."

"Who wouldn't?" Lila bit her lower lip. She understood guilt. That's why she relied heavily on this woman. With her experience as a psychiatrist, Janelle helped Lila keep her own fears at bay. "Will she be, okay?"

"Josie's one of the defiant, like you. She's struggled, but she passed all the tests. A team leader deserves trust. If you can't give it, there's nothing to do but choose another Blackbird."

"I just don't want her to—you know, kill someone."

Janelle's blue eyes narrowed. "Is that how you assess Josie's behavior? Or is this your own fear raising its ugly head?"

Lila chewed her lip. Josie's history threw her in a different category from most of the other Blackbirds. She'd killed her abuser. Her recent flare ups made Lila uneasy. The last thing she wanted was for Josie to have a setback. "My own stress is showing through. Silas has faith in me to make this shelter work. I don't want to fail either."

"We've talked about this before, Lila. You may only be twenty, but your life experiences take you way beyond your age. Life is filled with challenges. We can provide support to these women, but the individual must choose to accept what we offer."

"I'll talk to Josie."

"Great. I'll give Josie a ride home. I won't be here until after ten tomorrow unless you have a rescue. We poor psychiatrists need to make a living too, you know."

Lila rolled her eyes toward the heavens and returned the sarcasm. "Like you're going to the food pantry in order to eat." She wrapped her arms around Janelle's soft round body. "I'm so lucky to have you in my life."

Janelle hugged Lila back. "No, my dear. I'm the one who is lucky."

After the psychiatrist left, Lila trudged into the third bedroom. She cared about each Blackbird, but a conflict between admiration and protection arose where Josie was concerned. For that reason, she hadn't divulged the details of the earlier call.

The girl's voice echoed on an endless playlist of one in Lila's mind. She kicked at the pile of torn wallpaper.

There had to be a way to find those two kids.

CHAPTER EIGHT

At least I'm not guilty of murder for hire—yet.

My gaze slides around the room, taking in the soft tones of gray and ivory, the high-quality furniture, and the heavy window treatment. Not a speck of sunshine from the clear summer day sneaks past the thick fabric. A hollowed-out emptiness possesses my chest as I approach the woman in the bed. The doctors say, "Mary is less agitated when she can't see what she's missing." I find this gloom depressing and resist the urge to fling back the curtains and let the sun burn away this myth, along with the despair inside of me.

If only it were that simple.

Kansas City's Sunny Hills Care Center is designed to make a person's last days beyond comfortable—for a price. No cracks in the tile floors here. Odor digesting chemicals have eliminated the old people smell. The near perfect ambiance consoles me.

A shadow moves in the corner of the private room. My breath hitches. Leah has a habit of turning up when I least expect.

"Miss me?" Leah whispers in her secretive way.

That's the way our relationship is now. Secret.

"What is it, dear?" Mary's voice is weak and fluttery. "You have that tightness about your mouth. You're worried about something."

I take her hand, a bunch of bones so barren of flesh they threaten to rattle. The bedside lamp shows her olive skin-tone, typical of a

Vietnamese woman, is driven back by a sickly gray. Her name is not originally Mary, but like so many others, she'd been encouraged to go by an American name.

"Nothing," I lie. "Work is stressful right now, that's all." That part is the truth. Each day I wear a mask for the outside world, and each day a piece of my soul dissolves to float away.

The notice, from Sunny Hills, ghosts through my thoughts. Neat columns of numbers show a deficit, and a date that is careening toward me at a dizzying speed. If the two collide, there will be an eviction notice next. I shudder at the thought of Mary in a place that reeks of neglect. "You know, you're all I have left."

"And I have only you," Mary whispers.

"Don't be silly," Leah chides from the shadows. "You still have me. You'll always have me."

"I know," I whisper back. "Sometimes, it's hard to be sure."

Mary's faded brown eyes dart around the room. "Who are you talking to?"

As usual, Leah stays out of sight. "No one, love," I say, hating Mary's bewilderment, and that I'm the cause. "You're hearing things." I press my lips against the tissue-paper skin of her cheek.

I don't like lying to Mary, but she disapproves of my relationship with Leah. To protect Mary's health, Leah and I have agreed, it's better not to upset her.

"I bought a new book. I'll read to you for a while?"

"You're changing the subject." Mary's fingers pluck at the covers tucked under her chin.

I pull a chair close to the bed, turn on a reading lamp, and crack the cover on the latest publication from her favorite author. After hearing a few pages of words, her hands quiet. I glance up. Her lips tremble and she manages a smile. All the reward I need for the risks I take, comes in that simple expression of pleasure.

For a moment, I breathe in this room and picture the abandoned house and the girls locked inside. They are the commodity that guarantees the next payment to Sunny Hills Care Center.

CHAPTER NINE

The sound of screeching metal brought Silas's head up with a snap. His eyelids shot open. The House of Audrey rose on the other side of the gate, but the cruiser's bumper rested against a concrete wall. He ground his teeth. Why hadn't he listened to Hadley? His partner had tried to convince Silas not to drive, but he'd been too stubborn.

It was midnight, three weeks after Rose's narrow escape. Silas hadn't slept in forty-eight hours. In a city turned upside down by abductions and murders there was no time to rest. At least that was his excuse.

His head was thick from exhaustion, and even with his arms down he smelled. Under the protective sleeve of his prosthetic hand, his stump itched. It wasn't like him to risk an infection. The invisible burden of regret had made him careless.

Guilt, the psychiatrist called it.

When Rebecca Haze covered the serial killings two years earlier, she'd used the term failure. Back then, the reporter's public ridicule burned, and even though she retracted the statement, he couldn't turn from the truth.

Now, he'd worked himself into oblivion, never quite able to bury those memories. Through bleary eyes, he peered up at the House of Audrey. During his darkest moments, the shelter's purpose kept him from walking himself into a bullet.

The scars on the retaining wall flashed a message bolder than a skull and crossbones. He needed a reset. An idea had been in the back of Silas's mind for months. Did it make him an irresponsible coward? Maybe. He shrugged. Better a coward than a killer by negligence. He was well known for that already.

The gate opened at his verbal request, and he drove into the garage. A beep from his phone verified the reengagement of the outside alarm.

Camellia met him inside the door, sniffing his pant legs and purring a welcome. The calico was one legged and one eyed, non-critical, except when her food container was empty, and devoted to keeping his feet warm at night.

Silas followed the calico to the kitchen, checked her food and water, bent over to stroke her back for a moment, then trudged into the bedroom, tapping Sydney's number as he walked. Sydney Franco was one of the reasons life mattered.

"Hi, Babe," Sydney answered right away.

"You still working?" Silas kicked off his shoes and flopped across the bed. He visualized the petite medical examiner in her white autopsy gear, dark eyes even darker, reflecting the serious nature of her job.

"I am. Those last three homicides will keep me here all night. Did you hear? There was no match in the system from the DNA on Josie's baton?"

A yawn forced Silas's jaws wide. "Damn. We can't catch a break. Between the rash of murders and the abductions, I'm maxed out." His eyelids drooped. Camellia jumped onto the bed, startling him back awake. He heard Sydney say something about a hair. "I'll read the report myself, tomorrow," he interrupted, pretending he hadn't missed a word. "Get some rest when you can."

"Not possible tonight. Too many bodies. But I have high expectations for the weekend and our get-away. Oak Hills Resort is going to be the perfect place to relax. Can't wait to listen to country music in those hills of southern Missouri. The motorcycle still in the plan?"

"If you want it to be."

"Are you okay? You sound—different."

Silas rubbed the back of his neck. Sydney's radar was fully functional. "I just need to know you're good. You're working long hours."

"So says the man who most likely clocked fifty in the last three days. I'm doing what I must do. Same as you."

Sydney was right, but he wasn't in the mood for encouragement. "If you say so," Silas muttered. "I'm putting my phone on silent. Goodnight." His eyelids drooped.

"Night, Babe. Love you—even when you're grouchy."

Silas switched off the device. He settled in, remembering at the last moment to remove his prosthesis. He didn't need a skin ulcer. Sydney's words eased his troubled thoughts, and sleep faded the world away.

* * *

A cold nose nudged Silas's ear. He cracked one eyelid open. "Camellia, one of these days I'm going to throw you out." Silas reached out and scratched the calico between the ears. "I'll get an old tom cat who'll be too lazy to check if I'm alive."

He swung his legs over the side of the bed and sat up. After a bit of searching, he located his prosthesis on the floor and his cell under his pillow. According to the device he'd slept four hours. Twenty messages waited in his inbox.

"What the hell?" He groaned. The urge to smash the phone to pieces roared in his chest. "Why does everyone have to be so damn needy?"

He stomped off to the bathroom leaving the cat behind on the bed. "Nobody gets a piece of me, yet." Bloodshot eyes stared back at him from the mirror. He knew he should work out, swim twenty laps in the pool, replenish those lagging endorphins. He escaped into the shower instead.

Five minutes under the stinging hot water and Silas had mentally created his notice to the mayor. He stepped from the shower, dried off, and pulled on underwear and jeans. No angry spots of inflammation showed on his stump. His frame of mind moved a hair beyond phone-smashing level. He tapped the cell to life. Before he turned the corner on the next stage of his life, there was work to do.

"Bertha."

"Good morning, Silas. How can I help you?"

Back when he'd developed Bertha's personality, he'd been full of optimism and up for early morning pleasantries. Somehow, he had to get that mindset back. "Please play all messages from the last four hours." In the moment that passed, Silas attached his prosthesis, and then put the phone on speaker.

"Requested information available. Have a pleasant morning, Silas," Bertha withdrew into the banks of her computer brain.

Silas lathered his face and undertook the challenge of shaving. Whiskers whirlpooled down the drain. Updates from the homicide unit droned in his ears. In addition to the usual incidents that measured societies diminishing respect for life, another theme filtered beneath the words. Half the messages confirmed a dark cloud hung over even his best detectives. Any day, his team expected the kidnapper to cross the line from abduction to homicide.

"Detective Albert, it's Rose, you know from that night a few weeks ago." Silas's razor halted mid-stroke. "I need to talk to you. I'm scared. Please call me. Please."

Silas hit redial and zipped the remaining stubble from his chin.

"Hello."

"Rose, this is Detective Albert. What's happened?"

"He found me. You've got to do something."

Rose's words tumbled out fast, but there was no doubt who *he* was.

"Okay, Rose. Slow down. Where are you now?"

"In my room."

"Where are your parents?"

"They've gone to work, but I locked all the doors. I put a chair under my door handle. I've got a ball bat."

"Good girl. Is someone inside the house now?"

"No. But I heard a noise by my window. I'm really scared."

"What makes you think he knows where you live?"

"I—I got a note yesterday. He slid it under the door after my parents went to work. Somehow, he's found out the cops are involved. He threatened me, Mom, and Dad. All of us."

Questions peppered Silas's tongue, beginning with—why did you wait until today to call, and why didn't you tell your parents? The idea of her folks leaving her alone didn't sit well either. He kept those thoughts to himself.

Instead, he said, "Rose, I'm glad you called me. Tell me exactly what the message says."

Paper rustled and Silas gritted his teeth. Each crackle of paper equated to the contamination of fingerprints and physical evidence. Rose's abductor knew her and where she lived. During life or death moments like this one, forensics took a back seat.

"'You called the cops. Big mistake. Keep your mouth shut or you and your family are dead'."

Silas's brain seized on the word cops. So much for a discrete investigation. "When did you get this note?"

"Yesterday. But there was another one. I got it a couple of days after Josie found me in the park."

Three weeks had passed since that night. "Read the first message. Word for word."

"'This proves I know where you live. Be quiet or I'll come for you'."

"Your parents haven't seen these threats, have they?" The silence held for a long moment.

"Uh no. I thought this would—like —go away."

"Rose, I'll be there in five minutes. I won't be in uniform. Don't answer the door for any other reason." He considered telling Rose to go to a neighbor's house until he arrived, but it was too risky. The perp was privy to more than casual details about this victim. Protocol dictated notifying the kidnapping team. His pulse pumped. There was no time for a lengthy explanation. The fallout from not following the rules—again—would, well, fallout later.

"Okay," Rose replied.

Silas ran down the hall, asking questions as he went. "Where do your folks work? I'll have them picked up."

"Mom is a cook at I-HOP." Rose sniffled. "She didn't want to go in, but we need the money. I convinced her I'd be okay."

"Which one?"

"The one on Rainbow Boulevard. Dad does maintenance at the VA." Her voice shook. "Please hurry."

"Stay on the line. I'm on my way." He shrugged on a shirt then grabbed personal items and his gun from the dresser. Rose's address was familiar. She lived one block from Clarence Rochester. Silas cringed. He already had a meeting scheduled with the man for later that morning. To cross paths with Clarence twice in twenty-four hours was the sign of a really bad day. God willing, he and Rose would be long gone before the commissioner ever had his first cup of tea.

"Should I keep talking?" Rose whispered.

"Hang tight for a minute."

"Okay."

The detective thumbed an urgent text message to his partner. Eyes glued to the screen, Silas stomped his bare feet into boots and raced for the garage. "Stay with me, Rose."

"I'm here."

"Good. You're doing great." He bypassed the old freight elevator for the stairs. At the bottom he hit the emergency door release. The door swung open. A response from Hadley flashed on his phone. Silas stopped long enough to confirm the rescue team was rolling.

"Rose?"

"Yes."

"I'll be there before you know it." He started for the SUV, eyed the Harley, and changed directions. "Don't bring anything with you. We'll send someone back for whatever you need." He slammed on a helmet, fastened the strap, and checked the wi-fi transmission.

"What about my cat?" Rose's panic chattered through the built-in headphones. "I can't leave her here alone."

Of course. Silas couldn't count the number of times victims thought of their pet before themselves. After twelve years, given the same situation, he wouldn't leave Camellia either.

He shoved the phone into a bracket mounted on the bike's frame. "Bring the cat with you." He brought the Harley to life, remotely opened the security gate, roared past the fresh scars on the concrete wall, and rolled out onto the street.

"Thanks. I don't want her killed because of me."

Given a choice, Silas's bet was on the cat choosing homicide over a motorcycle ride. The bike hugged the white lines as Silas weaved through light traffic. "What's your cat's name?"

"Tilly," came the tentative reply.

Silas kept Rose talking, but his brain spun back to the night Josie rescued Rose. Silas had called in a favor, asking a lieutenant he trusted to manage a discrete investigation. Not a shred of evidence was found in the park, and so far, Rose's memory wasn't cooperating.

Based on the note, her assailant wasn't privy to that information, but somehow, he knew about the cops' involvement. A sketchy criminal profile was coming together, and the detective didn't care for the implications it brought along. He shrugged it off. In a few minutes, Rose would be in a safe house and Silas would go into the office, type up the letter to the mayor, and think about a weekend at Ozark Hills Resort with Sydney.

But until then, Silas needed to keep Rose calm. He passed a closed Italian restaurant. "What's your favorite food?"

"Fried chicken."

A red light had cars backed up, blocking Silas's path. He steered right and the Harley barreled down the sidewalk. Illegal as heck but at this hour there were no pedestrians. A welcoming green ushered him back to the road and through the intersection. Open pavement ahead, he talked to Rose about music. Her favorite was country. That made him question her Vietnamese heritage. She giggled. Tilly yowled in the background.

"Shush, baby. I'm taking you to a safe place," Rose soothed.

Silas wanted Rose's words to be true, but the situation was fluid. He scanned the block ahead. "I'm on your street now. You won't see me for a minute or two. I won't be talking either. Stay in your room. I'm going to make sure you don't have company."

If one and one still made two, Rose's subconscious could hold facts vital to identifying the kidnapper. Details important enough to get her killed.

Rebecca Haze had been right when she reported Silas as a failure in the Killer Surgeon case two years earlier. It was still hard for the detective to accept that the police chief of Kansas City, also known as, Silas's past lover had been a serial killer.

Silas gripped the handle bars tighter.

He might have failed in the past, he wasn't going to fail Rose today.

CHAPTER TEN

The neighborhood is quiet. I push myself away from the computer, my head aching from eyestrain. The dark web is a hellish place and addictive as cocaine. My attention strays to the desk. A cup of tea sits alongside a half-eaten sandwich. Putrid mayonnaise congeals along the edges of the bread. The sight sets my teeth on edge. I can't afford to keep losing track of time.

I go to open my office door, but it's not closed. My body goes rigid. I never risk this kind of exposure. The dishes clink together as I carry them to the kitchen and scrape the food into the garbage disposal. The smell of leftover takeout, I don't remember bringing home, ticks my pulse upward.

No sign of Leah. I hate it when she doesn't trust me and runs back to Paul, but I'm glad she can't see me in this state. Our genes tie Leah and me together, but her vanishing acts do get old. Paul's her husband, but he's no good for her. If she stays, he'll make her sick, like before. I can't go get her. There's that damn restraining order.

I load the dishes into the, already packed, dishwasher, and start the cycle. Anger pricks at my bones. Paul could be a problem. But I know all about his troubles, and when I'm ready, they will get a whole lot worse. He's already in over his head. Soon, his silly restraining order will be of no consequence.

When Leah returns, she'll be impressed. Thanks to me, there are more funds in the offshore account. I've been careful. No trail to the money, and no clues for the police.

Still, a knot forms in my stomach. Before I finish ruining Paul, I am determined to take back from him what is rightfully Leah's. But I don't quite have enough financial cushion. The dark web is the answer. A few more sales and we will escape this sham of a life.

I walk to the window and stare toward Rose's house. The night is dark and still. Her parents left for work hours earlier. She is alone. My threats should have her lying in bed with the covers pulled over her head.

The rumble of a motorcycle engine breaks through my thoughts. The driver has the motor throttled back. I snatch up binoculars from a nearby table and point the lens toward light pooling beneath the streetlamp.

A second passes and then the bike rolls into sight. The rider swings his head side to side, searching. He wears jeans and a short-sleeved shirt untucked and riding up his back. I don't have to see his face to confirm Silas Albert's identity. The artificial arm is proof enough. I'll never forget the stir he caused when he fought city hall to keep his job after the meth lab explosion took the one he was born with.

My insides quake. *How did a homicide detective get involved with Rose?* I lower the glasses and press my nose against the window, focusing on the single taillight. One, two, three, the fourth driveway belongs to Rose's family.

I will the red dot to disappear into the night, taking with it my fear of the reason the detective is here in the first place. But it's not to be. The motorcycle pulls in at Rose's house.

Rose rushes outside, lugging a container. Even at this distance, I hear the cat yowl louder than a beast possessed. Silas lifts Rose aboard the bike and fastens the crate behind her. The detective glances around, nervous, hand close to his waistband. He removes an extra helmet from the backrest and secures it to Rose's head. He climbs on board and the motorcycle roars off.

Leah is right. I shouldn't have shown Rose kindness. I should have left that stupid girl on the park bench and called the buyer.

There can be only one reason for Rose to behave this way. The little twerp is after attention. She'll show the police the notes, and she'll pretend to remember something important. No matter. The real me is impossible to match to the crime. Even Silas Albert isn't that good.

CHAPTER ELEVEN

Behind Lila the knob to the kitchen door rattled. *No one should be here at this time of day. It's four o'clock in the morning.* She whirled away from the entryway, crashing her crazy bone into the countertop. The tingle set her teeth on edge.

"Lila, it's me Woody. Woody Mendez."

"Woody?" She edged next to the door. "What are you doing here? Did my uncle put you up to checking on me?"

"Silas? I haven't seen him since—well you know."

Lila did know. Night patrol was Mendez's punishment for hiding his personal connection to a murder victim. The secret had made him a suspect in the killing. Woody had been cleared of everything except stupidity. For that he was on the late shift.

"I was driving by and noticed your car outside. Unusual for this early in the day. Thought I would make sure everything was all right. Aren't you going to let me in, or do I have to stand out her fighting off the moths till dawn?"

Unusual. How did Woody know what was unusual? Unable to sleep, Lila had been up for an hour, stripping wallpaper. She'd come down for a glass of cold water. She sighed, fluffed her hair, and surveyed her grubby clothes. He did have to do his civic duty when she was wearing worn out yoga pants with paint stains. No lipstick, no eyeliner—she must look twelve years old.

She unlocked the door and swung it open. "Sorry. Come in." As he passed by, she admired the way the uniform stretched across his broad shoulders, and how the light glinted from his black hair. "I can't offer you a chair since we don't have furniture yet. I do have soda. Want one?"

"No thanks, can't stay but a minute. I'm finishing an overtime gig. Officers are out sick, so I volunteered to work over to cover. The public's stressed about the abductions. We've increased night patrols, hoping to catch the perp, before someone shoots their neighbor."

An uneasy tingle wiggled up Lila's spine. If she understood Woody at all, he would take her personal investigation into those crimes as a slam at police procedure.

Woody's gaze fastened on Lila's face, took in the rest of her body, and then slid around the room. "You've transformed this old house. But it's still dark outside. Are you by yourself?"

A different kind of tingle traveled through her blood. *Stop it. He's just being a cop.* "That's why I had the door locked."

"You might want to think about replacing it." Woody pecked on the glass pane. "Easy for a person to break in."

Now he was treating her like a twelve-year old. She bit her tongue and attempted an adult response. "I know. It's on my list. The alarm system will be installed next week. I've still got tons of work to do here."

He stepped away from the door a smile in his eyes. "This is an important thing you're doing here, Lila. Could you use help? I would come by on my day off and give you a hand."

The offer came out innocent enough, but those twinkling peepers sent Lila's imagination into a tailspin. "I uh—I might take you up on that." She grinned up at Woody. "Sanding, painting, yardwork, hauling furniture. Sound fun?"

This invitation was going to upset Silas. But she'd learned from

49

living with her uncle for over twelve years, forgiveness was easier to get than permission. She was twenty and he couldn't take the keys to the Studebaker from her the way he had when she was sixteen. She'd convince Silas that Woody's offer was innocent, and the young officer had no intention of jumping her bones. On second thought, she'd better not mention bone-jumping.

"Right up my alley." He smiled and twenty-thousand volts zapped through her veins.

"Want to see what we've already done?"

He checked his watch. "Have to make it quick."

"Right this way, Officer Mendez." Cell in hand, she motioned for him to follow.

"Are you expecting a call?" Woody nodded at the phone she carried. She frowned. *What if I am?*

"Sorry, none of my business. After you, Lady Lila."

Lila tucked her phone into her waistband. "This house is loaded with mystery." She showed him the bullet hole in the banister.

In true police fashion, he paused to examine the entry and exit points. "Twenty-two caliber."

"Very good, Officer Mendez." When they reached the second floor, his hand cupped her elbow.

"Do you think you could go back to calling me, Woody?"

Warmth spread up her arm. What was wrong with her? She yanked her world back into normal rotation and backed a safer distance away. She wasn't afraid of him, but they were alone, and she didn't want to send the wrong message. "Sure, if you'll tell me how you got such an unusual name."

"Maybe—someday." Mischief danced in Woody's eyes.

"Let me guess. You passed your driver's test in a Chrysler Woody?" Her love of classic cars was showing again.

He laughed. "No. Guess again."

"I'll wait until you find the right time to tell me your deep dark secret." Lila led the way through the bedrooms, her curiosity about all things Woody Mendez bubbling like a witch's cauldron.

In the second bedroom, Woody gave a low whistle. "Wow. This is clever. A great imagination was at work here."

"I can't take the credit," Lila admitted. "Josie, from the women's shelter, is a fabulous decorator."

"I'm surprised you were able to get this house," Woody said, as they entered the hallway. "I heard a speculator was buying up chunks of real estate around here."

Lila's stomach clenched. The house was a gift from Janelle, but Lila's vision resonated from every corner. The thought of starting over didn't go down easy.

"Why would anyone be interested in buying up old houses?"

"A new sport's complex. One of my brothers is an engineer. I'm not supposed to know, but I—sort of—peeked at the model on his computer." He winked. "This area is targeted for hotels, restaurants, and retail shops. Someone is trying to get a head start."

Lila frowned. "Isn't that illegal?"

"Sure is, but it's done all the time."

"You don't know who is behind this?"

"No. An insider, I guess. A person with access to the city's big development projects. I did a little investigating, but the transaction history stops at a shell company."

"No one has approached me, and I don't know what I'd do if they did. I've fallen in love with this place."

She finished the tour, and Woody followed her downstairs. "How did you know I was here?" She asked over her shoulder.

"The Studebaker." He flashed two precious little dimples. "I picked up one of the shelter's pamphlets in a Quick Stop, while I was out on patrol a while back." Woody pulled a brochure from his back pocket.

"One of the things that piqued my interest to the point of stopping."

Lila dared to imagine that she was the second reason. It was an exciting thought.

Woody laid the leaflet on the counter then propped his tall frame against the granite. "Have you had anyone ask for help?"

"Only one that wasn't a prankster." She told Woody about Elsa and Gordy. "If I'd had one more second..." Lila's attention drifted downward to rest on her disgustingly grubby flip flops.

"Hey! This isn't your fault." Woody pushed away from the counter. "We'll find them. Do you have an audio copy of the conversation? A fresh set of ears might be helpful."

We? Did he say we?

Lila hurried to a corner of the kitchen and gathered her purse from the floor. "All calls here at the shelter are recorded." She pulled a flash drive audio player from inside the bag. "I've listened to it in my car," Lila said, responding to Woody's raised eyebrows. "I keep hoping I'll hear something that will tell me how to find them."

Woody slipped the device into his pocket. "I''ll get this back to you, but I've got to go. Thanks for the tour." His hand was on the doorknob, but he faced her again. "Tomorrow's my day off. I could drive over and help you strip wallpaper?" His expression reminded her of a little boy asking for ice cream.

"I uh, err, I'm busy tomorrow." Heat spread up her neck.

"Really?" Woody's eyes narrowed to a point where the lids almost touched. "I understand." He swung away and yanked at the door's handle. "I'll be getting back on duty."

She hated to tell him, but a person needed to turn the knob to release the latch to get the door open. "Wait."

He spun away from his escape route, dark eyebrows puckered in a glower. "Lila, you don't have to hit me with a hammer. Silas Albert doesn't want me in the same room with his niece. Don't worry, I won't tell him you let the big bad wolf inside."

"It's not that," she interrupted. "I'm twenty. You're not an axe murderer. I'll talk to you if I want." She placed a verbal exclamation mark behind *talk.* Resisting the dangerous attraction of a dark handsome man six years older who wanted to protect her required ridiculous willpower. "I'm going to the cemetery." It was a feeble explanation, and one Lila didn't expect him to believe. Before Woody's cop wheels turned the wrong way, she clarified. "Tomorrow is Elizabeth's birthday."

"Oh." Concern replaced the glower. "That'll be tough."

"I could use a ride-along friend."

So much for self-control.

Silas wasn't going to like this. He wouldn't have appreciated the times she and Woody met for coffee together either. Lila didn't plan to keep the friendship a secret from her uncle, but she wasn't quite sure how to tell him.

Woody gaped as if she'd grown horns, then a broad smile spread across his face. "What time, and where?"

"Ten. Right here."

"Are you driving the Studebaker?"

"Why?"

"Wanted to know whether to take my anxiety medicine or not. I know about your street-racing capabilities."

Lila laughed and gave Woody one more favorable mark. He hadn't assumed, because he was a man, he would do the driving. "I'd take a double dose if I were you." She closed and locked the door behind him.

Logic told her the kids would be impossible to find in the dark, but the delay frustrated her.

Tomorrow, God willing, they would rescue Elsa and Gordy. In the meantime, she planned to get Bertha investigating the sale of property around The Elle.

CHAPTER TWELVE

The next day at the station, Silas swirled dregs of coffee long gone cold, seeing only the frightened faces of Rose and her family in the bottom of his cup. Other detectives shuffled papers and scanned computer screens in the bull pen outside his office. The investigative machine never stopped humming.

As it turned out, the detective in charge of the abductions treated Silas with respect, thanking him for taking immediate action to protect their one and only witness. It didn't hurt that Silas had known him for ten years and that Special Agent Archie Hamilton made an appearance to vouch for the Silas.

A swath of sunshine cut through Silas's window, reminding him there was a report to file and a letter to complete. He set his cup down. Typing was one skill not mastered by his prosthetic hand, but thanks to audio conversion technology it wasn't necessary. He finished the incident report and forwarded it to the necessary departments.

Thirty minutes later, he completed his notice to the mayor. When Silas attached this document to an email and pressed send, there would be no turning back. Cyberspace didn't have a change-your-mind key.

Having lost the trust of my team and the city I took an oath to protect...

The letter sealed Silas's decision, but the expected relief didn't materialize. No great weight lifted from his shoulders. Kansas City's homicide unit would be better off without him, but the thought brought little consolation. This wasn't how he expected to go out.

"Ready to go, Boss?"

Silas startled at Detective Hadley Barker's uncannily pertinent question. No one knew his plans and for the moment, he preferred to keep it that way. His actions would be hard for those closest to him to accept. He hit save and powered down the computer.

"Sure." Silas followed his partner to the department cruiser, a bitter taste in his mouth. "Don't want to keep the commissioner waiting."

Hadley pulled into the hum of city traffic. "The Berger Nest is sure a strange place to meet. Rough neighborhood. I hope Rochester isn't planning to shoot you."

"What, and eliminate his favorite punching bag? I should be so lucky."

The remark warranted a sharp glance from Hadley. "Aren't you bursting with pleasantries today? I guess if Rose's cat screamed in my ear, and I had breakfast scheduled with Clarence, I'd be in a bad mood too."

"I'm sure Clarence has heard all about the ride from hell by now."

Hadley chuckled. "I would have had to schedule a shrink visit, after that one." He raised an eyebrow. "By the way, how are those going for you?"

Silas grimaced. "I stopped. Wasn't helping."

"So says the man who keeps a psychiatrist on call at his women's shelter. Guess it works for them, but not you?"

"Drop it."

"Yes, Boss."

"Thanks." Silas encouraged small talk as the cruiser slid through the city, hoping his partner would stay off the subject of his mental health. He caught his friend's scrutiny at each pause in the flow of traffic. Ten minutes later they arrived at the Burger Nest.

"Grab me a breakfast burrito, a side of hash browns, and a big OJ."

Hadley leaned back in the seat. "My presence among those patrons tends to overwhelm."

Silas smiled despite his negative mood. "Shouldn't take long." He climbed from the car and headed inside the diner. The only pleasure he expected to gain from the meeting was in telling the commissioner, no. He owed Rochester, but the paybacks the man deserved wouldn't come in the form of a favor.

Two years ago, Silas had been seated at the foot of a long walnut table surrounded by a group of accusers, of which Clarence Rochester was the spokesman. The results that day had cleared the detective and embarrassed Rochester. Humiliation was not something the commissioner wore well.

Yet, he'd asked for Silas's help. And to make things more interesting Rochester had suggested they have a private discussion away from city hall. The strangeness of the request had prompted Silas to agree to listen.

The proposed meeting place was a clean but well-worn haunt in a ragged part of the city. He'd been surprised when the commissioner agreed to slumming it. The detective pulled the door open, setting off a jangle of bells. Inside, patrons swiveled toward the sound. A few acknowledged him with a nod as he crossed the threshold. Others returned to their food and conversations. The smell of all things grilled and greasy filled the air.

Silas's surveyed the room. He had history with a share of the occupants seated at the scarred tables. Some good, some bad. On occasion the detective was rudely reminded some folks carried a grudge.

From force of habit, Silas checked the non-verbal language that could speak a thousand words. The sight of a serpent tattoo turned him cold. Even with his back to Silas, there was no mistaking the ex-con, Wade Rowland. His companion was a stranger. Deep in conversation, neither person acknowledged the detective. That was fine with him.

The hostess approached, wearing a welcoming smile, jeans in the trendy 'ripped' style, and a flaming red tee shirt that said *Hot Tamale*. Under normal circumstances, he would have teased about taking up a collection to buy her new jeans. For which his niece Lila would have called him a Boomer. Even though, he was more of a Gen Xer. Wherever he fell, he just wanted to get this meeting over.

"Hey there Detective Albert. How've you been? Haven't seen Lila in a while, how is she?"

"I'm doing fine, and Lila is as well. Thanks for asking."

The Burger Nest replicated a smaller town's atmosphere amid this city of thousands. Everyone was always fine, even when the blackest cloud hung over their heads. Silas agreed with the tradition. He had spilled his guts to a psychiatrist, and what had it done for him? Nothing. He was clear on one thing—sharing his troubles hadn't removed the cloud.

"The guy in the corner is expecting you." The hostess pointed toward a table near a swinging door to the kitchen.

"Thanks." From across the room the top of the commissioner's head was barely visible.

Silas took a step but paused when the man with the tattoos rose from his seat. A slow strut carried him across the tiled floor, where he stopped at Clarence's table, and leaned in close. When Clarence didn't draw away, Silas's cop instincts twinged. These two men engaged in a friendly conversation went against the grain of savvy politics. Clarence certainly knew Wade Rowland's history.

It wasn't so much the robbery Rowland had been convicted of but the rape of a child he'd gotten away with that made the meeting so unsavory.

The Burger Nest didn't have a fake rubber plant to hide behind, and Silas wasn't the cowering type. He strode across the restaurant. "Hello,

Clarence."

The commissioner jumped to his feet. His eyes darted from the detective to the ex-con and back. "Uh, hello, Silas." He stuck out his hand. "Thanks for coming."

Dressed in worn kakis and a casual polo shirt, Silas figured Clarence didn't want to bring attention to himself in such a lowly establishment. The detective didn't recall ever seeing the commissioner wear anything but a suit and a starched white shirt. Angry red scratches on Clarence's neck were a novelty as well. Fingernails made similar marks, but then so would a dog's claw.

Silas pulled out a chair and sat. He ignored Clarence's outstretched hand and locked onto the wintry stare of the tattooed man. Static electricity buzzed at the roots of Silas's hair. When that happened, life was about to get lively. He hadn't come in expecting an explosion, but he was more than willing to play his part if Wade made a move.

"Clarence, you need to change your cologne. You're attracting flies." Silas jerked his thumb in the direction of Clarence's visitor.

The scales of the serpent rippled. "Screw you, Albert. I'm not fallin' for your little tease. You're not getin' me to break my parole. But one of these days..." He smacked a fist into his hand, whirled, and stomped back to his table.

"Excellent. Now we won't be bothered by silly conversation. You called this meeting, Clarence. What's on your mind?"

Rochester sank to his seat, the welcoming expression traded for one of stony displeasure. The man's Asian ancestors would be proud of his restraint. No doubt, they'd also be honored by his success, but not his path to achievement.

The Kansas City Police Commission of which Clarence was a commissioner, had been established in 1939 to halt the corruption generated by the Pendergast Political Machine. Even in today's political climate, an Asian in a position of authority in the Midwest was a rare bird. For some, scars left behind after the Vietnam war needed another hundred years to heal. But Clarence had managed to worm his way into the good graces of Kansas City's mayor.

Now the proposal underway to bring control of the police by the state back to the city threatened the commissioner's job. If adapted, the KCPC was history—followed by Clarence's aspirations. The slightest hint of misconduct placed a live grenade in the hands of the opposition. A heyday for the reporter who connected a felon like Wade Rowland to a commissioner. The image of Rebecca Haze, her red hair streaming, spirited through Silas's thoughts. One phone call was all it took.

"Was that really necessary?" Clarence threw a glance over his shoulder.

A waitress approached, holding a pot in one hand a mug in the other. "Coffee, Detective?" She waved the cup in Silas's direction.

"Yes, please." Silas beckoned. Steam rolled from the black liquid.

"Would you like a menu?"

"No thanks, I won't be staying long. But I will place an order to go." He reeled off Hadley's request. "Have the cook go ahead and start it now. I'll pick it up at the register on my way out."

On swollen ankles, the waitress shuffled off to the next table. He'd be sure and leave her a hefty tip. Her interruption had reduced the tension in the air.

"I'll get right to the point." Clarence refreshed his tea from a white ceramic pot. "You've seen the news. Girls not much younger than your niece Lila are missing. The most recent last night. Families in this city are terrorized. The FBI is involved, but we need to improve the local leadership."

Silas blew on the hot coffee. Rose and her family were in a safe house. Access to their incident file limited to a "need to know" basis. There was a slim chance the commissioner wasn't aware of Silas's late-night motorcycle ride—yet.

"Go ahead," he said.

Clarence studied his hands. When he started talking, it took less than thirty seconds to blow Silas's mind. The commissioner was clearly a desperate man. The knowledge was more than a little gratifying. But the proposal on the table smelled rotten.

"Not interested," Silas forced a calm reply. "And using Lila as a guilt tactic is in poor taste, even for you." The index finger of his prosthetic hand clicked against the Formica between them. "In case you didn't know, I have ten active murders in the homicide unit." Heat rose in his chest. "And—you—you don't even like me. You've tried to have me arrested for aiding and abetting a serial killer. Before that, you deemed the loss of my hand a department embarrassment. Special task force—humph. Don't try to kid me with your *special* offers." He glared at Clarence. "Besides, I've scheduled vacation."

It was clear to Silas now. The commissioner wanted three things, the journalists off his back, a token for the mayor, and a person to blame. No way that trifecta was happening. Rochester should know better. The mayor wasn't like the old car washes that once took tokens, and Silas wasn't dumb enough to be a scapegoat. Journalists were unpredictable, that chip would fall where it fell.

Silas scraped back his chair. "Are we done here?"

Rochester glared. "Not even close."

CHAPTER THIRTEEN

Mourning doves cooed from the crooked spine of the garage roof. Walter enjoyed the peaceful sound. He hurried to roll up the tattered sleeping bag then slung it over his shoulder. He'd slept later than usual. Another night of unwelcome traffic had disturbed his routine. The kids would think he wasn't coming. Later today, he would find a safer place to camp. Moisture dampened his eyes. His spot behind the old house had been a good laydown. Now the property gave off evil vibes. For weeks now, he thought he was being followed.

A sharp pain gripped his spine. He winced. Damn shrapnel never stopped moving. An airport metal detector would overload if he tried to pass through. No matter, he wasn't a traveling man, anyway. Two tours in Vietnam took that need right out of his system. Loud noises and crowds left him a tangled-up mess of nerves. He'd worked once and been successful too. Now he mostly kept to himself.

Or at least he had, until those two pitiful kids showed up.

That day, God offered Walter a chance for redemption, and he accepted. Walter's own kids didn't even know who he was. He was glad for that, considering what he'd done. Years earlier, he would visit their neighborhood to keep up. For a moment he tried to recall where they lived. He shook his head. Time took that from him too. Time and Agent Orange.

Once, he'd been arrested by Kansas City's finest for stalking his own kids. At the time, he didn't even know what the term *stalker* meant. The cops released him after four hours in the slammer. Something about Walter being a war hero. True, he'd received medals, but he damn sure wasn't no hero. Heroes slept in beds with white crosses for headboards.

Helping that little girl and her brother, though, that had blown fresh air into his lungs for the first time in years. He didn't have many days left. For some reason, those two made him want to make amends.

Walter cocked his head and listened for the wing whistle of the mourning doves. No whistle, no intruders. Withdrawing a worn wallet from an inside coat pocket, he opened it, slow. A yellowed plastic cover protected the photo. The smiling faces made him ache with regret. How many years had it been since he'd seen them?

Agent Orange was hammering nails in his coffin at a thunderous pace. Impending death had a way of giving a person clarity. The lawyer already knew Walter's burial plans, and after today he'd know what to do with Walter's money too. He pulled a folded index card from next to a twenty-dollar bill.

He squinted. Yes, he'd written the names of his two new friends and those of his children.

CHAPTER FOURTEEN

Across from Silas, Clarence Rochester's eyes bore the gleam of a shark. "It's my job to protect this city, detective. I won't apologize for asking the tough questions." Clarence threaded his fingers together in a grip that turned his knuckles white. "Make no mistake, the board wants this to be your choice."

"And by you taking this position, it will be a positive political move. You've helped a person with a handicap." Silas sneered. "That's quite a reversal from your stance a few short years ago."

"All I'm saying is, don't put your career in jeopardy."

A poorly veiled threat underscored the last sentence. "What's that supposed to mean? Will you try to get the board to fire me if I don't accept?" Silas bared his teeth in a taunting grin. "Go ahead, see how far that gets you."

Rochester's nostrils flared. "Silas, can't we put the past to rest?" He reached across the table and placed a hand on Silas's arm. To a passerby, the two men were close friends.

Silas shrugged away the offending touch. "I'd like to, Clarence, but I don't trust you. What happened to you, anyway? You used to be a decent guy. I respected you. Now I'll bet your own wife doesn't turn her back on you."

Clarence's mouth went tight. "My family is none of your concern. I have my problems. You have yours. Maybe I've given you more credit than you deserve." Scorn clung to his words. "I thought you were smart enough to know, heading up this task force *could* make you a shoo-in for Chief of Police."

Strong emphasis rode the word *could*. "Clarence. Not sure if you intended that as a threat or a bribe. Either way, I'm not your man."

"Why are you being so blind?" His voice raised, Clarence glanced around as though hoping no one noticed. "This offer is a gesture of confidence. The mayor recognizes the board's actions toward you in the past were—umm—somewhat shortsighted. What will you say when your bullheaded thinking costs one of these girls her life? Or am I to think you support hate crimes against certain groups?" Rochester folded his arms across his chest.

"Hate crimes?" Disbelief rolled off Silas in waves. He shoved himself from the chair, sending it clattering to the floor behind him. The table wobbled. Coffee and tea slopped from the cups and painted a blend of browns across the red.

The detective loomed over the board member. "I'm sorry these girls are Asian, but I'd be sorry no matter their ethnic background. Tell the mayor you've got a problem. You've waited too long." Behind the two men, conversations faltered. Silas bent close to Clarence's face. "Statistics say the victims are already dead. You're hunting for a fool to absorb the blame when the bodies are found. Well thanks, but no thanks."

He turned his back and stalked out, ignoring the customers' wide-eyed stares. The tattooed man's table was empty. Silas expected those two men planned a surprise for him in the parking lot.

Outside, the heat and blinding sun struck the detective in the face. He shielded his eyes. No sign of trouble. The police cruiser was parked under a line of elm trees, the engine idling. His partner was focused on a chattering squirrel. Silas cringed at the idea of a passerby snapping a cellphone photo. The department took enough grief without being criticized for animal watching.

Silas stepped off the sidewalk. A white Toyota rolled toward him. He lengthened his stride. From the corner of his eye, he saw an arm covered in tattoos. A muted clunk, a beer bottle at his feet and Silas went down as a blur of white rushed by.

Doors slammed. Feet pounded against the concrete. The scent of stale garlic swooped up Silas's nose. Ned, the owner of The Burger Nest, poked his head in the detective's line of vision.

"You alright, man?"

"Yeah. Yeah." Silas struggled to his feet, sucking air, and holding his head.

"Do all cops have this many enemies?" Ned put out a steadying hand.

"I hope not." Silas gave the bump a tentative touch. "I'm going to have a monster headache that's for sure."

"What the hell happened?" Hadley panted to a stop by Silas's side. "I heard a car tearing out of the parking lot then you were on the ground."

"A gent with serpent tattoos doesn't like me. Sound familiar?"

A frown crawled between Hadley's brows. "Thought Wade Rowland was in prison."

"Guess not."

"Amazing how fast five years goes by. Would be nice to oblige him with a go back to jail free card. I'll put out the net."

"Rowland had a buddy with him in the Berger Nest. My bet he is the driver."

Hadley peered at Silas's head. "Don't think you need an ambulance. I'll see if anyone inside can identify Rowland's wheel man."

Silas waved him on his way.

"You're not bleeding." Ned helped him to his feet. "But you've got a lump big as an egg."

"Aren't you going to thank me for keeping the action outside?" A shot of sarcasm was all Silas could muster to cover his embarrassment.

"Why? You make good on the damages. Every few months, I get new pieces of furniture. How can I complain?" Ned slapped Silas on the back. "I can tell you're all right, even though you've used up another one of your nine lives. I've got to get back inside. Glad you're okay."

Silas wobbled over to the cruiser. The *Hot Tamale* hostess appeared with a bag of crushed ice. After twenty minutes, another officer arrived and took over for Hadley.

"Nothing on the driver," Hadley said, as he climbed in with Silas. "The waitress had already cleared the table, so no prints." Hadley dropped a grease-stained white bag on the console. "You forgot my breakfast." He grinned. "I'll give you a break since you were distracted." Hadley's face turned serious. "You think Clarence put the ex-con up to this?"

Silas considered the question. "Clarence was pissed, but he didn't have time to take that kind of action." He rehashed the scene for Hadley. The retelling didn't make it prettier. "Wade Rowland took offense at my remarks."

"You think? That's becoming a pattern in case you hadn't noticed."

Silas had noticed. He fastened his seat belt, saying nothing.

"How would Wade even know Clarence?" Hadley put the Dodge Charger in gear, steered around potholes, and drove into the street.

"Not hard to meet a guy like Wade if a person needs dirty work done. I interrupted a conversation that wasn't casual, that's for sure."

"Wade will be glad to share his secrets when we arrest him. What did Clarence want with you?"

Silas explained the commissioner's offer. "After what he's tried to do to me in the past, he must think I've gone soft in the head to even consider an offer from him."

"I have to say, your shrink would agree. Oops, I forgot. You're abstaining. But I did think you aspired to be Chief."

"Not anymore. I don't even know what I'm doing in homicide." Silas glanced out the window as the cruiser passed Kaufman Stadium. He'd watched his favorite team win the AFC championship twice from one of those red seats. That was right before he'd screwed up, big time.

"Then get out."

Silas's jaw went slack. "What?"

"My friend, letting that punk Wade Rowland take you out with a beer bottle is not your style." Hadley flipped the turn signal and changed lanes. "You're acting.

"Acting?"

"Yeah, like you want to get yourself killed."

"Maybe I'll win an Oscar," Silas said sourly.

Hadley wrinkled his nose. "Don't give me that crap."

"I'm not an idiot. I know I'm not safe to work with."

"More crap."

"And I need to shovel through it. I'm taking a few days off to think about how to do that."

"What, and mope around, The House of Audrey?"

"Damn man, ease up. Sydney and I are going to Branson."

Hadley nodded approval. "Now that is a commendable idea. When?"

"You're worse than a nagging old woman. I'm meeting Josie at the women's shelter, and then I'm checking to make sure Lila is okay. We'll leave in a day or two."

"What's wrong with Lila?"

"Elizabeth's birthday is coming up. Lila visits the grave on that day. I offered to go with her, but you know Lila, she does life her way."

"Yeah. She does do that."

Silas fell quiet thinking of the woman he also grieved.

Police Chief Elizabeth Cartwright—alias serial killer.

Would he ever be free of the guilt for the lives lost at the hands of Elizabeth? He forced his thoughts back to Lila. "The new children's shelter is Lila's elixir. Bringing that old house back from the dead keeps her focused on the future."

"Change can do that," Hadley said. "Maybe while you're in Branson you might reconsider Clarence's offer."

"No way."

"Why not? Lila has the instincts of a profiler. She told me she's checking out the abductions in her spare time. She's got Grandpa Charlie involved, too. With you in charge of the investigation, and Lila connecting the dots—voila. Problems of the universe solved." A mile long grin spread across Hadley's face.

"Forget it. My dad and Lila in this equation doesn't make Clarence's offer more inviting."

The cruiser slid through traffic and into the tunnel leading to I-35. Vehicle noise boom-a-ranged from metal and concrete walls at a maddening level. Hadley twirled the steering wheel and exited at Twelfth Street. To Silas's right, the gold leaf cupola of the Cathedral of the Immaculate Conception taunted him with its shiny optimism.

"Well at least you're taking a break," Hadley said. "Don't worry about a thing here. I'll make sure Lila's all right while you and your love are savoring country music—Ozark style." Hadley cleared his throat. "Umm, there is one more thing."

"What's that?"

"Do we need to have the safe-sex talk?"

Silas's eyebrows shot up. "With Lila?"

"No dummy, with you."

"Barker, you're disgusting."

"Maybe a little." Hadley chuckled.

A red light brought Hadley's foot to the brake and the cruiser rolled to a stop. He turned serious. "You do know you shouldn't stop the counseling?"

"She wanted me to take anti-depressants and anxiety drugs." Silas's guttural admission was acid in his throat.

"Oh, so that's it. Pride." Hadley's nostrils flared. "What's the big deal? Think it will hurt your sex life? You know better than anybody, half the department takes something these days. What makes you tougher than them?"

"Now you're a therapist?"

"No Silas. I'm your friend. You're not a shouter and you're not an internalist either, but your moods are swinging worse than a woman in menopause. And you can't help yourself any more than she can. Taking a break is great, but dammit, man listen to your doctor."

"If I reconsider, will you calm down?"

Hadley gave him the side-eye.

Silas changed the subject. "Today's meeting with the commissioner was odd. I haven't been face-to-face with him for a while, but the conversation had a desperate quality. Like his back was against a wall. City politics can be brutal, but that's never bothered Clarence before."

"If you're sorry for him, why didn't you take him up on his offer? Help him out."

A storm of reasons thundered through Silas's mind. The one bigger than all the others he couldn't admit, even to his best friend. He came back with a smart remark instead. "I'd have separation anxiety if I didn't see you every day."

"Ha." Hadley pulled to a stop in front of The House of Audrey. "I've seen you screwed up before, my brother, but what happened because of Elizabeth has you in a strangle hold. For now, Sydney is your best hope. Take care of you and your lady."

"Count on it." Silas climbed from the cruiser a secret truth bludgeoning his heart. The man others looked to for support feared failing another human being the way he'd failed Elizabeth Cartwright and her victims.

This detective had lost the one thing a cop couldn't afford to lose—trust in himself.

CHAPTER FIFTEEN

L eah is back. She sits outside the ethereal glow of the LCD screen. "I told you not to leave that girl in the park," she complains. "Now see what she's done."

Her condemnation grinds against my bones.

"So I have a heart. What about it?" I lash out. Pressure builds inside my skull. I wish for an upper, but resist. I won't take one in front of Leah. "Control my emotions, that's what you're thinking isn't it? Remember this, I'm the one with connections. I'm the one who knows what the cops are doing. You abandoned me." I bite my tongue, before I say something I can't take back.

"We could have both been arrested," she whispers, so low it could be imagined. "There was Mary to think about."

My temples throb. "Trust me, Rose is not a problem, and I've got Mary's well-being covered."

"If you say so," she mutters.

After a while, I cool off. "I've made progress on the Dark Web. Want to see?"

She nods.

The chair squeaks as I get comfortable. "Think of this as an onion. There are layers and layers of encryption. I had to use a special browser to peel back the skins." I finish explaining how the trafficking site works as I tap the computer keys. My wrist is almost healed, but still a bit stiff. "This is an absurd idea, but the perfect supply and demand chain was a mere finger stroke away. No more leaving girls on a park bench for a couple hundred bucks."

Her silence worries me. I want her on board. "What do you think?"

Her words are soft-spoken, but I'm sure she responds, "Genius."

"Watch this." The site comes up. A collage of photos spirals in and out. Guitars scream and drums pound. Leah leans in. "The process is designed to protect user identity," I explain. "People all over the world participate." Then, I show a photo of a person minus their head.

Leah gasps.

"That's what happens if terms of the contract are not met. Don't worry. I've got everything under control." The music reaches a crescendo then falls silent. I touch a finger to my lips. "The auction is about to begin." One image moves to the center of the screen. My mouth goes dry. I recognize the girl as one of ours.

The bidding starts low at one-thousand dollars. Seconds drag by. Then a feeding frenzy explodes. Numbers flash across the top of the screen at lightning speed. Five, ten, fifteen, twenty, twenty-five. SOLD. The second girl brings forty thousand and the third sixty. The screen goes dark. I lunge to my feet. "Unbelievable." My shout bounces off the walls. Not the first of our girls I've seen sell, but the result still leaves me in a state of amazement.

"Impressive," Leah says.

I gloat a little. Then, I turn off the computer and go to the laptop used only for the offshore account. "I've been busy while you were gone." I wave her over.

She studies the screen. Her head shakes back and forth. She backs up.

Her reaction surprises me. We've come too far for her to gain a conscience now. I hasten to reassure her. "Here's the way to think about this. These are streetwalkers. We're doing the community a favor by relocating them. These girls don't care about their work zip code." I smile reassuringly. "I promise, we won't do this long. Just until we have enough money to take care of Mary."

At last, she nods. "Good."

I release pent-up air. Leah can't know the secrets I keep. She won't understand. The buyers on the dark web don't want street walkers. The product they demand is fresh faced and innocent.

High quality girls bring a steeper price. Soon, we'll have enough money to leave the country. Right after a special reunion. The kind reserved for family.

CHAPTER SIXTEEN

"Hello. Anyone home?"

Lila recognized Silas's voice coming from downstairs. It was late afternoon, and she hadn't been out of the house all day.

"Up here." Lila ran to bend over the railing. "Wait till you see what Josie created." She waited for her uncle, noticing a slowness in his step and lines of fatigue etched across his face. Silas was only forty, but he moved like a man twenty years older. "Hey. What've you been up to? Solved any murders today?"

"Nope." He paused on the steps to touch the bullet hole in the walnut banister, or was he covering a need to rest? "I did have an interesting meeting with Clarence Rochester."

He joined Lila on the landing. The bruise on his head hadn't been there yesterday. "What happened here?" She leaned in for a closer examination.

"I ran into a door."

"Guess you didn't see a doctor?"

"Nope. But I did get a job offer."

Her uncle discouraged questions about his injuries. Lila allowed him his pride and listened to the bizarre story.

"I politely declined," he said.

Lila gave him the side eye. "Sure, you did. I bet you told him to stick it where the sun don't shine. Although, when you hear what Grandpa Charlie and I uncovered about the abductions, you may wish you'd accepted."

"I doubt it."

"Did you know there was another teenager taken last night?"

"Rochester informed me."

"Then he knows these aren't hate crimes. The missing girls have all been Asian. At least those that have been reported. Vietnamese mostly. Like Rose." Lila paused for effect. "But not now. The last victims have all been white. That detail isn't even in the news. But you know as well as I do, Clarence Rochester is privy to all the latest info." She paused, expecting at least a raised eyebrow. More questions. Something.

"He didn't mention it."

Worry shivered through Lila's brain. She pretended not to hear the disturbing note of disinterest. "There's more. The department checked out local sex offenders. That was a long shot anyway. Sex offenders don't usually take more than one or two at a time. Since no bodies have turned up either, we placed hate crimes at the bottom of the list of motives too. I've been suspicious of a child trafficking operation. Now I'm convinced."

She paused. Here was where Silas would drop a word of encouragement, constructive criticism, even offer a cop joke. He didn't even shift positions just stared over the railing. He'd shut down.

"We used Bertha's AI and dug into the dark web, working from the premise the missing girls are sold out of Kansas City. Don't ask me how, but between Grandpa and Big Bertha, they found a trail. Silas, you've got to shut these predators down."

"Lila, I'm in homicide."

"Are you being serious, right now? You said that like you were deciding on steak or fish for supper."

"I take care of my own business. Give the kidnapping info to Archie.

The FBI is better equipped."

"Right. That's why we've been assigned to them for the last five years. And for your information, I already sent all of Bertha's data to Archie."

"Good girl."

Lila was speechless. Had somebody stolen Silas Albert and replaced him with a zombie? She considered a different tactic.

Lila was determined to make the children's shelter successful, but Silas would know if its existence was threatened. "Did you know there's a new sports complex in Kansas City's future?"

"Maybe ten years down the road."

"Maybe sooner. I heard a speculator is buying up property around here. I had Bertha do a little investigating."

"And?"

"Bertha checked real estate transactions within a ten-block area of The Elle. Found over twenty sales recorded in the last six months." She waited for Silas to respond, show an interest—something. "To the same buyer. That takes bucks."

He blinked. "The city could be involved."

"Through a shell corporation?" Lila frowned. "Don't you think it's odd no one has approached me?"

"Not if it's illegal. You are well known and connected to the police." Silas drummed his fingers on the railing. "Are the purchased lots next to each other?"

"Mostly. These properties are run down and would have sold cheap. But twenty is a drop in the bucket compared to the needs of a project of this magnitude. Even a small-time buyer in on the ground floor would make millions."

"Let's not talk about crime. I came by to tell you Sydney and I are going to Branson for a few days."

Lila sighed. He had deftly changed the subject. "What did she do, threaten you?"

Silas shrugged. "Thank God I have Sydney in my life. At least she has patience. You should take lessons. You should also lock the door when you're here alone."

"You worry too much." Lila stood on her tiptoes and kissed her uncle's cheek. "Better check the weather before you go. I heard there's a major storm on the way."

"You sound like, Grandma."

"Ha. Ha. Tell me all the things you plan to do. Are you going to stop at DeShawn and Ada's place?" She didn't burden him with Josie's behavior from earlier in the day. It was up to her to make her peace with the Blackbird on her own. Her failed rescue of Elsa and Gordy wasn't going to be part of the conversation either. She didn't want Silas to think she couldn't do her job. The item she kept the tightest lid on was her visit from, Woody Mendez. Her conscience twinged. It wasn't a habit to keep so many secrets from Silas.

As Silas talked about the upcoming trip, Lila was happy to see his features brighten. Three days alone with Sydney would soothe his battered soul. "Well come look," she invited. "I want to get you in a good mood before you are off on your wild adventure. Josie has created the eighth wonder of the world with paint."

She led Silas from room to room, hoping the renovation progress boosted his spirits. They paused, as Silas studied Josie's mural. A daughter couldn't be closer to a biological father than Lila was to Silas, and she knew big trouble rode her uncle's back. She'd witnessed similar signals from traumatized women. He needed help, but Silas was one to give not receive.

"Josie did an amazing job and so have you." Silas squeezed her shoulder.

"Thanks." Lila glowed. "The Blackbirds worked together. Josie and Janelle really busted their butts. I don't know how I'll repay them."

She talked to Silas over her shoulder, as he followed her to the kitchen.

"Helping children will be payment enough for those two. The Blackbirds need another team leader. Have you decided who it will be?"

"Pretty much." Her answer was a bit evasive for a reason. She hadn't totally made up her mind, and he already had enough on his. "I'm thinking Josie is ready."

"It's your call. She's come a long way. I know the two of you have been cross ways of one another in the past. Are you on solid ground now?" He studied her face.

Lila fiddled with a strand of hair. Silas knew his Blackbirds well. "We're good. Our goals are the same. She's impatient with me sometimes, but I guess that comes with the territory. She's sure pumped up about those new night goggles."

"Archie said we can keep the pair she tested."

"She'll appreciate that." It aggravated Lila that Silas was more interested in Josie than he was in the kidnappings. Lila had wasted her time talking about insider land speculation. "Did you know she wants to get a cat like our Camellia for the shelter?"

"A one-eyed cat. Can't see it."

Lila grimaced. "So *not* funny. It's a fabulous idea. Cats are cuddly and comforting. When you brought Camellia home after my transplant, she was my best friend. She listened to all my troubles and never criticized me one time. Having only one eye made me love her more. These kids will need a friend who isn't picking their brain."

"Okay. Okay. Have Josie get the cat, but you better draw the line at a pony." Then his speech took on a more serious tone. "I'm proud of you, Lila. You're bringing out the best in your team."

Her team.

The shadow of a grimace passed over Silas's face. The lighthearted banter of the last few minutes disappeared. "Be sure and let Grandma know when you plan to spend the night here. You're all grown up and all, but she still worries about your safety and your health. I guess you know Grandpa has a dual purpose in helping you work the abductions. He also wants to protect you."

"I know. He asked me to do an extra session of martial arts." Lila stepped into a defensive stance, elbows askew, arms protecting her chest. She hoped for a return of Silas's smile, but it didn't happen. She slung her arms to her sides. "I hope you're not using the abductions as an excuse to have one of your cop buddies check on me all the time."

"Would I do that?" He batted his eyes innocently. "Regardless, I'm only a phone call away—excuse me—a text away."

"I'm not texting you. And don't be checking on me every hour either." She put her hands on her hips. "I want you to have fun. You worry about me too much."

"Well, I can't text you anyway. I ruined my phone today."

"Bummer. But no worries, I've got this place under control. And I do know who to call if I need help, and it's not my grandparents. They are going out of town too, in case you forgot. They would be a close second, anyway." She winked mysteriously.

Silas's one eyebrow shot up. "Who?"

"Ohhh, I'd call Officer Mendez. I'm sure he would race to my aid." Lila forced a straight face, testing the ice. Woody needed to be a topic of conversation sooner or later.

A muscle twitched along Silas's jaw. "Mendez is not the best option. I'd recommend Hadley. He's got more pull. But if you get another traffic ticket, you're on your own." A silent moment passed between them. "I trust you to do the right thing."

Silas's words had the effect of cold water on a pair of mating cats. All intriguing thoughts of Woody Mendez evaporated. But she wasn't about to let Silas know. "Oh my God, you're trying to guilt trip me." She clamped her head in her hands, pretending a proper level of aggravation. "Well, it worked. Don't worry. If I get in trouble, I'll call Hadley."

"A much better choice," Silas agreed. "One I hope you don't have to make."

"Me too. Give Sydney a hug for me and promise you'll try to have fun." Lila followed him outside, blowing a kiss as he climbed aboard the Harley. Apparently, for Silas, crime didn't have the appeal it once did.

But mention Woody Mendez and Silas's attention was razor focused.

CHAPTER SEVENTEEN

Silas waved to Lila and pointed the Harley down the road. Wind whipped his cheeks and blended the surroundings into the background. From the seat of the motorcycle, the world resembled an I-MAX vision. He was on the inside with no true destination, the bike his medium for meditation. This time, he hoped to figure out how to protect his niece from a broken heart. A job not listed under responsibilities of a guardian.

Helping Lila develop toughness and teaching her to think for herself had been no problem. He'd been sorry only once or twice. Then he'd trained her to be a Blackbird, and now she was stepping out on her own. He was determined to give her the responsibility and trust she deserved, but his mind revolted at her mention of Woody Mendez.

The problem wasn't with Woody as a cop, or his Mexican heritage. The young man had all the makings of a valuable homicide detective. Silas even liked the guy. But Woody had a reputation as a *Romeo*.

Lila was no help either. She pretended to tease him about Mendez, but her obvious intent was to measure the level of Silas's resistance. Right now, it was damn high. But doubt sidled right along beside his resolve. Lila needed to know Woody's history, but if Silas stepped over the line between guidance and interference Lila would defy him for sure. The situation made his head hurt.

Someone needed to talk to her. Not the best discussion for a grandma to have with Lila, and this kind of girl talk wasn't meant to be navigated by men.

That's it.

The answer was so simple it made him giddy. He'd ask someone he and Lila both trusted. The list was short. Janelle, Josie, or Sydney. Lila might consider Janelle too grandmotherly and Josie too condescending. But Sydney—Sydney was perfect. Beautiful, smart, tactful, and Lila respected her. Silas grinned into the wind. Problem solved. A woman-to-woman discussion was what his niece needed, and Sydney fit the textbook definition to a T.

Silas rolled through the gates of Columbus Park, the turns in the road a vague memory. He drove slow whistling a little tune. A far different approach to his last visit when he rescued Rose.

There was history here. In the mid-seventies, after the Fall of Saigon five thousand Asian refugees started life over in Columbus Park. The neighborhood still included a tight knit population of Vietnamese Americans. One of which was Clarence Rochester.

He rode on. A hint of incense teased the air. Olive-skinned children kicked at a ball in the center of the street. Years earlier, when police business brought him here, the kids stared in shy curiosity. Now there was a wariness in their dark eyes. Times had changed. The shadow of hate crimes, drugs, and gang influence hung over this neighborhood too. The boys parted, allowing the Harley passage but followed along on either side. Silas saw a face he knew. He pulled in, stopped, and pulled off his helmet.

"Cop," one boy said.

"Shut up," another ordered. "You'll get us in trouble."

"You shut up. See that fake hand. Bad ass." The last word hissed between white teeth. "He's a cop, but he's no trouble for us. That's Silas Albert. I know him." The boy puffed out his chest. "He stopped a bunch of guys from beating up my grandpa. There were six of them.

He never pulled his gun."

Silas's recollection was slightly different. There'd only been four. But what boy doesn't embellish a fight scene to impress his friends?

"Hey there, Jay." Silas waved. "How's your grandpa?"

Jay shook his head. "He doesn't get out much anymore."

"Tell him I'll stop by and visit soon."

"Okay."

"Bet you can't pop a wheelie," another boy yelled.

"Pop a wheelie. Pop a wheelie. Do it. Do it." A chant started slow, then rose in volume.

Silas's ego stirred. "Hold this," he said, handing Jay the helmet. He saluted with his prosthetic, started the engine, cranked the gas, and engaged the clutch. The rear tire grabbed pavement, the front end lifted, and the bike rolled down the street on one wheel. The kids raced alongside. Delighted cheers rose above the roar. Gravity brought the bike horizontal, and Silas braked.

"Can I have a ride?" Jay asked.

"Me too."

Silas hesitated.

I really shouldn't.

It's only a little thing.

I don't have parental consent.

What the hell?

"Here put this on."He pulled the extra helmet from the backrest and handed it to Jay then tugged the other one on. He showed the boy how to use the built-in intercom.

"Cool." Jay swung on behind.

Another thought had added weight to Silas's decision. Living in the neighborhood, Jay was a wealth of information. He could save Silas time. Silas raced the engine to spark a little envy in the other kids, then burned rubber. At the first corner he slowed and spoke into the intercom. "Guess you know just about everyone within a couple of blocks."

"Yep. Lived here since I was born."

"How about Clarence Rochester? You know him?"

The boy hesitated. "I know him."

"Is he a good guy?"

"Guess so. I used to see him walking around the block with his wife. He bought us kids popsickles off the ice cream truck."

Silas was having a hard time imagining Clarence sparing a minute or a dime on a child. "Do the Rochesters seem to get along?"

Jay was quiet for a second. "They don't talk bad to each other. Never smile either. But I haven't seen them together since last summer. Is he in trouble?"

"I hope not." Silas motored around the corner and made a right on to the commissioner's street.

"He lives right there." Jay pointed.

Silas slowed the Harley, taking note of the yard. An American flag drooped from a tall flagpole, and tired potted petunias resisted the heat in a panorama of purples and pinks. A silver BMW sat in the drive. A sticker on the rear bumper flashed Support Kansas City Police Commissioners. Silas barely noticed. He zeroed in on the Corvette Stingray parked next door. "Sharp car."

"Oh yeah. Belongs to Rebecca Haze. She's a reporter on Channel Fourteen. Man, does she drive a sweet ride—or what? Sebring orange. Retractable hardtop. 495 horsepower mid-engine configuration. Eight speed dual clutch transmission." Jay reeled off details in a fashion that would put a good car salesman to shame.

Silas drove around the corner and stopped, pretending to adjust the mirrors. Rebecca Haze, right next door to, Clarence Rochester. Interesting coincidence, that.

"Man, this helmet is dope. Can you play music through these

speakers too?" Jay interrupted the detective's thoughts.

"Sure. I download a playlist to my phone and connect through the bike's radio."

"Wow. I need one of these things. Your Harley's cool too, but to be honest, I like Rebecca's Stingray better."

Silas chuckled. "A man likes, what a man likes. I respect that. You know enough to sell Corvettes." Silas imagined Jay's chest puffing with pride. "How'd you learn so much?"

"Rebecca and me, we're friends. Sometimes when Becca's sad, she takes me for a ride. I checked out the car on Mom's computer. It gives us something to talk about."

From what Silas knew about the reporter, the story didn't fit. Jay loved to impress, and he'd already lied about the incident with his grandpa. As far as Silas was concerned, Rebecca was mad not sad.

Before he agreed to doing the documentary, he really should check her background. In the meantime, Silas would bet fifty dollars the boy could tell him why a redheaded white woman was in a Vietnamese community. "Smooth. How'd you and Rebecca get to be friends?"

"She's lived here all her life, same as me. That's her mom's house, where she grew up. Her mom's in a nursing home now."

Silas mulled that over. No wonder she'd been so chummy with Clarence Rochester. They could trade yellow journalism over the back fence. He put the Harley in gear and drove on down the street. Another thought popped up. "But she's not Vietnamese?"

Jay laughed. "Yes, she is. She may have a red-headed white daddy, but her momma looks like me. My mom says it don't matter the color of your hair or skin. Our heritage is in our blood."

"Your mom's a smart lady."

"Mom and Becca've been besties since high school. They hung around with Clarence's daughter too. Even with she moved away, they still visited Mrs. Rochester. Becca and Mom were both real sad about what happened to their friend."

"What happened?"

"You're kidding, right?"

Goosebumps prickled Silas's skin. "She died?"

"Yep."

Silas gulped. "Sorry."

"That's okay. You didn't know."

"Was that about the same time Clarence and his wife stopped taking walks?"

"Hmm. It might have been. Mom don't hang out with Rebecca anymore, and she quit visiting the Rochesters. Rebecca left for a while, too. When I asked Mom why, she said it was none of my business. I'm smart enough to know when to let a thing go."

"I'll bet you are." Silas's brain whirled. Odd. Two women had abandoned the mother of their best friend and each other. The Vietnamese culture supported caring, not indifference. But he knew all too well, grief did terrible things to a person, split families, and drove friends apart. "Anything bad go on around here?"

"Some. Gangs. Drugs. Two or three girls ran off a while back. They'll turn up one of these days. Just wanted attention if you asked me."

Silas cringed. When Rose was abducted, she wasn't seeking attention. "What does your mom say about the missing girls?"

"Not much. But she won't let me go to the Quick Stop by myself anymore."

"Hope she doesn't call the cops on me."

Jay snickered. "She wouldn't do that. She knows you helped Grandpa."

Silas stopped the Harley in front of the other kids.

Jay crawled off. "Thanks for the ride." He removed his helmet and handed it to Silas.

"Tell your grandpa I'll stop by soon."

One by one, Silas hauled kids to the end of the block and back, while he mulled over what he'd learned from Jay. When the last passenger crawled down, Silas thought he understood what had changed Clarence Rochester. The loss of a daughter would leave a void, a festering open wound.

For Silas, it wasn't beyond the realm of possibility for Clarence to soothe his grief with power and money.

Embezzlement would fit in that picture too.

CHAPTER EIGHTEEN

Silas stood at Sydney's front door, holding a box of Pappy's oven-roasted pizza. He didn't use his key but out of courtesy rang the doorbell. The sight of her through the window made life worthwhile. He loved her, and he needed to say the words more often. A missing eyebrow, and an artificial arm clearly said, no one knew what tomorrow might bring.

She opened the door dressed in a yellow t-shirt knotted at the waist and white jeans, tight, and rolled up just enough to showcase a slim sexy ankle.

"Hey."

"Hey yourself." He handed her the pizza and followed her to the kitchen. "Hope you have a beer or two. It's been a day."

Sydney set the box on the counter. "I tried to reach you earlier, my call went to voicemail. Nothing important. Just wanted to say hi."

"Really, I don't think it even pinged." He pulled the device from his pocket. "Damn." He showed Sydney the cracked glass and dark screen. "I hate to think of buying a new one. It'll take a week to upload all the Blackbird programs."

Sydney scrutinized the damaged cell then Silas's latest beauty mark. "What happened?" Worry tinged her dark eyes.

"Later. Lend me your phone and I'll let the world know I'm off-line."

Sydney handed over her unit. He made a half-dozen calls, and then tapped a general text to his detectives.

Sydney raised her eyebrows when he finished. "Eat, or talk?"

"Eat first then maybe a little time to wind down." He shot her a suggestive grin.

"Put a little ice on that bump. You have a fever."

He washed his hands at the sink, then unboxed the pizza, while Sydney set frosted mugs and Samuel Adams beers on the kitchen island. He rolled a can across his brow. "Got a fever all right."

He set the brew down and before she could protest, he pulled her into his arms. "I love you, Sydney Franco." He kissed her long and deep. The softest lips in the world kissed him back. The thought of the discussion they needed to have made him pull away. "My fever's dropped, let's eat."

"What? Hold on, while I refer to my medical books. A head injury is not known to affect a man's lust." Her eyes gleamed with mischief. "You wait. I will get even."

"That's exactly what I'm counting on." They settled on stools around the kitchen island. He handed her the first slice of pizza. "Are you all packed up?"

Sydney poured the beer. "All the necessities, right there." She pointed to a bag not much bigger than an over sized purse.

"Not many clothes can fit in that. Makes me anticipate this trip more and more."

"Humph."

The banter with Sydney relaxed him. "Went by to talk to Lila earlier," he said around a bite of pizza. "Remember, I told you we worked out a plan for when I'm not available and the Blackbirds need help?"

"Right. She would call Agent Hamilton."

"Now she wants to call Woody Mendez instead."

"But Woody doesn't even know about the Blackbirds." Sydney put down her food. "She wouldn't have told him, would she?"

"No. We're careful who's in our inner circle. Lila tried to pretend she was teasing, but it was more about preparing me for what I don't want to hear. I was hoping I could get you to talk to her. You know, warn her about his reputation."

The corners of Sydney's lips tilted. "She's twenty, Silas. He's cute, smart, and a challenge. Did you ever think she's looking for someone like you? Besides, why should I do this instead of you?"

He swirled a thumb through the condensation on the beer mug. "Women know how to talk to each other about this stuff. I'll just make her mad."

"Lila's quite aware of Woody's history, and your opinion needs an update." Sydney sounded put out. "He's a good man and from what Hadley says, he's settled down. He's not even seeing anyone."

How had Sydney become informed about Woody's goodness and Lila's awareness? Even Hadley was taking sides against him. "Guess I've been living in a cave?" Silas chomped into his pizza.

"Don't take it personal, my love. This won't be the last time she makes a choice you don't agree with. You should know that by now."

Silas thought about Lila's determination to visit Elizabeth Cartwright's grave. He hadn't wanted her to go alone, but she was. His gut twisted. Sydney was right. Doubting Lila's judgment was about him, not her. Supporting her was his job, and if she needed him, he'd be there. Broken hearts happened, and if Silas had to help his niece pick up the pieces of hers, he would do that, too. The choices belonged to Lila and no one else.

"When did you get so smart?" He wiped a smudge of sauce from Sydney's cheek. "You may have saved me from myself."

They finished their beer and food. Sydney brought out fresh, iced mugs and two more beers. She set them on the table and then straddled his lap. "Tell me about your interesting day."

"Are you kidding me?" He patted the stool next to him. "I can barely talk with you in this position, and I have something important to discuss."

Fine black eyebrows rushed together in a delicate frown. "Are you breaking up with me?"

"Not hardly." He lifted her from his lap, kissed her on the lips, and deposited her on the stool closest to him. A golden stream of Samuel Adams slid down the inside of Sydney's mug as Silas poured the beer and gathered his thoughts. Facing Sydney with his decision was more difficult than staring down head hunting commissioners. This time he wasn't sure where he stood. He poured his own beer and took his seat. "I'm getting out of police work."

Tears glistened in Sydney's eyes. "Is your mental well-being at stake?"

Heat rushed up his neck. Did everyone think he was going crazy?

"Don't act so surprised, Silas. I know you maybe—better than you know yourself. If leaving police work will help you heal, then I'm on your side." Her soft compassionate tone was one she used when preparing a person to identify the remains of a loved one.

Kind of fit, since leaving the force would be like a death to him. Or losing a limb. No, already done that.

"Have you given notice?"

"Wrote the letter this morning, and submitting it to the mayor when we get back from Branson." His chest heaved "I'll give them thirty days for transfer of duties if he wants, or I'm gone immediately."

"Why the mayor and not the Board of Commissioners?"

"The mayor's earned my respect, and I don't want Clarence Rochester to think he influenced my decision." Silas told her the details of what led up to the knot on his head and his visit to Columbus Park. "It's amazing what you can learn by taking a kid on a motorcycle ride. Did you know Rebecca Haze is half Vietnamese?"

Tiny lines formed between Sydney's brows. "I had no idea. She's a beautiful woman, but I would have credited the Irish for those red tresses. I figured since you're working on the documentary, you knew everything about her."

Silas kept his expression blank. "I haven't agreed to anything, yet. I'm more curious about why Clarence keeps his daughter's death a secret than I am Rebecca's ancestry. I've been in his office multiple times. He doesn't have a family picture of any kind on his desk. That's not normal."

Sydney sipped her beer. "A person should never have to bury their own child. A photo would be a painful reminder. Gives credence to why Clarence turned into a Grade A jerk."

Silas gnawed at the inside of his cheek. "I can see that. But Clarence was sure touchy about his family today. For some reason, he mentally buried his daughter long before her death last year."

"Maybe it's the way she died. Death by drugs or because of an STD could have dragged on forever and would be difficult for a parent. Do you know what happened?"

"I didn't even know Clarence's daughter was dead until an hour ago. Something about her death drove him to keep it secret. In any case, the daughter seems to be at the center of Clarence's bad attitude."

Silas gathered the pizza box and shoved it into the trash compactor. "Clarence and his troubles have taken us a bit off the subject of me turning in my badge."

Sydney's eyes narrowed. "Have you told your family or Hadley you're resigning?"

"Not yet. I planned to talk to you about this in Branson. But tonight seems better. Give you an opportunity to change your mind. If you don't want to go with me it's not a problem. Shirking my responsibilities..."

"Stop it. You're rambling." She pressed a finger to his lips. "Taking care of you, doesn't brand you a failure. However..."

He braced himself. One of the many traits he admired about Sydney, she never sugarcoated the truth.

"I'm not convinced you've bought into your own decision. Talk of weakness or dereliction of duty is not your MO. The Silas I know chose to use a prosthetic hand when it wasn't acceptable in police work, but it was right for him. He charged ahead and to hell with what anyone thought. If you were sure, you'd do that here too."

"That was different."

"Was it?"

"I'm not that guy anymore."

She rolled her eyes. "How long have you been a different person?"

"Don't be a smart ass."

"Sorry. But don't expect me to accept a reason that isn't logical. What changed this week that wasn't part of the job last month or last year?"

Silence hung between them thick and heavy. Silas's stomach churned. He didn't know how to explain the fear, depression, and anger. "I don't trust myself to do the job the way it needs to be done."

Sydney pursed her lips. "Have you considered taking a step back? Not three days in Branson, but a leave of absence."

He was confused. She said she was on his side, but it sure didn't sound that way. "You think I'm running away, don't you?"

A tinge of pink brightened her cheeks. "That's not what I said. This is your decision, but it's a life event too. Have you asked yourself what it will take to replace your adrenaline addiction? Three to six months of R&R would let you know if you can survive without the rush."

Silas swallowed hard. He wasn't dependent. Was he? Had he been so caught up in building a cross and nailing himself to it, that the rush was more important than the job. "What would I do for three months?"

A sly smile tinkered with the curve of her lips. "I could say, what are you going to do for the rest of your life after you resign, but here's another idea. I've accrued vacation. You have too. We could backpack into the wilds of Canada and expand our life of sin. Or, how about this? Rent a house on a remote Caribbean Island and swim naked in the ocean every day. Rejoin the defiant."

"Are you kidding? You wouldn't do either of those things." He studied her face, searching for a sign of mockery. *Damned, if she isn't serious.*

"Try me," she said.

"Would you marry me first?"

Sydney's eyes widened. "Yes. Umm—no. I mean yes when the time is right. I want a proper proposal, a white-gown wedding, and a honeymoon in a place we'll never forget."

"I was afraid of that." He tilted her chin, and kissed her first on one corner of her mouth and then the other. "At least Mom will be happy."

Sydney slid off the stool and cuddled in his lap. "So you will consider taking a leave of absence?"

"Your ideas are irresistible." He nibbled at her ear. "Maybe, just maybe, you do know me better than I know myself." This time he didn't hesitate. He lifted her in his arms and carried her down the hall.

A warm sigh brushed his neck. Was it his imagination, or was relief in that pent up release of breath?

CHAPTER NINETEEN

I leave Leah asleep, load supplies in the car, and drive to the collection depot. Beat up and road weary, the Mazda blends well with other vehicles when I park in front of a row of run-down houses. Boarded up windows, and rotting porches speak to the loss of hope here in the inner-city. I pull on a pair of gloves, grab the bag of supplies, and step out of the car. The cool dampness of early morning mists my skin.

I cross the street. Ahead, the uneven sidewalk is empty. Over my shoulder, no one follows. Street thugs don't get up at this early hour, and to the average observer, I'm another wretched street person in a poverty-stricken area of Kansas City.

A patchwork of dawn leaks through the tops of trees, but the abandoned house remains shrouded in gloom. The hole in the fence is barely visible. I push my upper body through the opening. The bag snags. My brain freezes. Then I realize it's only hung on the fence and yank it free. The scene resembles a dark comedy, where the crowd laughs at the actor's stupidity. No one is laughing here.

The yard is the same as when I was last here. I freeze at the sound of scuffing feet. Shadows move near the trunk of a tree, exposing the brim of a beat-up sombrero. A burst of air leaves my lungs. *It's only Walter.*

Walter peers at me from a distance disapproval in his stance, like I'm the one trespassing. Today, he seems suspicious, moving closer than usual. Even though my disguise fits the part, a true homeless person won't be fooled. My smell is too clean. I don't talk to myself, and I don't sort trash with my bare hands like so many.

Daylight has stirred his boldness. I'm not worried. I know he doesn't see well and could never identify the true me. But I am curious as to what he will do next.

I turn my back, slip the key into the padlock, and release the chain. Pushing the door open releases a stale musty odor. Inside, the deadbolt grates into place. I drop the bag and rush through the rooms and out a side door. Tall grass whispers against my ankles as I creep to the corner. A mass of climbing vines camouflages my vantage point.

Walter stands at the back door, an ear pressed against the wood. A red rose pokes jauntily from the sombrero's hatband. The dangling chain receives an inspection, and the knob a firm rattle. Incoherent mumbles drift across the yard. He bends down and plucks an object from the ground.

A bracelet.

My heart thrashes against my ribs.

He brings the piece of jewelry close to his face, turning it left then right. Charms glitter when a splinter of sunshine flashes against the metal. He removes a square of paper from his pocket, smooths it against the door, and dangles the bracelet alongside. The sombrero moves up and down, riding an almost imperceptible nod.

A web of cold spreads the length of my spine. I have to get that bracelet back.

Walter tucks his treasure and the square of paper into a pocket. If he gossips about his find every vagrant in the area will come nosing around. The police will take notice. In the blink of an eye, the revolver is in my hand. I won't let a vagrant ruin my life.

Don't kill him here.

My brain whirls. Each time I've watched Walter, something will catch his eye. He focuses then loses interest. He always moves on to stop at a trash bin two blocks west of the abandoned house. After that, he goes on to the soup kitchen. He's learned how to be first in line.

I sneak back and lock the side door, glide across the yard, and climb out through the hole in the fence. Minutes later I reach the old warehouse and hunch into the deepest shadows.

Time crawls. My joints ache. Doubt swirls in my head. Have I underestimated the level of Walter's curiosity? Is he at this second, breaking into the abandoned house? Has he found the padded room?

At last, my patience is rewarded by the shuffle of feet. I cock the gun. Walter stops at the dumpster. He pokes and prods, stirring the stench. A rat scurries for cover. I force myself to focus.

"Sorry, Walter."

Slipping from my hiding place and in the deep shadow of the vacant warehouse, I pull the trigger. Walter's sombrero tumbles to the side. He crumples to the asphalt in a heap that resembles a lump of dirty clothes.

"Nooo!"

I twist toward the scream. Two young faces stare, mouths gaping, eyes wide and round. I know them. I've observed them hanging around with Walter.

They've seen me kill their friend.

The girl shoves the little boy behind her. She backs up, forcing her brother to move with her and away from me. I take a step, gun in hand, but can't do it. She takes advantage, grabs the boy's arm, and drags him into the shadows. Again, I stop. Those two are street wise. I'll never catch them. I whirl back to Walter.

Blood leaks from beneath his head. For the first time, I notice his hair is red, streaked with white. I tear my gaze away, grab Walter's legs, and drag him to the back side of the dumpster. The thump of his head against the pavement echoes in my brain strong as the beat of the shaman's drum in the villages of Vietnam.

I kneel, jam my hand into one of Walter's pockets, and paw junk out onto the sidewalk. No bracelet. I lean in, dig deeper, come up with a wallet, and shake it open. A twenty-dollar bill follows a business card and a blue piece of paper to the ground.

My fingers fumble, and the billfold falls on top of the pile of trash. Two faces in a photo smile up at me. The world spins. I know the picture well. I snatch it up and yank at the yellowed plastic. Men's voices freeze me in place. I jump to my feet. The Mazda is nearby. I could be far away in minutes. Walter can't talk now, and those two kids will remember my disguise, not me.

But there is the contract.

My mental vision is splashed with the technicolor memory of the headless person. The broker will hunt me down if I don't deliver. I tuck the wallet into an inside pocket and rush into the shadows. When I emerge on the sidewalk moments later, the sun perches atop the horizontal ridgeline of nearby roofs.

It is the time of day the ragged homeless appear from their camps, bridges, and vacant buildings. One passes by without a glance, but a second stops and points a dirty finger at my face.

"Ketchup. You splattered the ketchup." The old man accuses. "Go wash your face." He giggles to himself and totters on.

Crazy old fool. Or does he mean...?

My gloved hands flail at my cheeks and forehead. The fingertips come away smeared in red and something else worse. I pull myself together and wipe my face with the bottom of my shirt. Tucking my head low, I force myself to walk. The rumble of an awakening city trails my steps. Sirens shrill in the distance, draw closer, and roll on to a more distant emergency. Gloom settles over me. *What else could happen?*

I shake it off and check the front door. The entry is secure, and I return to the side entrance, slip into the house, and gather the bag of supplies from where it was dropped earlier. In a bathroom off the hall, the marks of murder disappear down the drain. Walter was a demented old man. No one will care that he's gone. He shouldn't have been snooping around.

In the bag is a mask. I cover my face, draw my gun, and hurry to the bedroom with the supplies. An odor slides under the door. Seconds pass as I struggle with the lock and then shove the door open. The stench slams up my nose and crawls down my throat.

"Help. We're sick."

I breathe through my mouth and scan the room. Girls are curled into knots or stretched out flat on the floor. Yesterday, they complained of the stomachache. Today, the smells tell me my list of problems just grew.

What if they're contagious?

The contract can't be fulfilled with sick girls, and a delivery is scheduled for tomorrow. I toss the bag inside the room.

"There's food in there and medicine for vomiting and diarrhea. I'll be back tomorrow." I shut and lock the door pulling a flip-phone from my pocket.

"Hello," the lackey answers.

"Plans have changed. The package scheduled to fly to Chicago tomorrow is no longer available. Pick up the next on the list tonight. That bundle will fit nicely on the same flight. Deliver to the original address. Got it?"

"No problem."

"Call when the task is complete."

I disconnect. If these girls aren't better soon, I'll be forced to take action.

CHAPTER TWENTY

The next morning, Silas stopped at an AT&T store where he bought the latest in cell phone technology and a cheap old school flip phone. The thought of uploading programs from Big Bertha to regain Blackbird proficiency made his head hurt. He sent a text to Hadley noting the temporary number.

Minutes later, Silas stood outside the Quick Stop, listening to gas gurgle into the motorcycle's tank. He was still trying to absorb last night's discussion with Sydney. For the first time in months, he sensed a change to his outlook on life. Too bad he'd wasted all those counseling sessions. He valued psychiatric treatment, but until now guilt had blocked the way to accepting help for himself. Stubbornness, too, if he were honest.

The detective topped off the tank and went inside. He spent a minute searching for Sydney's favorite treat. When he found the fig cookies, he stepped in line to pay. A TV screen flickered behind the counter.

Bulletin. Homeless man found shot.

Silas's ears perked up. The local news anchor read off the name of a nearby street.

"Glad I'm carrying." A red-faced customer in front of Silas patted his hip holster.

Silas kept his face blank, personal opinions to himself, and focused on the breaking story. A red mane of hair blowing in the breeze made

Rebecca Haze easy to recognize. Her ivory skin bore no signs of the Vietnamese heritage Jay had mentioned.

The line of customers inched forward, breaking Silas's attention. When his focus returned to the screen, David Reagan, another reporter, identified himself. Where was Rebecca? She'd be furious if another journalist stole the limelight.

"According to officers on the scene, the shooting victim was found in this parking lot right behind me." The camera panned the area, catching the gleam of yellow crime tape. Silas recognized his partner, Hadley in the background. "Rebecca Haze, action reporter from our own station, discovered the body." The redhead stepped into the spotlight. "Tell us what happened?" David positioned the mic to pick up her words.

She dragged a hand across bone dry eyes. Manicured fingertips never came within an inch of her TV ready makeup. She'd happened on a murder. Was the woman really that cold? What was she even doing in such a bad part of town? One of these days chasing a story was going to get her killed.

"David, this is the worst experience of my career. I'm familiar with covering homicides, car accidents, and deadly fires, but this..." The camera zoomed in on Rebecca's face. Her lower lip trembled, and she batted her eyelashes. "I've never discovered a body before. The poor man."

Silas's rated her acting at an eight. He'd give her a nine if she cried, a ten if she brought tears to David Regan's eyes. The redhead deserved credit. She was an expert at working the TV audience.

"Do you know the victim?"

"Oh no. I'm working on a story related to the serial abductions that have plagued Kansas City. An anonymous caller claimed he had a tip and to meet here. The tipster couldn't have missed my car." The news camera swooped in for a closeup of the orange Corvette. "I'm sorry,

David, the police have asked that I not share specifics."

"Of course. Did you alert police in advance of your meeting?"

Tiny lines creased the smooth skin of Rebecca's forehead. Lips highlighted in coral tightened at the corners.

Of course, she didn't.

The redhead covered with a smile. "No need to waste their time until the information proved solid. As you know David, our leads are often from crackpots. I waited, but no one showed. I don't believe in karma, but the signage on this warehouse may be the last thing this poor man saw." She pointed and the camera focused.

Abernathy Casket Company.

Well, that was over the top.

"I almost tripped over the victim. There was no doubt the man was dead. Not wanting to contaminate the scene, I ran to my vehicle and called police."

"Rebecca, do the police have reason to believe the anonymous call and the murder are connected?"

"I'd rather not speculate. But David, I am shocked at the number of unsolved murders here in Kansas City. Over twenty to be exact. Not to mention the serial kidnapper abducting children from their own homes. Speaking from a citizen's point of view, this is intolerable." Rebecca stared straight into the camera lens. "Crime is out of control in our city. The police need our help. Call Clarence Rochester on the board of commissioners and demand results."

She had presented the facts. She hadn't bashed Silas, and her remarks were slightly less incendiary. He wanted to believe the advice he'd given her in the coffee shop had sunk in, but it was too soon to tell.

The camera cut back to David Reagan. "Thank you, Rebecca. Channel Fourteen News will continue to update the public on the latest shooting fatality in the center of Kansas City. Please call the Tips Stop Crime Hot Line if you have any information that could help police." He reeled off the number. "This is David Reagan reporting. Now, back to you at the station."

Silas swiped his debit card and left the Quick Stop with the fig cookies. He tucked the treat inside a saddlebag and mounted the motorcycle. The twinge in his stomach made itself known. *Leave it alone, Albert. In a few days you won't be a cop anymore.*

The bike rumbled away from the gas pump. At the edge of the parking lot, Silas gave in to his instincts and called Hadley.

"Hey, Boss. No face timing. What am I to do?"

"Yeah. Flip phones came right after two ten cans and string." Silas said sarcastically. "I caught the news report. Not often we have a homeless person shot to death. Usually, they die from a beating."

"Thought you were tired of police work?"

"Last I checked, I'm still on the payroll. Seriously, this one caught me as odd. Have you identified the victim?"

"Walter Stone. No criminal record. Seventy-five. Vietnam War Veteran. Awarded two Purple Hearts and a Silver Star. Damn shame what happened to him."

"Had he been beaten too?"

"No. At least no marks on his hands or face. Who knows what's under all those layers of clothing? The body is at the morgue now, but I'm not seeing this as a person with a beef against the homeless."

Silas considered the information. "Suicide?"

"The entry wound is to the back of the head. The spatter pattern indicated Walter was digging through the dumpster when shot."

"What about robbery?"

"That part is a little strange. From all appearances, someone was going through Walter's pockets but got interrupted. Officers found a mound of junk on the sidewalk by the victim. Twenty dollars right on top."

"Walter had something personal the killer wanted."

"That's the puzzle. The crew found a slew of weird items in Walter's pockets, including a charm bracelet along with a handful of posters of the missing girls."

"What about Walter as the kidnapper?"

"Can't rule anything out at this point, but I think he was pretty feeble, and as far as we can determine, he didn't have a car."

"Time of death?"

"Six o'clock this morning, give or take. Rebecca Haze found him about seven. That woman's always in the middle of police business," Hadley groused.

"Reporting the news is her job."

"Since when does Silas Albert defend the Red Haze?"

"She cut back on the drama, today. I'm holding out hope she's found a new direction."

"Oh yeah. She's cozied up to you for a story about the women's shelter. You better watch out. Sydney won't appreciate competition."

"A documentary," Silas corrected. "And there's no competition. Who'd you hear that from anyway?"

Hadley chuckled. "My sources are protected."

"I'm headed into the office. Got paperwork to finish." Silas paused. "You know, I haven't had a premonition for a while, but I have a gut feeling about Walter." Silas had given up trying to figure out what brought the sensations on, but he'd learned not to ignore them.

There was a void of silence. Silas imagined Hadley twirling a pencil. The incessant habit drove Silas crazy.

"The last time your stomach gave us guidance, you got shot."

"Guess that can't happen if I'm not working the case."

"Sure, you're not." Hadley cleared his throat. "Here's a bit of news you can chew on to satisfy your cop fix. A buddy over in the Crimes Against Persons unit gave me an update on Rose's case. She's getting her memory back."

Silas's pulse pinged. "And?"

"She drew the investigators a rough sketch of the front of the car. The emblem in the grille showed wings enclosed in a circle."

Silas's brain clicked. "A Mazda."

"Right. She went through a computer collage of vehicles and identified the logo."

"Color and year?"

"Black or dark blue. An older model but she couldn't nail down the year.

"At least that's something for the CAP team to go on."

Conversation in the background filtered through the helmet speakers. "I've got to go, Boss, but I'm convinced Rose's abductor has more screws loose than the usual crazy."

Silas snorted. "Outstanding revelation, Captain Obvious."

"Listen. Rose remembers her abductor arguing with another person in the car. A person named Leah. But it was a one-sided argument. No other voice. Think about that. I'll call you later."

In the silence left by the disconnect, Silas grappled with the concept of a psycho and an imagined co-conspirator. Dangerous, if one attempted to control the other. There was also the possibility Leah was a real person. Rose's recall from her encounter had to be flawed at best. Either way, Silas had to agree with Hadley. The abductions carried the signature of insanity.

CHAPTER TWENTY-ONE

A blackbird's squawk of alarm stirred Lila from a deep sleep. The unique sound indicated Big Bertha had intercepted a request for help. Lila rubbed her eyes and crawled out of her sleeping pallet on the floor of The Elle.

She switched the signal off and waited for the supercomputer to analyze the information and assemble a mission. The time marker showed 1:05 a.m. Seconds passed. Another squawk. Lila took a moment to review the details of Big Bertha's plan. According to the log, the computer had picked up the signal from a teenager's emergency app.

Lila considered her options for team leader. A child's life hung in the balance of her choice. *Was Josie ready?* Lila blew out a puff of air. The two Blackbirds didn't always agree, but skills mattered most here. She made the assignment and released her approval for Bertha to send the Blackbird team with Josie in charge.

* * *

"Hello." Josie checked the time—1:06 a.m.

"Hold for your assignment." The faintest of clicks and then the computer communicated the details in a warm motherly tone. "Lila has been notified," Bertha announced when she finished. "Please acknowledge."

"Mission understood. Thank you, Bertha."

"That is all. Be safe." The last detail of Bertha's AI message gave the computer an even more human quality. A reflection of the nature of Bertha's creator.

Josie's thoughts flew to the detective. He was the reason dozens of survivors of abuse re-invented themselves. Josie was a prime example. The Elle was Lila's project. This initial mission for the children's shelter was Josie's chance to prove she'd overcome her past. She gritted her teeth.

She could do it.

At 1:10, Josie settled behind the wheel of a dark gray van dressed in tight black clothing. She tossed her vest, mask, and the new night goggles in the back.

"Okay sisters," she said, using an electronically patched connection. "Get your gear on." Josie swung the wheel to the right and pulled onto the street. "Owl, I'm picking you up in four minutes. Red Bird you get seven. Don't make me wait." She didn't elaborate, knowing the computer had supplied each responder the necessary info. She was aware of each team member's real identity, but once the assignment had been made, they stuck to code names.

At this point, the operation was blind. A young girl named Macy Franklin had activated a 911 call from an emergency app on her cell. To Josie, this meant the girl either accidentally sent a call for help, or she was unable to speak. The Blackbirds responded no matter what, but considering the early hour of the morning and the girl's age, there was no time to waste.

Josie sped down Meyer Boulevard, turned left at Paseo, and tromped the accelerator to beat a changing traffic light. Moths and lightning bugs splattered against the windshield, leaving a mixture of guts and glow.

"Eagle?"

"Yes Bertha."

"Shooting in progress. Location. The Vibe, corner of Twelfth and Central. Multiple injuries. Estimated time of arrival of police and EMT to the Franklin address is twenty minutes."

"Understood. Thank you, Bertha." Eagle spoke to the computer with the same respect the team leader gave any deserving human, but a fist of resentment tightened around her heart. The Vibe was a popular night spot inside an upscale hotel in downtown Kansas City. For Eagle, the world should never be a place where a child's life didn't take priority. But she also understood the weight of the decisions surrounding a hundred lives inside a crowded bar compared to one. The police would do the best they could.

The Blackbirds operated on the fringes of the law to fill these gaps. Eagle tightened her grip on the steering wheel. In her mind there shouldn't be a void in the first place. But the reality existed, and she was glad of Lila's faith in her as this mission's team leader.

At 1:18, Eagle slid the van to the curb. Owl stepped from the shadows and climbed into the passenger side of the vehicle. A slug of August humidity bullied its clammy heaviness inside before the door closed.

"I heard Bertha's update. We're the first responders, this time." Owl twisted to face Eagle. Owl had not donned her headgear, and her blond hair was a ghostly shimmer under the streetlights. "Can I ask you a question?"

"Sure."

"Are you okay with this assignment?"

A black, extended cab truck rolled by the gray van. The vehicle was common enough, but the Tennessee Titan's bumper sticker was damn ballsy in the middle of Chief's Kingdom.

Eagle considered how to answer. Owl's question was a fair one. Blackbird teams relied on their leader to be in control, no matter what painful memories a mission stirred. "You mean because this rescue involves a child?"

"Yeah."

"I asked Lila to make me a part of her new project." A lump formed in Eagle's throat. "Each child we save, helps me live with the loss of my own. Don't worry, I can keep a clamp on my emotions."

"Okay." Owl settled back in the seat. "I get that. Just know, you don't always have to be the strong one."

"Thanks." The team leader reached across the seat and squeezed the blonde's hand. Owl rarely spoke on a personal subject. Her encouragement warmed Eagle. "I am worried about all the kidnappings. I hope this isn't another one."

"According to the news, less time has passed with each abduction."

"That's what worries me."

Three minutes later, Eagle turned down a side street and stopped alongside a twenty-year-old Buick with the rear fender bashed in. Eagle drummed her fingers against the steering wheel as the final member of the Blackbird team exited the battered car and folded her tall frame inside the van.

"Go," Red Bird ordered.

Twenty-five registered on the speedometer before the vehicle's door slid shut. The team leader's feet flew between the brake and the accelerator as they sped around a corner and back onto Paseo.

"Bertha?"

"Yes, Eagle."

"Are there police units between here and our destination?"

Bertha's programs whirred. "Negative."

Red Bird's seat belt clicked, and Eagle challenged the horses under the Ford's hood. Precious seconds often made the difference between saving a life and losing one. Eagle was familiar with the latter.

"This is the layout of the Franklin home." Owl verbally walked the team through the details as Eagle drove. "Any questions?"

Silence in the van gave the answer. "Okay," Eagle said. "We're five blocks from landing. Here's the plan."

The van rolled into the upscale neighborhood. Each ten-acre estate was hidden from the next by tall trees and thick shrubs. The street ahead was empty of vehicles. Light glimmered a beacon of cheer from an occasional window.

An object the shape of a spare tire entered the plane of her vision. She wrenched the steering wheel, but it was too late. The front end of the van bounced. The impact vibrated through her hands and the vehicle veered to the right.

"What was that?" Red Bird yelled from the backseat.

"Don't know, but I can barely steer." Eagle limped the vehicle to the edge of the street. "We'll go the rest of the way on foot. Red Bird, check out what we hit and get a backup coming this way. I'll communicate details when we know what we have." She and Owl exited the van.

"On it." Red Bird slid the door open and jumped from the vehicle.

Eagle and her teammate slung on their equipment and sprinted down the sidewalk. Soft soled shoes designed for stealth, softened the slap of the Blackbirds' feet. Keeping to the shadows, they crossed the first intersection, then the second. Ahead of them, a vehicle pulled onto the street. Eagle grabbed a low-hanging limb of a nearby tree and swung herself into its protective branches. Owl flattened herself against the trunk. A black Dodge van flew by.

The team leader dropped to the ground, running hard the remaining half-block. A huffing sound measured Owl's proximity. Eagle stopped at the Franklin drive, pulled her head gear into place, and donned the new night goggles. She gave the sign to clear the perimeter.

Owl returned a thumbs up. Her silhouette slid from shadow to shadow then blended into the surroundings.

The night was silent except for an occasional call of a whippoorwill.

A distinct smell of lawn chemicals explained the missing whine of mosquitoes. Eagle glided down the shrub lined drive. Dim light from deep inside the house, seeped through the windows in deformed rectangles and squares. A click—once—twice. *Door latch. Heavy. A truck.* The sound repeated. *Two people, or two vehicles?* A starter motor ground, clicked, ground again. The engine fired.

A vehicle rolled from behind the house its headlights dark. Eagle dove for the hedge. *Was a child inside?* She hugged the ground. Heat from the vehicle's exhaust fanned her cheeks. She snapped a picture, tapped a code, and hit send. Bertha was the only hope of keeping the truck under surveillance.

No, it wasn't.

She rolled to her feet, slipped her cell into a pocket, and burst into a dead run. Her vest rattled and rasped. A deaf person could hear her coming. She wasn't taking a chance on a child's life ever again. The Blackbird peeled off the vest. The older model truck braked at the street. A car sped toward them from the right. *One second. I only need one second.*

Eagle stepped up on a stone gate marker, hoped the passing vehicle distracted the driver, and crawled soundlessly over the fender into the bed of the truck. She huddled in the corner trying to be invisible.

The truck passed under a streetlight, and Eagle spotted a green tarp. She dragged air into her lungs. Sliding down into a prone position, she stretched out her arms, gripped the canvas with her fingertips, and dragged the thick material over her body an inch at a time.

For a minute, she lay still as the dead. The truck increased speed and her rush of adrenaline faded. All the team leader needed to do was send the computer a different code and Bertha's programs activated the rescue.

Eagle reached for her phone. She found only an empty pocket. Her gut twisted.

CHAPTER TWENTY-ONE

No phone. No taser. No help. I'm on my own.

* * *

Owl emerged at the rear of the house as a truck rolled around the corner. Was the driver a Franklin family member or were they too late? No lights visible in the house. Owl braced for the worst.

Poised on the balls of her feet and prepared to take out a knee or a collar bone, Owl advanced. The door to the three-car garage gaped wide. One parking spot was empty. A boat and an SUV filled the remaining spaces. Eagle would not enter a house alone, unless she feared a life-or-death situation required immediate response. *Where is she?*

Owl rushed to the corner of the building in time to see a truck pull into the street. She hesitated then sent Eagle a text. "Where are you?" Seconds crawled by. No response. Owl whirled back toward the house. Her first responsibility was to Macy Franklin. She hoped when she found Macy, she'd find Eagle, too. Alive.

Holding the baton in one hand and a flashlight in the other, Owl entered the garage. She slid the torch's switch to the on position careful to keep the beam sheltered from the outside. A glimmering trail of dark droplets led Owl across the concrete floor. She avoided the stains, crossed through a door, and glided into a dimly lit kitchen. She cleared the first floor in thirty seconds and returned to the stairs where the trace led upward.

A low whine filtered down from the second floor. *Dogs don't whine in the middle of the night. A dog barks—unless they're hurt.*

Owl took the steps two at a time. She hesitated at the first room. From Big Bertha's original instructions this was Macy's room. A note taped to the wall read, *Macy's woman cave.* The bed was rumpled but empty. *Bad sign.* The Blackbird moved faster, clearing the bathroom.

Again, the whine. The urge to rush toward the sound boiled in Owl's chest. She returned to the hall, sliding soundlessly along the wall.

The next door opened into an expansive bedroom. A sophisticated design integrated gold, black, and cream colors, creating a warm inviting atmosphere. The comforter on the king-sized bed was wrinkle free, the pillows undisturbed. The bathroom proved unoccupied.

Owl followed the sound of the dog. A strong smell of exploded gunpowder tainted the air. She lowered her profile, tightened her grip on the baton, and slipped into the last room. The fan of light exposed a dresser cluttered with bottles of nail polish, photos of a girl in a volleyball uniform, and the same girl holding a vaulter's pole. Another shot showed two girls, their arms wound around each other's waist. One wore braces and held a basketball. Despite the difference in age, the girl's features mirrored one another.

Sisters!

Tangled sheets trailing from yet another empty bed sent a terrible message to Owl's brain.

We're too late.

A chain of events formed in Owl's mind. The parents gone. Older sister left in charge. Macy awoke to a scream. She stayed calm enough to use the emergency app to call for help. Then, she came to her sibling's aide.

A soft thump spiked an electric current up Owl's spine. She edged around the end of the bed. *Please let me find somebody alive.*

The beam of her light caught the droopy face of a St. Bernard. The dog tried in vain to raise its muzzle. A pitiful whine sawed at Owl's heart strings. She dropped to her knees and ran the beam of light down the length of the dog's frame. A patch the size of a saucer darkened the magnificent white chest.

"You tried to save your humans, didn't you? Hang on baby," she whispered. "We'll get you help, and we'll find your girls." Owl stroked the silky ears. She couldn't carry the St. Bernard down the steps without risk of greater injury. Her fingers searched and found a weak but steady pulse. There was nothing Owl could do for the dog until help arrived.

"I hate to leave you, but I need to find my friend." Owl gave the dog a final stroke, jumped to her feet, and raced down the stairs. She connected with Bertha as she ran.

"Bertha. Advise arrival time of the pick-up team."

"Three minutes to reach you."

"Communication from Eagle?"

"Eagle activated a drone search for a silver 2020 Chevrolet Canyon."

The same truck Owl watched leave the Franklin property. "Results, Bertha."

"In process. Success probability low. Unable to confirm Eagle received the last update."

"Bertha, locate Eagle's phone?" Owl stopped in the garage and waited. She studied the blood trail, noting a different pattern. Thinking of the hole in the dog's chest, these droplets suggested a different type of wound. The Blackbird hoped the drops proved the St. Bernard left a painful impression on the intruder.

Bertha's program whirred in Owl's ear. "Eagle's phone is located fifty yards east of Owl's position."

"Engage the finder signal." The Blackbird jogged east. Eagle would have been moving west, down the drive, while Owl cleared the perimeter. She scanned the nearby shrubs. Six feet from the street she caught the sound of steady ping. *This is all wrong. Why is Eagle going this direction?*

At the edge of the drive the Blackbird spotted the vest. She picked it up. The team leader was nowhere in sight. A sinking sensation took hold of Owl's stomach. She'd once witnessed Eagle take down three grown men. It would have been no easy task to restrain the woman. Only a gun would make her stop fighting, and maybe not even that.

Unless.

Owl scanned the ground. There in the dirt at the edge of the gate marker was the phone, and a footprint. There was no doubt. Eagle was in the bed of that truck.

A white van turned into the drive pulling to a stop alongside, Owl. Red Bird lowered the window. "What've we got?"

"A mess." Owl explained the situation as she connected to Bertha. "Bertha, we have two missing girls believed to have kidnapped. Two separate vehicles sighted leaving the scene. Eagle is with one of the kidnappers. We also have an injured, St. Bernard. Notify Hawk and tell her we need Agent Hamilton's help. Have her call the vet Silas uses and tell him to be ready to treat a St. Bernard for a bullet wound. Condition serious."

"Instructions received and understood." Bertha responded. "Police car approaching."

Nothing more for The Blackbirds here. Police would take care of locating and notifying the parents. Owl raced to the passenger side of the van.

"The FBI will take over. One of the agents will take the dog to the animal hospital." Inside the van, Owl glanced through the side window.

"When those girls are found, they'll need their dog."

CHAPTER TWENTY-TWO

A black carpet of lawn stretches beneath the window. I have managed to make it through another day. I circle my office, avoiding my image in the glass. The sight of me—the murderer—makes me sick. I shouldn't have shot Walter. And those kids. I'll never forget the fear in their eyes.

Despair draws my chest tight in a dangerous way. I press my hands against my skull, swear, and kick at the furniture. The room spins. I slump into a chair. Buried images pass before my eyes. A woman rests beneath still white sheets. I stand by her side my fists knotted. A nurse takes me by the arm and guides me from the room.

"It's time for Leah to go..." The nurse chokes on the last word.

I hear the gurney bump across the floor. Then the vision changes, and it's me on the stretcher. I wear a white jacket. For some reason, I can't move. I scream for Leah, but it does no good. A stranger takes me away.

The dream memory is as dangerous as shifting sand. I resist the pull, forcing my mind to reclaim the solid ground of the present. A ticking clock centers me. I focus on the time—two a.m. The package pick-up should be completed by now, but the lackeys haven't called. I stand, pace back and forth, then glare at the picture of Leah. I don't like her accusing stare and flip the frame on its face. The glass shatters.

A favorite melody grabs my attention. I answer the ring tone, remembering at the last moment to turn on the voice modulator. "What took you so long?"

"We had a minor problem, but everything's under wraps."

I rub my temples. "What problem?"

"There was a dog big as a damn horse. He bit me. Had to shoot the mutt. But we got a bonus."

"I told you not to steal anything." A sharp edge curls through my voice.

The lackey snorts. "I'm not stupid. There were two packages."

His arrogant tone disgusts me. Five years in prison is not a mark of superior intelligence. "How old is the bonus?"

"Twelve or thirteen."

My pulse thumps. According to Facebook, the younger girl is supposed to be at camp. I hope she's not sick. There's plenty of that to deal with already. "Where are they now?"

"One is with me. I'll deliver that package to Chicago tomorrow, the way we originally planned. Clyde didn't know if you were ready for another bonus. He took that package to his farm in the Ozarks."

"Good." I picture the old shed in the woods. Clyde had taken me there, long before the need for his brother arose. My prior acquaintance with Clyde may prove useful if Wade gets out of hand. "The next delivery is in two days. He'd better not screw this up."

"He won't. Anything else?"

"I need more product to choose from."

"No problem. I'll tell Clyde." He disconnects.

I swallow back a sarcastic laugh. My head will remain where it belongs.

I straighten Leah's picture. "Don't be mad. Walter was a liability."

She smiles back at me. Leah knows my intentions are honorable. But for now, the focus remains on what to do about the problems in the padded room. An idea spins round and round in my head, gaining shape and weight.

What if I did nothing? The bodies wouldn't be found for weeks, maybe never.

CHAPTER TWENTY-THREE

C entrifugal force tugged at Josie as the truck swung onto an unpaved road. The Blackbird peeked from beneath the tarp. She estimated they'd been traveling over two hours. According to her knowledge of Missouri geography, and glimpses of overhead signs, their location was between Springfield and Branson. The last billboard had featured a big white chicken and the words, *Ada and DeShawn's Convenience Store.* They had passed the business before the last turn. The truck slowed.

A lemon wedge of moon peeked over the tops of trees. The crunch of gravel receded, replaced by the soft whir of rubber against dirt. A thread of a power line tracked their path through the night. But it was the creak of old metal and loose floorboards that sent the Blackbird's hopes plummeting. She had crossed old bridges before. The middle of nowhere was where they ended.

The truck traveled a short distance, climbed an incline, and stopped. A door opened, bathing the interior in a dim light. Josie slid the goggles in place and raised her head. Headlights fanned across the front of an old farm building. Small saplings grew along the rock foundation. The driver jumped out and shut the door.

Metal scraped against metal. A light deep within the building switched on. The Blackbird's pulse surged. Electricity meant houses, people, and options. She slid across the truck bed and skimmed over the side. A thump marked her contact with the ground. She froze in a crouched position.

Footsteps drew near, then stopped. *Had he heard her?* She waited. A door latch clicked. A moment later the kidnapper shuffled backward, the girl slung over his shoulder. A kick of a boot closed the door.

Josie clung to the edge of darkness, gliding behind her prey. Strands of a spider's web fell across the lens of the glasses. She dragged in air through her nose, eased the urge to paw at the sticky threads. She crept past the hulk of a tractor and a hay baler.

Ahead, the girl groaned. The sound raked up bad memories. Three more feet and she would have the advantage. Then the world tilted. Josie's mind spun her to another time and place. *Celia.* Her daughter lay motionless on the ground. *I'm too late.* Under clammy skin, her muscles refused to cooperate.

Not a flashback. Not now.

Josie squeezed her eyelids tight, fought to stop the scene, and regain control. A minute passed—or an hour. Time bore no authenticity.

A scream blasted Josie fully into the present, as the girl slammed her bare feet into the kidnapper's chest.

The man grunted and fell back a step.

Josie charged, grabbed his arm, and twisted. But the angle was wrong, and he slung her to the floor. She rolled to her feet to find a pistol an inch from her temple.

"Don't," the girl screamed.

"Look what's growing wild in these here Missouri woods—a damn-sure ninja warrior." A mirthless sound came out of his mouth. "If you've got a gun, better give it to me now."

The Blackbird scanned the room. An old metal cot sat along the far wall covered in a thin stained mattress. A two by six board lay lose on the floor nearby. No help. Not now anyway.

"I'm not armed," she said.

"Damn, I forgot. Ninjas don't need guns. Get over there next to her and take off those glasses. I want to see what I'm dealing with here."

Josie trudged across the room. The girl sat on the cot, defiant as a child could be when barefoot, dressed in pajamas bottoms, and wearing a tank top.

The toe of Josie's boot caught the two by six, she stumbled, but righted herself. Facing the kidnapper, she tossed the goggles to the floor. If he made the mistake of bending to pick them up, she would render him an unconscious fool.

He stepped out of range. "Kick them over here. Take off that hood too."

Josie did as she was told.

"Holy shit, you're a woman!"

If the scene hadn't been so serious, Josie would have laughed. Instead, she lunged forward, snapped the hood like a whip, and prayed to connect with his eyes. For a big man, he was quick. He dodged, grabbed her wrist, and yanked her forward. When she came to a stop, they were chest to chest, the cold barrel of a gun planted against her temple, and no place to turn from the stink of whiskey breath.

"Who are you? What are you doing here?"

She made her voice hard and tough. "You'll find out soon enough. The police are following me."

"Yeah. Sure. That's funny." But he didn't laugh, and he shot an uneasy glance into the darkness.

Josie's muscles throbbed. She wanted to take him out, but the gun was an edge not in her favor, and wild bullets couldn't be trusted.

"You're no more leading the police here than I am running for sheriff. But you are a problem. Back up."

She slid her feet backward until her calves touched the iron cot. Not having a gun at her temple eased the tension in her lungs, but dread descended as he lifted the goggles with his toe and flipped them into his hand.

"Hi tech. These might come in handy." The kidnapper sized Josie up. "A shame you're too old to meet the boss's standards. You have the right color skin. He likes your kind. I might give him a call and see if he's interested in another bonus, or if you need to disappear."

"What? This girl's white and blonde." She pointed.

"He's broadened his horizons. Ain't life filled with surprises? I got little Macy here, brother Wade's got her sister, and now we got you." He dragged restraints from his pocket and tossed them in Macy's lap. "Fasten those around her wrists. Nice and tight."

Staring down the bore of the gun was a clear reminder of the limited options. Fighting was one, but if he shot her that left the girl alone. Josie wasn't about to do that. She chose to bide her time, find his weakness. The Blackbird faced Macy and stuck out her hands.

A fist came from the side. Stars exploded across her vision. She would have fallen, but Macy caught her by the arm.

"Don't test me, woman. Hands behind your back."

Josie adjusted her position. "Do it, Macy. We can't escape if we're dead."

"She's right, little sister."

Macy's face faded in and out, but Josie recognized defiance in the girl's glare. A tough accomplishment considering the tears streaming down the child's face.

"Don't call me that. Kin of yours would have horns and a tail."

"Bite your tongue, kid. Unless you want bad things to happen to Odessa. That's right isn't it. Her name is Odessa."

"You better not hurt my sister."

"Shush Macy, just do as he says." The Blackbird stuck her hands out behind her. "I'm Josie, and we're going to be okay." The zip teeth chattered.

"Now the ankles."

Macy scooted to the right then stood.

Now or never. Josie stared the kidnapper in the eye. "What's your name?"

A flicker of surprise winked across his face. "Why?"

Adrenaline pumped through the Blackbird.. "When we meet again, and I take you down, I don't want to just call you dumb ass."

Raucous laughter was not the response she expected.

"You're just like my old lady. You think you're smart. Well, consider this, ninja bitch." He winked, pretended to pull the trigger, and put the bore to his lips and blew imaginary smoke from the bore. "Get my drift." He bared his teeth. "Now that we're on friendly terms, you can call me Clyde."

For God's sake, he thinks he's being cute.

"Kiah!" Josie screamed and launched the full force of her body into a head butt. Macy lunged too. The crunch of bone smashing cartilage sounded good. Knees or nose, it didn't matter. Three bodies hit the floor in a tangle of arms and legs. Then silence shrouded the room.

"Josie?" Macy's whisper split the quiet.

The Blackbird's words slurred as her brain absorbed darkness. "I'm—all—right."

CHAPTER TWENTY-FOUR

I stretch and roll over, touching bare feet to the floor. Another uneasy night left behind in a tangle of sheets. My parched tongue swabs at a cottony mouth.

God, I hate the aftereffects of sleeping pills.

I peer at the clock. A weight lifts from my shoulders. By this time, the food poisoning will have solved three of my problems.

I dry swallow a pill. Maintaining a balance in two worlds takes a toll, and I need a little extra punch to keep my brain sharp.

My episode of guilt over Walter's demise is a distant memory, but I can't get the photo in his wallet out of my mind. The puzzle picks at me, aggravating as a sliver of glass stuck in my heel. How could something so personal fall into the hands of a vagrant? Is Mary's daughter the culprit? Did she use it for spite?

I never understood her anger. She hurt those who loved her most, and then turned her back on everyone. She even caused Leah to shun me for a while. But the common thread between Leah and I is too strong. A forever bond brings her back to me over and over. I'm the one person in her life who does what's right.

For a second, faces of the sick girls flash before my eyes. There's something wrong about leaving their dead bodies to rot. I won't go back in that house but leaving them will give Leah another reason to criticize.

An idea weaves its way through my brain cells. Their stupidity should be a lesson. A tingle spreads along my spine. Leah will approve. Channel Fourteen News will love a scoop, and Rebecca is the one to do the story justice.

A hot shower, pot of tea, and a hard boiled egg later, I'm ready to make the call. The plane bound for Chicago will be on the ground by now. Another girl ships out tomorrow. The sun is shining bright when a real person answers at the news station. I turn on the voice modulator.

"This information is for Rebecca Haze," I say. "Tell her. Three of the missing girls are locked in a padded room at the following address." The predictable gasp sends a shiver through me. The street and house number slides off my tongue. I wish to be a mouse, witnessing the chaos in the newsroom. I hang up, not bothering to tell them I know Rebecca's not there, and there is no need to hurry.

The story will be the same in one hour or two days.

CHAPTER TWENTY-FIVE

Silas arrived at the station the following morning, having decided to do a cursory review of the Walter Long case. The detective trusted his team and especially Hadley, but there was that annoying stomach thing. Life got out of hand when he ignored a gut-feeling.

The detective pulled up the computer file and skimmed through what he'd already learned from Hadley the day of the murder. There was a smattering of added information from CSI. The lack of fingerprints earned a mention. A side note suggested the assailant wore gloves. Silas rocked in his chair. The crime had the components of premeditation.

Once more, he ran through the list of evidence and compared the photos taken at the crime scene. An expired driver's license from 1999 lay on top of a pile of odds and ends. A loose twenty-dollar bill indicated the murder wasn't about money. CSI had noted a crease in the currency resembled the mark from a folded wallet, but one wasn't found at the scene. Why?

The bullet had spared the man's face. The Army's rendition of Walter Stone from fifty years earlier bore little resemblance to the victim. Comparing the handsome smooth shaven Walter to the one crumpled on the sidewalk, made the detective want to turn away. But there was an intensity in the soldier's expression in the photo that held Silas's attention. He instinctively knew he'd seen those eyes before. The where and when escaped him.

The investigation had generated pages of additional information. His team was clocking the hours. Walter's work history after Vietnam and college had been steady as a rock. One job as an investment broker lasted from 1974 thru 1997.

The detective had been in high school in 1997. Girls were on his mind then, and he had zero interest in bond yields or tech stock. His parents had other ideas. They had expected him to learn to manage the inheritance he received from his grandfather.

If he remembered correctly, there was an Asian economic crisis in '97. The impact caused a global stock market crash. The recovery was quick, but from Walter's employment history not fast enough to save his job.

Had Walter been homeless for over twenty years?

The thought saddened the detective. Losing a long-term job would be a blow to anyone. For a PTSD victim—it would be devastating.

The detective read the interviews, searching for patterns. Walter had visited the soup kitchen on a regular basis. According to the notes, he was polite, never made trouble, and didn't seem to have any buddies. No one knew where he slept.

Silas was ready to close the file when a comment caught his attention. Clark, a volunteer at the kitchen, had witnessed two kids eating with Walter. Another anomaly.

There was no notation of a follow-up with the volunteer. Silas gritted his teeth. He reached out to Hadley, but the call went to voicemail. The detective chose not to leave a message.

The homicide department was stretched thin, but every person deserved justice, especially a person who'd served his country. A detective should have interviewed the two people known to interact with the murder victim. There should have been concern for the children. Silas only had hours left on the job, but he had time for this.

He was about to give the soup kitchen a visit when the flip phone pinged. He recognized the number.

"Hello."

"Silas. Archie Hamilton, here. There's been a development. Can we meet for a cup of coffee? The agency needs your help."

The FBI agent wouldn't ask if the situation wasn't serious. "Sure, but I'm going out of town tonight."

"I know. I'll explain at, Jorge's Place. Can you be there in an hour? This is important."

Jorge's Place was located a couple of blocks from the soup kitchen. "I'll be close by." Silas explained his meeting with Clark. "I can make that work." He had enough time to do the interview.

Fifteen minutes later, Silas climbed out of his cruiser and entered the building where volunteers served a morning and evening meal, no questions asked. A strong smell of bleach hung in the air. Stragglers lingered over egg-smeared plates. Silas approached the counter.

"Breakfast is over. All we've got left is coffee." The person continued to clean the grill. "You'll find the pot at the end of the counter. Help yourself."

"Thanks, but I'm looking for Clark."

The volunteer gave Silas the once-over. "That'd be me."

The detective held up his badge. "Silas Albert, homicide. I'm investigating the murder of Walter Stone. Need to ask you one or two questions."

Clark laid his cleaning tools on a worktable and wiped his hands on a towel. "I've heard of you." He grabbed a silver-handled cane and limped to the counter. For a brief second his attention focused on Silas's prosthetic arm. "How can I help?"

The volunteer's hair was military short. Muscular arms protruded from the rolled sleeves of a chef's coat. Above the man's wrist was a bold tattoo of four ivy leaves. Silas recognized the Army's 4th Infantry insignia. Printed below the ivy was D Co Steadfast and Loyal. Silas swallowed.

He nodded toward the ink. "Same company my dad served with. Vietnam."

Clark glanced at his arm. "Afghanistan." Moisture gleamed in the man's eyes. "If you can—tell him, welcome home."

The choice of words wasn't lost on Silas. "I can. Thank you for your service." He cleared his throat. "Understand you knew the victim. What can you tell me about him?"

"Not much. I've been here five years. Walter came in to eat twice a day. Sat right over there in the corner, kept his head down, never said a word. That is until a couple of weeks back, when a young boy and a girl started coming in with him."

"Did you ask questions?"

"You're the second detective to ask me that. I'm glad Walter's death is getting serious attention."

Silas was relieved one of his detectives was simply behind on filing the case posts and not negligent. "We're doing the best we can," he said.

"I'll tell you what I told him. This is a no-questions-asked facility. If a person is hungry, they get fed. But I was concerned. I talked to Walter about who the kids were. For once, he didn't ignore me. Claimed they were his grandchildren. They acted more scared of me than Walter. I let it go."

"You think they were homeless?"

Clark's lips tightened. "There's plenty of kids in this area who would pass for homeless but are just hungry."

"Have those two been back since the murder?"

Clark shook his head. "Thought they'd come back to meet their friend. I planned to try to help. Even told my wife about them. The girl is only about twelve, the boy close to eight. That's the wrong age to be on the street."

Silas nodded. "Sorry for the duplicate questions and thanks for not blowing me off." He handed Clark a card. "For obvious reasons, I hope Walter's friends show up."

"I hope so too." Clark followed Silas to the door, where they shook hands.

The detective made his way back outside, squinting against the streaming sun. It was hot as hell even for August, but at least the sky was blue. A choked scream caught him off guard.

"Help! Please help."

Silas twisted toward the sound, shielding his eyes, one hand on his gun. "Holy Jesus." A girl tottered down the alley toward him. Naked.

She wobbled, righted herself, and staggered forward, something white clutched in her hands. "Help. We need help."

We.

The door to the soup kitchen slammed open. "What the hell?" Clark growled.

"Give me your jacket," Silas ordered.

The volunteer shucked off his chef's coat.

The detective raced into the alley, head on a swivel, hand on his gun, the garment tucked under his arm. Clark jog-hobbled along behind him, ignoring his bum leg. As Silas closed the distance, the girl's strength seemed to fade. She stumbled. A jagged hunk of white porcelain fell from her hands. The detective caught her as she collapsed. His stomach heaved at the stench of human feces.

"He kidnapped us," she babbled, eyes wild. The other girls—they're dying."

Silas draped her in the coat. "Call 911," he said. "She's got a raging fever. Tell them to follow contagious disease protocol."

Clark held up his cell. "On the line with dispatch now."

The girl's body shook inside the circle of Silas's arms. "I've got you.

Where are the others?"

A trembling hand snuck out of the too big sleeve, pointing. "Two blocks. A blue house on the corner."

Clark updated the 911 dispatcher with the additional location. "This is a kidnapping situation. Send multiple ambulances and the police."

"How many girls?" Silas lowered his ear close to the child's lips.

"Two—I—I think."

"Did you get that, Clark?"

The army veteran gave him a thumbs up. "One female victim age approximately fourteen is at the first address. Condition serious. High fever, possible dehydration. At least two more females at the second location. Age and condition unknown."

Silas brought his focus back to the girl. "Is anyone else there?"

She shook her head, dark eyes dominating a pale frightened face.

Silas met Clark's grim stare. "Stay with her. Don't let anyone touch her but a paramedic. I don't know what we're dealing with here."

The veteran paled but didn't hesitate. "Go," he said, trading places with Silas.

Two blocks became a long way to run in August. The detective's lungs pumped fire. The house came into view. The boarded up windows matched a dozen others on the same street.

He steeled his mind for what he might find inside.

A chain link fence surrounded the property. Silas located the gate down the side street. "Damn it." A five-foot sapling blocked any chance of pushing it open.

The detective slid to the left and slammed his gun into its holster. Wire cut into Silas's hand as he vaulted over the top support. On the other side, the detective pulled his weapon, wishing for the protection of a tactical vest.

Profile low, he darted across the yard, feet stirring the smell of decay. Ahead, a door hung open above a crooked step. Hunks of what was once the porcelain lid from a toilet tank, crunched beneath his heel. He imagined the girl battering her way free. Curses bit at his throat.

The detective stopped left of the entry. Years on the street told him, this stretch of houses, built in the fifties, all had the same floor plan. Two bedrooms to the right, one to the left, bathroom just beyond, dining room straight ahead, living room at the front, and a kitchen in the rear. No attached garage. Entry to the basement would be from the kitchen.

Silas crossed the threshold and flattened his back to the wall. One foot assessed for rotted floorboards before the second moved. Using the light from his cell for guidance, he passed by open doors, the space behind them empty.

The stench curdled in his mouth. If the victims weren't dead, they were close. The pale skin of an outstretched arm stopped him mid-step.

The child lay across a long narrow rug. Silas recoiled at the sight of bare buttocks.

Her moan pumped hope through Silas's chest. There was still a life here to save. The detective shined the light into a room to the right. Another naked girl lay in the middle of the floor. *God Almighty, what was going on here?*

CHAPTER TWENTY-SIX

At 1:32 a.m., Lila had tried to call Special Agent Archie Hamilton. When told he was unavailable, she gave the code word and was quickly forwarded to another agent. Communication back and forth all night with Agent Mason Croy had left her eyes burning from lack of sleep. Each passing hour lessened the chances of Josie and the two Franklin girls being found alive.

She would have called Silas, but he'd ruined his phone. He must not have linked with Bertha yet, or he would have been there. She had a responsibility to alert him, in case Josie was...

Lila blocked the thought. She could get a message to him, but what would he do that she wasn't already doing? If she hadn't heard positive news by the time she and Woody returned from the cemetery, she would contact her uncle. *And then there was Elsa and Gordy.* She bit her lip. This was not how rescues were meant to go.

As Lila turned away from the counter, the pamphlet Woody had shown her the night before caught her eye. She picked up the brochure. What was it Woody had said about where he picked up the advertisement? *The Quick Stop.* She grabbed her phone.

"Bertha."

"Good morning, Lila. How can I help you?"

"A couple of days ago, a girl called The Elle, asking for help. I need that recording." While she waited, she rolled up Bertha's latest data on the kidnappings.

As she expected, the facts showed a change to the victim selection. Prostitutes and girls of color had been replaced by white girls from upper middle-class families. Lila's skin prickled. Young white girls in the world of trafficking attracted dangerous clientele to the table. These types would do anything to keep their identity hidden.

The latest abductions occurred while the parents were out of town. In each situation, the parents had booked accommodations with the same hotel chain. A solid lead. Lila sent the information to Archie Hamilton. Occasionally, Big Bertha was faster than Archie's sources.

She opened the audio she had requested from Bertha. "There was this paper at the Quick Stop."

It wasn't much, but how many Quick Stops could there be? And how many abandoned houses near a Quick Stop would have a tree house in the back yard?

Lila googled Quick Stops in Kansas City. A dozen markers popped up. She saved the map and called Bertha, giving instructions to assign two Blackbirds to The Elle and alert the psychiatrist. She added specific instructions in case the kids turned up. She itched to jump into the Studebaker and begin the search immediately, but Woody would be there in five minutes. She grabbed a glow pink, gloss stick from her purse and slicked her lips. How would she keep from telling him about the missing Blackbird?

Promptly at ten o'clock, Lila opened the door to Woody's knock. Dressed in charcoal gray cargo shorts and a Kansas City Royal's t-shirt, damp strands of hair escaped from under his simple gray cap with a tiny American flag stitched to the front. He could have stepped right out of a sports magazine. A cooler swung from his right hand. Was she having a dream, or was her lack of sleep taking its toll? She eyed the cooler but grabbed Woody's arm and tugged him inside.

"What's wrong? What's going on?" Woody exclaimed.

"Remember the kids who called here asking for help?"

"Sure. I listened to the recording."

"I know how to find them."

"You do?"

"The shelter's brochure you picked up at the convenience store. It reminded me of where the girl said she got the number to call. It gave me an idea."

"Really? What?"

"Check this out." She pulled up the map of Quick Stop locations and explained their significance to the vacant house, on a corner lot, with a treehouse.

Woody studied the screen. He glanced up eyes gleaming. "Good detective work. I'll make a call, shouldn't take us long to check your idea out." He handed her back her phone and palmed his own.

"For real?" Lila shrilled. "You'll hunt for them? What will happen when they're found?"

"Don't get your hopes too high. Kids living on the street often fall victim to predators, or the system may have already picked them up. If we find them, I'd have them brought here, but the shelter's not ready."

"It's ready enough," Lila blurted. "Furniture will be delivered later today. I already called two staff members. One is a nurse. I have a psychiatrist available if we need her."

"Go figure." A grin flashed across Woody's face. He made the calls. "We need to give the officers two or three hours to conduct the search."

"That sounds like forever. Isn't there something else we can do?"

Woody remained silent for a moment. "From what I could pick up in listening to Elsa, she's smart. I'd say, she's been taking care of her brother and herself for a while now. Don't underestimate her. The best thing we can do is keep ourselves busy." He lifted the cooler and swung it back and forth in front of Lila's face. "Aren't you even a little curious?"

"I just want to find those two kids."

"Momma Mendez taught me that food helps to take a person's mind off their problems. But, under these new circumstances, I understand if you're not interested."

Lila bit her lip. She had her phone. She could rely on Bertha and Agent Croy to reach her if anything changed. Good or bad.

Woody's face fell. "Sorry. I should have asked first. We don't have to..."

"Stop." Lila held up both hands. "It's all cool." She forced a smile.

"Are you sure? Cause I don't have a problem if we don't eat at all."

"You're right, keeping busy is better than sitting here, thinking the worst. When they find the kids, I'll make the Studebaker fly home."

Lila grabbed her purse and keys from the counter. "Did you take your anxiety medicine?" She cocked an eyebrow.

"Don't worry about it. But don't get us thrown in jail. I need my job."

Moments later, Lila pulled the Studebaker onto the street headed east. A wreath covered in purple and yellow flowers rested in the back seat where Lila had placed it earlier. She fought the urge to squall the tires and let the power of the Corvette engine hidden beneath the hood of the deceptively demure car rattle Woody's bones.

Woody relaxed in the passenger seat. "You cut your hair. Nice. Sort of jagged—sophisticated."

Slow heat crept under Lila's skin. "Thanks." She lifted the short strands with the tips of her fingers. "Just trying to fool the reporters."

Woody's description sounded nice, but sophisticated was not what Lila considered herself to be. She was a Blackbird. Trained to enter situations requiring both toughness and compassion, fashion rarely mattered. Short hair was harder for an assailant to get a grip on and easier to keep under the headgear.

"I know that feeling." He drummed the tips of his fingers against his bare knees.

"Do I make you nervous—ur—I mean does my driving make you nervous?" Woody didn't laugh and his expression was so danged serious.

"You do know your uncle's going to have a coronary?"

Lila almost laughed. "I can manage Silas. I asked you, not the other way around. He really didn't want me to go to the cemetery alone, but I insisted. I simply decided to take his advice and invite a friend who understands the situation."

"Hope you're right. I don't want to spend the rest of my career on the night shift."

"Sooo. It's a 'big ole' fear of Silas Albert that has you worried." Lila gripped the steering wheel, punched the accelerator, and left two plumes of black smoke behind the Hawk. Woody's shoulders slammed back into the passenger seat. She sped by three cars, wheeled a sharp left, and a sharp right. Her feet danced between the pedals as she shifted gears.

"Damn it, Lila you're going to kill us both."

The Studebaker blew down the entry ramp onto I-70. "Made you stop worrying about Silas, didn't I?" Lila grinned at her passenger. Woody no longer tapped his fingers against his knees, but his jaw was tight as a bowstring.

"Hey! Keep your eyes on the road."

"Oops." She urged the Studebaker back between the dotted lines. A trucker honked as he passed. The draft from the semi rocked the car and left the smell of diesel in its wake.

"Do you do this to all your friends—or am I special?"

"What? Didn't you take your anxiety medicine?" Lila let up on the accelerator.

"There's not a drug in the world with that kind of power." He blew out a soft whistle. "Smooth shifting. Who taught you?"

Woody didn't strike Lila as the type to be impressed easily, but she detected no hint of sarcasm. "There's an abandoned air strip south of Lee's Summit. Part of an old military base. Silas took me there. We spent weeks practicing. Silas had to replace the clutch twice before I got speed shifting right."

"Your uncle is a unique guy. Protects you like a grizzly bear one minute and teaches you how to kill yourself the next."

"Not true." Lila tilted her chin. "He taught me to survive. But more than that, he taught me to live." Her fingers caressed the grooves of the steering wheel and guided the car into a different lane. "Silas understood I needed a way to be different that had nothing to do with my transplant. Racing this old Hawk helped me." She sighed. "I don't street race anymore."

"Did you know I watched you race once?"

"You did not." *He was kidding—right?*

"Witnessed you leave the driver of a fancy blue Mustang sniffing Studebaker fumes."

Lila's throat went dry. The owner of the blue Mustang was Hunter Morgan, and their relationship was a whole different chapter in her life. She silently prayed Woody didn't want to talk about the half-brother she'd discovered two years earlier. The rumble of the Hawk engine and the hum of the tires filled the dead space. "And you didn't arrest me. That must have taken restraint."

"I wasn't on duty. I wanted to get to know you, not make you mad."

Check. Another positive mark in her book for evaluating men. Woody was handsome, and she was attracted, but there was more, and Lila wanted to explore. "Why would you be interested in me? I'm so much younger, and my life is complicated."

"I could make a cute remark here, but you might make me walk home. If you must know, most women my age aren't as mature as you, Lila. You have a deep strength. You do things your way, yet I've seen your compassion. I'm surprised you don't have an animal shelter too."

Lila shot him the evil eye. "You sound just like Silas."

Laughter burst from Woody's throat. "Worse things have been said about me, but don't tell Silas."

Lila smirked. "Tell me about your family."

"That will take the rest of our lives. I have dozens and dozens of relatives. They're a rowdy bunch, but they have big hearts. You would fit right in."

There was a bit of an assumption in Woody's words, but Lila let it slide. She wouldn't object if today was the beginning of a deeper friendship, or dare she hope—relationship?

Woody talked and Lila soaked up the interesting stories of his six siblings. His voice carried a subtle blend of strength and sweetness, like espresso with cream.

"Now it's your turn. Tell me about growing up in a women's shelter."

The question sounded innocent enough. But what did he really expect her to say? "When it's all you know, it's normal. I've seen bad stuff, and it makes me mad, but being a part of a woman's recovery creates a special connection. We form a sisterhood of sorts. It's hard to explain." Lila guided the Studebaker to the Highway 13 exit and turned south toward Warrensburg.

"That makes total sense, but your uncle has a reputation as a tough guy. Living at the House of Audrey doesn't fit how I picture him."

Lila smiled. "I get that, but here's a clue about Silas. Few are accepted into his inner circle. If you want to be there, you earn it."

"Guess, I've got my work cut out for me. Challenge accepted."

"I expect a progress report, Officer Mendez."

She couldn't wait to see what Woody did to get on Silas's good side.

CHAPTER TWENTY-SEVEN

Precious seconds flew by as Silas cleared the remainder of the first floor. He found the basement door nailed shut. He holstered his gun, retraced his steps, and dropped to his knees in the hallway. "I'm a police officer." The girl felt hot to his touch. "I'm here to help you."

Her eyelids fluttered. "Momma," she whispered, grabbing at his arm

Silas's throat went tight. He lifted the ends of the rug and gently covered her as best he could. "You're safe now."

The peal of sirens filtered through the old house. Silas feared the worst as he followed the light to the other girl. At first touch he felt the heat, the racing pulse. She wasn't dead.

"Hang on. Hang on." He lifted her into his arms, stepped around the first girl, and ran toward the sound of emergency vehicles.

"This is Silas Albert. I'm a police officer," he yelled. "I'm coming out with an unconscious victim."

Two figures dressed in hazmat suits, met him on each side of the door, guns drawn. "Anyone else in there?"

"There's another sick girl back there in the hall." Silas jerked his chin toward the scene behind him. "She's barely conscious. High fever. Evidence of severe diarrhea and vomiting." He angled his body, doing his best to protect the modesty of the child he carried.

Half-a-dozen personnel rushed past Silas into the house. Police and firefighters, dressed in hazmat suits, formed a human chain from the step to the street. The seriousness of the scene could have been scripted for an apocalyptic movie.

"Detective Albert. We've got this. You can put the patient on the gurney now."

Silas lowered his burden. "Hurry. She's in bad shape."

A male EMT quickly covered the girl's nakedness with a silver rescue blanket.

"Thank you," Silas said.

"I've got two daughters at home." The EMT nodded to his assistant. "Let's go."

Gentle hands raised the litter above the overgrown yard. The precious cargo passed from person to person, over the fence, and into a waiting ambulance. Bright lights inside the vehicle showed an oxygen mask drop over the child's face.

Moments later, the last victim traveled past Silas on a stretcher. Her eyes were open. She was breathing on her own.

"Detective." An EMT touched his elbow. "We need you to come with us to the hospital. Until we know what's made these girls sick, we need to follow contagion protocol."

"I understand." Silas followed the paramedic. As he stepped inside the ambulance, he caught a glimpse of red hair shining in the sun. Behind the reporter, a man shouldered a camera. The number fourteen identified the local news channel.

How did Rebecca Haze get here this fast?

A person wearing a yellow hazmat suit blocked Silas's view. Stamped across the front were the letters, FBI.

"Hold on. I'm Special Agent Archie Hamilton. I'm going with him." The statement wasn't a request.

"Yes sir." The attendants made room, and Archie climbed aboard.

Clothes wet with sweat, the cool air inside the ambulance made Silas shiver. The attendant checking his vital signs noticed and draped a blanket across his shoulders.

Archie's lips tightened. "You, okay?"

Silas nodded. "I hope we were in time."

The agent steadied himself as the ambulance pulled away from the curb. He fumbled with his phone, gloved hands awkward and cumbersome. "Hell of a thing, what the human race is capable of." He brought a series of photos to the screen. "Can you match any of these females to the victims you found? Each one was reported missing within the last few months."

Silas took the device and swiped through a collage of young faces. His gut twisted. There were so many.

"That one." He tapped one of the photos. "And her. She escaped from the house and ran down the alley to get help for the others." The detective's temples pounded as he showed Archie the last photo. "I put this one on the gurney."

Archie thumbs flew across the screen. "I'll get things rolling to inform the parents. Give me a minute."

Silas waited while Archie notified the other agents.

"It would help if one of these girls identified the kidnapper," Archie commented when he ended the call. "Even if they can't..." He hesitated, glancing at the ambulance attendants. "We're beginning to get one or two breaks. The bracelet your team found in a pocket of the murder victim, Walter Stone, belonged to Kelsey Springer. She's the girl you carried from the house."

Silas's shook his head. "Walter's not the kidnapper. He was too frail. My gut tells me the bracelet ties Walter's killer to the kidnappings."

Behind the face plate of the hazmat suit, Archie's eyebrows rose. "I agree. Don't know if you're aware, but forensics found red hairs on the clothes Rose wore the night Josie found her in the park. No match in the system, but they belonged to a female."

"If the drugs in Rose's system altered her memory, the Leah her abductor spoke to could be a partner. A red-headed accomplice."

"Exactly. We're getting closer, Silas. And thanks to Lila, we have a link between Clarence Rochester and the how. The timing of your weekend at Oak Hills Resort couldn't be better. The agency has an undercover assignment for you and Sydney."

Silas's defensive instincts jumped to attention. "No. Not just no, but hell no. Sydney's not going to be a part of..."

Archie cut him off. "Hold on. Hold on. Sydney's your cover enhancement. She is a fully trained Blackbird. I don't think she'd appreciate you making decisions for her. Besides, you're not going anywhere until this issue with contagious disease is resolved. We may not even need your help by then."

The sirens grew silent. "We're at the hospital. I'll tell you the details later." The rear doors of the vehicle flew open, and Archie disappeared in the flurry of activity, leaving a frustrated Silas behind.

Rushed into isolation, Silas fumed at Archie, but was more than a little curious about the assignment. Doctors and nurses entered and exited the room, asking the same questions over and over. A lull rolled into a timeless period of waiting. Silas raised his bed to a comfortable position. Figures moved across a muted TV on the opposite wall. He closed his eyes. His thoughts whirled around the plight of the missing girls, and the murder of Walter stone.

The bracelet tied Kelsey Springer to Walter. More than likely the homeless man had camped on the abandoned property. The kidnapper must have caught him snooping or saw him pick up the bracelet. The risk of Walter talking would have been more than enough motive for murder.

The ideas jived but didn't explain the missing wallet or how the kidnapper knew Rose. Clarence Rochester lived in the same neighborhood as Rose. But he didn't have red hair and unless Silas was blind, the commissioner wasn't a woman. The disconnect gave him a brain cramp.

Silas opened his eyes to find the TV screen filled with a panoramic camera shot of the crime scene. He located the control and turned up the sound. Only one ambulance remained, but a dozen police cars lined the street. Yellow crime tape chased the chain link fence. One officer moved left to right behind a leashed dog. Silas swallowed hard. His brain hadn't caught up to the possibility of a dead child.

Rebecca Haze stepped in front of the camera. Lines around the eyes and mouth deeper than when she'd met Silas in the coffee shop. Sunglasses rested on top of her head in a haphazard fashion. Makeup not perfect, she appeared tired, worried, or both.

"Channel Fourteen News, reporting live." The camera focused on a street sign as the reporter reeled off the address. "Within the last half-hour, an anonymous caller notified our station, that three children, victims of the serial kidnapper, were locked inside this abandoned house. The station immediately notified police. According to authorities here at the scene, all three children are alive."

Another anonymous caller. Silas pursed his lips. *What were the odds?* He waited for the reporter to unleash her usual drama. But Rebecca's tone was sincere, sensitive even. The positive change resonated with Silas.

"You will notice all responders are wearing hazmat suits. I am told this is not cause for alarm, but a precautionary measure taken at the advice of homicide detective Silas Albert. Detective Albert had cause to enter the house without backup or emergency protection. Unfortunately, the detective is not available for comment. Viewers take note. Detective Albert put himself at risk to initiate this rescue. If a person were to mention the detective's lack of concern for his own personal safety, he would respond, I was just doing my job. Channel Fourteen News will continue to bring you updates on this situation. To you, Detective Albert." Rebecca touched her hand to her brow in a mock salute. "Rebecca Haze, Channel Fourteen News back to the studio."

Silas perceived an act of concession in the acknowledgment. She'd given him what he'd asked for, solid reporting. But she wanted him to know, her style would be her own, and truth didn't pick sides. Silas would be okay with that.

Silas located his flip phone. After a couple of wrong numbers, he managed to connect to, Channel Fourteen News. "This is homicide detective Silas Albert. I need to speak with Rebecca Haze."

"Honest reporting, Rebecca," he said, when she answered.

"Thanks for noticing. I admit, leaving out all those lovely adjectives was uncomfortable, but at the same time the story came across stronger. Where are you?"

Silas recognized the reporter's fishing expedition. The hazmat suits would have any good reporter digging for the hot story.

"I'm hiding from the press." The detective chuckled. "I wanted you to know I read your synopsis for the documentary. The direction you've taken the story is agreeable. I'm out of town for three or four days. When I return, I'll call to set up another meeting."

"I'm a little surprised you agreed, but I'm pleased. Are you taking vacation?"

"Rebecca, do you ever stop sniffing for a story?"

"Are you hiding something?" There was a smile in her voice.

Silas considered how closely he and Rebecca would be working in the future. Best to set at least one boundary. "It's no secret," he said. "Sydney and I are going to Branson."

"She's a lucky woman." Rebecca's tone sounded wistful.

"One more thing." Silas guided the conversation back to business. "I noticed the synopsis didn't have a title."

"I haven't found one that fit."

"I have an idea."

"Really. What is it?"

"Inside The House of Audrey, a woman is offered tools to move beyond surviving their history. Never an easy path to choose. I'm thinking the title should be, The Defiant."

"A person's past does haunt them," Rebecca said. "I like it. I hear hope and strength behind those two words."

Silas's ear caught a note of sadness as though the reporter's opinion was based on experience.

"Good. That was my intent. I'll call you when Sydney and I get back."

Two hours passed before Archie returned. Missing the hazmat suite, he wore a broad smile. "Good news," he said. "No contagious disease—food poisoning. Kelsey Springer is in the worst condition, but they're all stable. The girl who escaped also heard the kidnapper talking to a Leah. That confirms Rose's story."

"Sexually assaulted?"

"No, but traumatized. Drugged, forced to undress, and kept in the dark in an ungodly hot room. Here's the surprise. Commissioner Rochester owns the house."

Silas's eyes narrowed. "What does he have to say about that?"

"Admitted he owned the place. Used as a rental until he got tired of the problems. Seemed shocked by the questions we asked. Claimed ignorance."

"That figures."

"We're not done with him yet. Thanks to Lila, we may be close to busting this trafficking operation wide open. She discovered a pattern that points to the method used to select the victims and how the kidnapper knows when the parents are away."

Silas's conscience twinged. "I knew she was working on a lead."

"That's where you and Sydney come in."

After sixty seconds, Silas gained a clear understanding of the implications between the hotel and the abductions. A picture of a young

Walter in uniform loaded with medals swirled in Silas's mind, followed by the image of the naked girl staggering down the alley. The memory of a will so strong to fight with only a jagged piece of porcelain in her hand sealed his decision.

"Tell me the plan."

CHAPTER TWENTY-EIGHT

J osie's eyelids fluttered open. Wood beams crisscrossed overhead where a bare bulb screwed into an old ceramic fixture. Even its dim light hurt her eyes. Her skull throbbed with the force of a jack hammer.

Was that humming, or...

She swiveled her head. To the right was a plank wall. The same on the left. She returned to center and lowered her chin. She gasped. She stared into the unseeing eyes of a dead man. She was hallucinating—wasn't she? The humming stopped.

"Josie. I didn't think you'd ever wake up. The sun's been shining forever. I wanted to go for help, but I was afraid I'd get lost and you'd die."

Josie sat up. She was nauseated, and her mouth felt watery. Macy was propped against the metal cot next to her. "Are you hurt?"

"I'm okay." Macy held out a bottle. "I found a six-pack of these."

The water was warm, but Josie guzzled it down.

"He's not so good." Macy nodded in Wade's direction her face void of emotion. "He's dead.

"I thought so."

"Your head butt knocked him out, but that's not what killed him." Macy stated in monotone.

"How do you know?" There was no smell of exploded gun powder. A gun had not been fired recently.

"I was afraid he'd wake up and come after us, so I got the zip ties."

Dear God, had this skinny girl strangled a grown man?

"Macy, what happened to him?"

"I didn't notice what was wrong at first. I rolled him over to fix his hands behind, like he made me do you. That board was fastened to the back of his head." Macy pointed.

The two by eight, Josie had tripped over earlier, lay slightly to the left of the kidnapper's corpse. Bits of pink and gray matter stuck to three nails protruding from the board.

"He never screamed once."

The words, cold as stone, struck Josie at her core. She wrapped Macy in her arms and pulled her close. "Don't think about him. You didn't do anything wrong." The sound of the girl's wounded soul was like a knife in Josie's chest. She gently rocked the child.

At last, the sobs quieted. Macy wiped her eyes. "But now he can't tell us where Odessa is." The raw bitterness was painful to hear.

"You can't help that. We're alive, and you'll be there when your sister is found. Let's get in that loser's truck and get out of here."

"Won't work."

"Sure, it will. Come on." Josie set Macy aside. The room tilted then settled. The Blackbird struggled to her feet.

"I already tried," Macy said. "The truck won't start. I turned the key, but it just clicked."

Bile crawled up Josie's throat. Rummaging thru a dead man's pockets for keys would be a creepy task for an adult, and a twelve-year-old girl should never have the experience. "Sounds like the battery is dead or the solenoid's gone bad."

"Can you fix it?"

"No." The Blackbird held out her hand. "Come on. We'll crawl out of here if we have to."

A glimmer of Macy's earlier defiance returned to her eyes. She took Josie's hand and climbed to her feet then scooped up the gun. "You better have this."

Josie took the weapon, checked the safety, and tucked the Beretta into her waistband. A moment later, the odd couple shuffled across the floor.

"Are you really a ninja?"

They had entered the room filled with farm equipment.

"Sort of," Josie replied.

"It's a secret group, isn't it?"

Josie frowned. "How about we focus on getting out of here?"

"I won't tell. I've read lots of books. I know how vigilantes work."

"My story is complicated. When we're safe, I'll share a little." An optimistic statement to have made when they had no transportation and no way to call for help. "I love afternoon walks. Don't you?"

"This is not funny. You're hurt. Do you even know which way to go?"

"Pick a direction." Josie's legs wobbled. She grabbed the rear wheel of an old tractor for support.

Macy's eyes widened. "You better sit down."

"Can't. A friend of Clyde's might show up at any minute." The Blackbird closed her eyes. She tried to recall her training. *What would Lila do?*

She caught a whiff of the rotten-egg-smell of sulfur. The odor emanated from the rubber tractor tire. A childhood memory stirred. What if she could get the tractor started? She was grasping for a straw, but it was all she had. She straightened and patted the tractor fender.

"We're going to see if this thing runs."

"You can drive a tractor?"

Josie managed a grin, ignoring the fact she'd been twelve when she last sat on her grandpa's John Deere.

Macy's eyebrows raised. "That's not a yes."

"They call these Johnny Pops because they make a funny popping sound when they start," Josie replied, as she checked that the brakes were locked. "If I remember right that long lever is a hand clutch. The little, short lever on the steering wheel works the same as a gas pedal. Forward for more gas, backward for less."

"How long do you think this Johnny's been sitting here? Doesn't gas evaporate?"

"Stop with the negative vibes, girl. Climb up there." Josie gave Macy a nudge. "See if you can find an ignition key in the dash. But don't turn it yet."

Macy stepped on the draw bar, grabbed the back of the green seat, and shimmied up to the metal deck. "I see it," she said.

"Excellent. Now pull that long lever back toward you." If Josie was in the presence of a priest, she'd ask him to pray for gas to be in the tank and the battery to be charged. Without those two additional items, the odd couple would be back to hiking out of these woods. Then prayers would be needed even more.

"Is this stick thing supposed to like flop around?"

"Yes. That means you've got it out of gear. Now on the instrument panel there should be a couple of gauges. Find the one for gas."

Macy dipped her head toward the dash. "I see it."

"Okay. The ignition works from two positions set by the key. One click turns on the power. The second starts the engine. Twist the key to the first click. If the fuel gauge is working and there's power in the battery, the arrow will move."

"Oh my gosh," Macy shouted. "We've got gas. The arrow went all the way over."

"Fantastic." Josie's pulse jumped. "There's one black knob. Find it and pull it out half-way."

"Got it."

"Now move the gas lever forward half, and turn the key to the second click. There'll be a grinding sound then a loud pop. When that happens, push the knob back in."

The starter turned. The engine popped once—twice. The silence after was deafening.

"Want me to try again?"

"Not yet. Let me think." For some reason, the engine wasn't getting gas. Josie walked her mind back to when she stood beside her grandpa thirty years earlier. In the memory, the slender Asian man had pointed to a glass bulb filled with orange liquid. A small shut-off valve stuck out at the top.

"Hang on." She called up to Macy. "I missed a step." If this didn't work, she was out of ideas. A moment later, she was back behind the rear tire. "The gas was turned off. Try it again."

"Come on," Macy pleaded. The starter ground, and then ground again. "Come on old Johnny, you can do it."

The engine turned over, hesitated as though dragging in a breath, popped once, twice, three times, and then settled into a steady rhythm. Josie clung to the tire treads in relief. "Thank you, Grandpa," she whispered.

"We did it," Macy shouted. "I'll get the door." She jumped to the ground and ran outside. A moment later she was back, panting hard. "Little trees are growing up in front. It won't open."

"It'll open." The room tipped and swayed as Josie fought through the pain and climbed onto the tractor. "Get back."

"Wait. Josie don't do it. What if you fall off?"

"It's our best hope for getting out of here." The Blackbird settled on the seat, released the brakes, and engaged the clutch. The wheels inched in the right direction. She braced her feet and shoved the gas lever forward. The tractor lunged. Metal screeched and wood splintered as the machine slammed into the door. Josie's butt lifted off the seat. She hung on. Hinges snapped and debris pounded the side of the shed.

The tractor bounced down an incline. Water sparkled in the sunlight, straight ahead. Josie yanked back on the gas and cranked the steering wheel with all her might. The old Johnny Pop veered into the hill, popping a little slower against the climb. The Blackbird pulled the clutch handle and tromped the brake pedals.

Macy ran up to the tractor as it rolled to a stop."You did it, Josie. You did it."

Josie released the steering wheel, mouth dry, and muscles trembling. Moisture trickled down her forehead. She swiped it away fingers coming away red. The hope in Macy's upturned face helped her focus. "What are you waiting for. Let's make tracks."

The draw bar clanged as Macy stepped up and perched on the fender. "Ready," she said.

"We should have walked to Kansas City," Josie muttered, then she giggled, but that hurt and she stopped.

"Josie, what's wrong with you?"

"Tired. It's hard being a clown. Need to rest." Josie was seeing in triplicate.

"Stop it. You're not a clown. Oh my God, this is bad. I don't know what to do. Josie, tell me what to do."

The panic in Macy's voice sliced through the fog in Josie's brain. "Concussion. Can't see to drive."

The climb down from the tractor became the scaling of Mt. Everest in reverse, slow and treacherous. Her arms and legs refused to follow orders. Dizzy was an understatement. When her feet touched the ground, her knees melted. Then there were arms around her waist.

"I got you." Macy sounded far away.

Josie forced her legs to lose their wet noodle feel. "Help me get in the shade." She took a step, but the ground did a slow roll. "Need a crutch."

Macy darted off up the hill. She returned carrying a rake.

The sun showed them kindness when it hid behind a cloud, but Josie was drenched in sweat when she collapsed under a tree twenty yards from the shed. Five minutes of rest, that's all she needed. Then she and Macy would get back on the Johnny Pop and drive across the old metal bridge to safety.

CHAPTER TWENTY-NINE

Miles slipped by, and the easy conversation between Woody and Lila tempted her to intentionally miss the entrance to Liberty Cemetery. Instead, she down shifted and maneuvered the '53 Studebaker through the open gateway. The engine's rumble softened to a dull growl. Following the narrow curving lane to the top of the hill, she parked under the limbs of a time-weathered cedar. Amber colored gum oozed from under the shaggy, reddish bark that had protected the tree's trunk for over a hundred years.

"It's peaceful here." Woody took in the grounds. "A troubled soul has a chance to be at ease here."

"Silas and I wanted that for Liz."

Woody pulled his cell from his pocket. "Maybe I can get an update on our kids."

The air-conditioner pumped cool air inside the car. Lila opened her own screen. She found one text from agent Croy. The agency was continuing to make Josie and the Franklin girls a top priority. Words. Just words.

Lila closed her eyes regretting every argument she'd ever had with Josie. Her phone pinged. The number wasn't one she recognized, but the caller ID showed Silas's name. She motioned to Woody she was taking the call outside and climbed from the car.

"Hi Silas. I see you got a new phone."

"Yeah. Can't access Bertha's resources with this one, but it'll get me by. Did you already go to the cemetery?

"I'm here now." She hesitated to blurt out the mission failure.

"I'm not checking up on you," he said. "Since you forwarded that information to Archie, he's got a serious lead. That was excellent work."

Lila tensed as Silas shared the horror of his morning. "Guess that's why I got shoved off to Agent Croy," she said.

"What are you talking about?" Silas's voice tightened.

"Silas, a Blackbird mission went bad. Josie is missing." Lila's stomach hurt by the time she finished her tale of failure.

"We've got this. Lila." Silas's tone softened to the one she'd heard him use dozens of times when she was grieving for her mother. "Don't worry, we've got the best tools at our fingertips. We'll find Josie. Stay in contact with Agent Croy. Do whatever he says. I'll be working closely with Archie."

"Okay. It's hard to believe Sydney is going undercover with you. Be careful. These people are dangerous." She disconnected and pulled in her emotions as Woody climbed from the Studebaker.

"The officers have eliminated about half of the Quick Stop locations." Woody said, sliding his cell back into his pocket. "Nothing yet."

Lila glanced in the direction of Liz's grave, trying to get her thoughts under control.

"If you need a private moment, I can wait over there." Woody motioned toward a seating area under the cedar.

"No. I'd like it if you'd come with me." Lila shut off the car, tucked her cell into her pocket, and gathered the wreath. Birds pecked at the blue seeds scattered beneath the cedar while Lila grappled with what to say. "Would you think I'm weird if I told you, I enjoy myself here?"

"Not in the slightest. This place would help me relax. I'll set the cooler by the bench." He grabbed the Coleman from behind the seat and carried it under the cedar where he placed it in the shade. He opened the lid and removed a small bouquet of daisies.

"Officer Mendez, you're amazing."

Woody offered his hand. "I know."

"And humble, too." There was nothing she could do for Josie, and she had to keep Woody from asking questions. She slid her palm into his.

Together, they wandered aimlessly from stone to stone reading the inscriptions. A squirrel chattered his disgust from his perch atop a moss-covered grave marker. One stone set for two brothers lost to the Civil War. Both killed at the Battle of Lexington, one a Confederate only eighteen and the other a Yankee two years older. Two tear drops had been etched into the stone under each name.

"This place is a history lesson." Woody slid his fingertips across the weather-worn marks.

Lila twisted two yellow flowers from Liz's wreath and left one on each side of the marker. "Can you imagine bringing two sons together for the last time in this way?"

"No. I can't" Woody placed his hand in the middle of her back. A warm tingle spread under her skin. He guided her forward as though he knew where he was going. Lila wondered if he'd visited here before. How close to Elizabeth Cartwright had Woody been? Someday, she might ask him. There was a great deal she wanted to know about Woody Mendez.

The absence of flowers across the cemetery indicated few visitors came here to pay their respects. Elizabeth's burial site provided protection in its obscurity. Despite the pain and guilt Liz had caused, Lila and Silas hadn't wanted the grave vandalized.

A few steps further and Lila stood before her friend's marker. A sharp breeze swept a smattering of leaves from the flat granite inscribed with only the initials, E.C. followed by a dates of birth and death.

"I remember you liked purple." Lila's words crept past a lump in her throat. She knelt and placed her arrangement against the base of the stone. A smaller wreath showed that one other person cared. Lila pictured Silas resting his prosthetic hand on the stone as he pressed the wire legs of the display into the dirt and tried to sort out how to move forward from a terrible betrayal.

Or did Woody leave the flowers?

Woody placed his daisies near the stone. "Rest in peace, Chief." He pivoted toward the cedar tree. "Let's sit in the shade."

Lila nodded, glimpsing a sheen of moisture in his eyes. She followed him to where a genius had placed a bench in the perfect spot to catch the cool breeze furling around the base of the tree. Lila positioned herself at one end of the seat, placing her cell phone beside her. Woody settled close, but not too close. Another positive check mark in Lila's mental log for evaluating men.

A woolly worm crawled across the toe of Lila's shoe. The old-timers claimed the color predicted the severity of the upcoming winter. Lila didn't know if the tale was true, but to her the bands of the little creature resembled Lila's own life. A black stripe on each end, represented the darkness of loss, and the pain and evil, attempting to smother her from every direction. For Lila, the bright orange bristles in the middle stood for her ability to survive in the darkest moments.

Woody took her hand. "Tell me what you're thinking."

"I'm thinking how lucky I am." Lila drank in the scent of cedar. "My life's been challenging, but I've always had family who cared. Liz never did. She's the reason I wanted to open a shelter for children." The wooly worm inched off the toe of Lila's shoe. "If one child can be saved from falling through the cracks the way Liz did, I'll be happy."

"I know." He swiped a stray strand of hair away from her forehead. "That's why you named the shelter, The Elle." He smiled into Lila's eyes. "I read that Elizabeth's sister called her, Elle. I made the connection."

Lila cocked an eyebrow. "Top notch detective work there, Officer Mendez. You better watch out. Silas Albert might have his eye on you to join the homicide unit."

A mischievous grin eased across Woody's face. "Silas has his eye on me alright, but he's not seeing my potential as a detective." He leaned forward and gently kissed her on the lips.

Lila's world spun.

He's so much older.

Silas doesn't like him.

His lips are so soft.

What's a girl to do?

She slid closer and kissed him back. The clean scent of his skin was intoxicating. Her ears hummed. The sound grew louder—an engine. She pushed away from Woody.

"What's wrong?"

"Someone's coming." Lila twisted toward the highway. The gravel thread leading up the hill was empty.

Darn her jumpy self, spoiling a most excellent kiss.

"Sorry, I'm still nervous about reporters." She pointed skyward. "Guess that's what I heard." A speck appeared from the south and morphed into a small yellow plane.

Lila tilted her head. The sound wasn't quite right. At first the heavens provided no reason for her unease, and then a tail of black trailed the plane. A message of doom scripted across the blue sky. She jumped to her feet, pointing skyward. "It's on fire."

Woody scrambled to her side. "I only hear one engine."

"He's flying low. Must be searching for a place to land." Lila snatched her phone from the iron bench and punched in three digits.

"911. What is your emergency?"

"My name is Lila Girard." She reeled off the information the 911 operator needed. The plane approached the cemetery. "There is a plane in trouble here. I'm not sure the pilot can clear the trees. He's flying with only one engine."

"Thank you for calling this in, but a Mayday call was received from the pilot. Emergency units are dispatched. If the plane crashes, there is a high risk of an explosion. Do not go near the site."

"Thank you." Lila disconnected from the 911 dispatcher. "Rescue units are on the way."

"That's a Cessna," Woody said. "A well-trained pilot can land her with one engine. The gusting wind is the problem. When he comes down, he may need help. I need to get closer. Woody ran toward the trees.

"But the dispatcher said..." Lila shoved the cell under her waistband. "Never mind." She raced after Woody. At a gate to the field, they halted, frozen in place by the terrible scene playing out ahead.

The Cessna's nose ploughed dirt, throwing clods into the air. One wing sliced hunks from hay bales as though they were loaves of bread. Failing metal screeched. At last, gravity dragged the plane to a stop.

Lila unlatched the gate, shoved it open, and sprinted toward the smoke. Woody ran beside her. White smoke curled from beneath the belly of the aircraft. At any moment she expected the plane to erupt into a fireball. She pressed forward faster.

When they reached the plane part of the undercarriage was torn lose. One wing curled backward toward the cabin. Lila's skin prickled at the pounding and frantic screams coming from inside.

"I'm Woody Mendez, a police officer. Help is on the way." Woody yanked the handle. "It's jammed," he yelled. "Are you the pilot?"

"The pilot's dead!" A man shouted. "Get me out of here."

"Try to stay calm. You're going to be okay." Woody spoke with control and authority. "You'll find a fire axe hanging in the cockpit.

Use it to smash the door open."

Seconds passed. "I got it."

Blow after blow slammed against the door until a gap appeared. A man peered through the opening. Long hair framed a face with eyes the size of saucers.

"It's loose. Hand out the axe," Lila shouted. "We can pry it open now."

The axe handle poked through the crack. "Hurry—the smoke—can't breathe."

Moments later the door hung free. Lila and Woody assisted the man down from the plane. Ugly tattoos of scaly creatures covered his arms and neck. His hair was none to clean. "Are you sure the pilot's dead?" Lila spoke first.

"No doubt about it. His head's all smashed."

"What about other passengers?" Woody asked.

The tattooed man snapped a glance at the plane, back to Woody, and then toward where Lila's Studebaker was parked. "Nope, just me. And I'm getting out of here. This plane's going to blow." He whirled and jogged off in the direction of the cemetery.

Doubt swirled in Lila's head. Any person worth a dollar would have stayed to help. "I don't believe him. The pilot may still be alive." She grabbed the edge of the opening.

"Lila, you can't go in there. He's right. This plane could explode any second."

"I can't live with myself if I don't check." She hesitated. "In case I don't make it back, you're an acceptable kisser."

"Wait." Woody reached for her arm. "What about your heart?"

Riding on a hunch, Lila avoided his grasp and pulled herself into the semi-dark cabin. She covered her nose and mouth with her shirt collar and inched forward. Visibility was poor. She tripped, regained her balance, and shoved a small bag out through the door.

Passenger seats ghosted through the smoke. She checked the first two. Empty. Behind her, she heard Woody climb inside the plane. Another sound made her gasp.

"Lila—are you hurt?"

"No." Lila stumbled forward to the next row. She stopped short at the sight of a girl slumped in the seat. "I found a passenger. You check on the pilot. I'll get her out."

She touched two fingers against the girl's neck. A steady pulse. But she had to hurry. She unsnapped the seat belt and encircled the teenager with her arms.

The girl's head lolled left then right. "Help. Please help." The trembling plea slurred in Lila's ear.

Keep calm. Complete the rescue.

She locked her hands together and dragged the girl backward to the door. The smoke thickened and crawled down her throat.

Woody shuffled through the haze the pilot draped over his shoulders. "Is he alive?"

"No, but I won't leave him."

"Hurry." She lowered the passenger to the floor at the exit and jumped to the ground. Her lungs gobbled fresh air. Then she took the first step, carrying her own burden.

Woody was out of the plane and on the move. "Get behind one of those big bales."

Sweat poured down her face. *How much strain would a transplanted heart take?* She passed the first hay bale, then a second, and a third. The wind shifted. The hairs at the back of her neck stirred.

"Get down." Woody shoved her to the ground behind the next bale. The hard dirt bit at her knees and elbows. The passenger she carried slid forward, coming to rest an arm's length away. Panic chewed at Lila's nerves. She shielded her head with her arms.

Woody let loose of the pilot and threw himself on top of Lila. The earth rocked. She squeezed her eye lids tight, praying not to be burned alive. The stink of melted rubber filled the air.

"Stay down," Woody shouted. "Keep your eyes shut."

Lila's eyes shot open of their own accord. The pilot lay next to her. His smashed, jack-o-lantern, face inches from her own. A jagged gash coursed from the top of the man's head to his upper lip. She twisted away, gagging a little.

"I told you to keep your eyes closed. Are you okay?"

"No." The memory of the pilot's face would be with her for a long time. "What about the girl?"

"She's alive. I heard her groan."

"Let me up." Lila ordered. "I have to see if I can help her."

"Do you want to die?"

"I said, let me up." She bucked and rolled out from under his weight.

"You're one stubborn woman," he growled.

On hands and knees, Lila crawled to the teenager. One side of her face was visible. Blood from a cut on her scalp had matted the shiny blonde hair. The half of her lips Lila could see were swollen and turning purple. "You're safe now. Help is on the way." Lila soothed the young woman. "What's your name?"

"Odessa," came the slurred reply.

The familiar growl of Lila's Studebaker rolled across the hayfield. "He's taking your car." Woody yelled.

"No," Lila shouted. "He's coming back."

The car herkie-jerked across the field, wheeling to a stop close to Lila. The driver jumped out. "Whoever owns this car, left the keys in the ignition. We'll use it and explain later. That girl might die before help arrives.

It's mine." Lila said. Alarm bells clanged in her head. *The girls name—Odessa.* Lila rose to her feet.

The man motioned toward the car. "Then you drive. I'm not that good with a stick shift."

"Hold on, I know yo...." Woody stepped in front of Lila.

The Studebaker backfired. Too loud. Too close. Woody staggered. A dark stain crawled across his shirt. His eyes widened as he fell.

"Woody," Lila screamed, dropped to her knees, and pressed both hands against the wound. Her peripheral vision caught the glimpse of a boot, and then pain exploded up and down her rib cage. Knocked to the ground, she tensed for another kick but all that came was mocking laughter.

"Get up, Lila," the tattooed man ordered. "Get up right now or I shoot her next." He pointed the gun at Odessa.

Lila struggled to her feet, sucking air between her teeth. "How do you know my name?"

He motioned toward the Studebaker. "A while back, when your uncle saved your sweet little ass, you and that car were plastered all over the news. Not happening this time. I've got a score to settle with the detective." His lips curled. "Business first. Then pleasure. When I'm done with you, Silas Albert will be sorry he ever knew Wade Rowland."

Lila's stare never left Woody. "Let me try to stop the bleeding. I'll do whatever you want."

"Yes. You will." A cold and menacing tone crackled in her ear. "I know you've got a phone. Hand it over. We don't want you found—yet."

Lila's stomach turned to ice. Emergency responders would be here any minute. She had to count on them to save Woody. This monster wanted revenge, but that wasn't the only reason he'd returned. He needed a driver. She tugged the device loose from her waistband and handed it over. He promptly smashed it with his boot and threw the disabled phone into the weeds. He motioned the girl, Odessa, toward the car.

"Take me but leave her," Lila pleaded.

"Not on your life. Get in the car."

"Help is on the way, Woody. Hang in there." She forced her feet to move. The salty taste of tears rode sharp on her tongue as she climbed behind the wheel.

Rowland shoved Odessa in the front. He pulled a zip tie from his back pocket and secured her hands, fastened the safety belt, and slid into the rear seat. "Drive." He tapped the gun against the back of the seat. "Don't try to be a hero."

Lila's body shook as she put the Studebaker in gear and drove back through the cemetery. The cooler waited under the bench as a stark reminder of Woody's kiss.

"When you get to the highway, turn left."

She wheeled the Studebaker onto the highway. Every move sent a wave of pain through her rib cage. A mile passed. The faint peal of sirens rolled toward them.

"Damn. They got here fast." He indicated a gravel road leading off to the east. "Turn there."

Dust kicked up behind them. The sound of emergency vehicles grew louder. *Please God, help them find Woody in time.*

Lila forced the image of Woody lying in a pool of blood to the back of her mind and focused on her Blackbird training. *Evaluate. Calculate. Execute.*

According to Owl, two men in different vehicles abducted the Franklin girls. Eagle managed to climb into the back of a GMC Canyon. Odessa was here with Lila. That meant her sister, Macy, had an Eagle to protect her.

If there was a hope to be had, it was two Blackbirds in a fight instead of one. Even if this one had an injured wing.

Lila struggled to focus on the road unable to blink away the sight of Woody, lying beside the dead pilot. A pale but alert Odessa held her bound hands locked between her knees. It would be hours before anyone questioned Lila's absence. The 911 dispatcher having Lila's name was their only hope.

Boiling dust tracked the Studebaker down the narrow gravel road. A ribbon of black trailed off to the right. "Turn there," Wade pointed.

Lila slowed the car and turned south.

"You can drive sixty. No faster." Wade tapped the gun on the back of Odessa's seat. "Don't be trying to attract attention. I figure we've got about an hour, maybe two, before they start the hunt for you. By that time, we'll be in the hills. I know how to keep us invisible there."

Lila's mind cleared a little. *A Blackbird never stops until she finds a way.* She glanced left and right. The ground was rough, dotted with rocks, wild blackberry vines, and multi-flora rose. A person wouldn't dare enter for fear of breaking a leg or being torn to shreds by the vicious thorns. Not one house in sight, no place to run after a crash.

The kidnapper prodded Lila's sore shoulder with the gun. "I see you looking all around. I know you're planning something. If you so much as veer the wrong direction, she'll pay." He stroked Odessa's hair with dirty fingers. "Young girls have such silky hair."

Odessa shrieked and jerked away.

"Leave her alone."

"What's the matter, Lila? You don't want me to have a little extra fun before I get to you?"

Anger swept through Lila in waves. "The police will hunt you down and shoot you, like a dog. What does that get you?"

"Humph," Wade snorted. "No city girl could ever understand the code of the hills. I tried it there. Got nothing but trouble. Silas Albert cost me five years. A gut full of payback is what I aim to gain." He trailed the sight of the gun along the back of Lila's neck. "Think about that, sweet thing."

She denied him the pleasure of even a flinch. The urge to slam on the brakes and take her chances roared through her brain. *No. No. No. Calm down.* He caught her checking the mirror and blew her a kiss.

For the next hour, the Studebaker followed a snaky trail around knobby hills and across rocky creek beds with ditches too deep to risk wrecking the car. Fifty miles passed beneath the car's belly. Then she heard Wade's phone beep as he used the keypad.

She took advantage of his distraction and squeezed Odessa's hand. The girl returned the pressure.

One eye on the road, Lila strained to hear Wade's conversation. One ring, but no voice. Another ring, still no answer. Then beep, beep, beep.

"Damned reception," Wade grunted.

Lila dared another peek in the mirror.

Wade glared back at her. "What're you lookin' at?"

"Thought you wanted something." Lila ducked her head. *Was brother Clyde not following the plan?* Lila guessed he was supposed to secure Macy and then drive to a designated location that would have a cell signal. Maybe, just maybe, he hadn't counted on an Eagle to get in his way. "Your brother's place in the middle of nowhere?"

"Yes. It is, but damn him. He only had to go two miles to that convenience store. That big black dude was smart. He opened his place on top of a hill. People can see that white rooster from both directions down the highway, and nothing blocks the cell frequency."

Lila bit back a gasp. *The general location was right. There couldn't be two stores, using a white rooster as advertisement in the Ozarks. It had to be DeShawn and Ada's place.*

"Maybe he never made it." Lila fed his anxiety. "He might have hit a deer. They're always crossing the road at night."

"Shut up. He didn't hit no deer."

"What if he broke down?"

"I said shut up," Wade's frustration vibrated the air. "The Boss must have called him and told him to stay put."

That didn't make sense. No one could reach Clyde if he didn't have a signal. She heard Wade dial again. Once. Twice. A person answered, but the tone was odd. Not distinctly male, nor clearly female.

"The person you are trying to reach is unavailable. Leave a message."

"Boss, it's Wade. We have a problem. I'll call you back."

Lila shivered. Time was running out.

CHAPTER THIRTY

The Harley rumbled down the road, carrying Silas and Sydney into the Ozark hills. The last few hours had altered his mental frame of reference. A change, he admitted, brought on by Sydney's perspective of the undercover operation they had agreed to work together.

Thanks to her, for the first time in months, Silas pulled his police training toward him embracing it as a strength and not a burden. He still needed a chance to pick apart and digest what this meant for his future, but a window was opening and the guilt he bore as punishment had a place to go. He understood he still needed separation, a fresh landscape. He also knew his problems would wait until the child trafficking ring was destroyed.

"You know, I would have been disappointed if you'd kept me in the dark about the new purpose of this trip," Sydney spoke through the helmet intercom.

"Archie warned me that would be a dangerous decision." Silas reduced the Harley's speed and leaned into a sharp curve. A wall of granite climbed high on the right. Yellow signs warned of falling rock. He couldn't help but glance up and a shift in Sydney's body told him she'd done the same.

A lane for slow moving traffic fanned out ahead, and Silas guided the motorcycle around a dump truck loaded with gravel. After a mile, trees reclaimed the roadside. A sign for DeShawn and Ada's Convenience Store caught Silas's eye. The white, metal rooster cut a strut along the top of the advertisement. 'WELCOME' blinked in red neon across the chicken's chest.

Silas pointed to the rooster and spoke into the helmet's intercom. "Pages' store. Remember, I told you about them?" He swallowed back a chuckle. He hadn't told her about Homer. "We can't check in at the resort until three. Do you mind if we stop?"

"I'd love to meet them. And—I need to use the lady's room."

A half-dozen live chickens performed a rendition of the Charleston Stroll across a grassy area, as Silas motored into the parking lot. Their crimson heads bobbed and one foot swiveled, creating an uneven motion of the body. DeShawn had taught Silas an imitation of the dance one night after they'd partaken of a beer or two. One part of their history Silas hoped DeShawn never shared. Especially with Sydney.

"Real chickens," Sydney said. "How fun."

Silas bit his tongue. *Little did she know.*

He'd met DeShawn and Ada Page in the city while working the drive-by shooting that had taken their only child's life. Charmed by the sweet couple, Silas recognized their need for a fresh start. He had helped the couple find this little store. DeShawn and Ada sold their house in the inner-city for the down-payment. Silas discretely backed the loan, and the couple moved into the living quarters in the back. He'd never been sorry.

Silas located a shady spot and parked. He surveyed the business as Sydney dismounted. "DeShawn told me Ada's selling her homemade sweet rolls. Can't wait to check that out."

"Mmm, me too. Let's go."

Silas followed Sydney inside, appreciating the sway of her hips, and anticipating the surprise that awaited her inside the convenience store.

"Oh my gosh!" Sydney gaped at the six-foot tall, white, rooster. A magnet couldn't have drawn her quicker. She extended her hand and touched the bird's golden claws. "How cu..."

The rooster sprang to life, flapped his wings, threw open his beak, and crowed loud enough to be heard all the way to Arkansas. Sydney shrieked and backed up, slamming into Silas.

"Hi, I'm Homer. Welcome to DeShawn and Ada's place." The rooster spoke in DeShawn Page's sultry voice. Silas roared with laughter. Homer had made another memory.

Sydney rolled her eyes. "It's not that funny. He scared the crap out of me. Hope your friends have insurance. I almost had a stroke."

A booming laugh drew their attention to the customer check-out station. DeShawn Page's six-foot-three frame towered over the cash register. "The sign clearly says, *Don't Touch*, but no one can resist Homer. First time customers are excused." A big grin spread across the smooth black face. "Well, I'll be darned. Silas Albert, is that you?" DeShawn signaled to an older man behind the counter to take over. "Give me a minute."

Silas gave Sydney a hug. "You've got to admit that rooster is a great gimmick. A person will never forget this place. Folks make a point to stop here, just to see Homer." He pointed to a blue arrow. "The restrooms are that way." Sidney hurried off, shaking her head.

"Go get Ada. She's in the back. She'll be thrilled to see you," DeShawn called out.

"Take your time." Silas wandered to the bakery. The scent of cinnamon turned his thoughts to Lila. She loved Ada's sweet rolls. Lila would be hurting today. He hoped she didn't get blindsided by her own emotions.

Silas checked the flip phone for messages. His scalp prickled. Janelle didn't text him often. He opened the message. "Hi Silas. We have our first two children at the shelter. They say Lila told them to come. The children claim they witnessed a murder. Tried to reach Lila first. No response. I've called Hadley but wanted you to know."

Janelle had done the right thing in calling Hadley. For Lila to have her cell off was a bit unusual, but the detective wasn't particularly alarmed. Silas had built the system. Now he needed to let it work the way it was meant to when he wasn't available. Movement in Silas's peripheral vision caught his attention. He casually switched position.

With the stealth of practice, a boy removed packages from a cooler and slid them under a ragged jacket. He hesitated, glancing toward the cash register.

Silas figured him to be about twelve. The age when boys are all arms, legs, and neck.

This one didn't strike Silas as the bold walk-out-the-front-door-with-his-loot type. The detective strolled outside and slipped around the corner. A beat-up bicycle leaned against a light pole. The rubber portion of the peddles had long since disintegrated. Duct tape covered the worn-out seat, and a frayed Chief's flag hung from the bike's handlebars.

Silas positioned himself by the rear exit. The sun bore down, ripening the contents of a green metal dumpster. Flies feasted on the refuse and buzzed a happy tune of delight at their luck. Sweat trickled in rivulets down the detective's forehead.

The door inched open wide enough for a skinny kid to slip through. Silas stuck out his foot and caught the little shoplifter before he hit the ground. "What's your hurry?"

"Let me go." A wild kick missed the detective's shins by a hair.

Silas held the boy at arm's length. "First, why are you stealing food?"

"Leave me alone. I'm none of your business."

Silas held the boy with his good hand and retrieved his badge with his prosthetic. He waved it under the boy's nose. "This says, thieves *are* my business. What's your name?"

The boy paled. "Bubba."

"Real name."

"Austin."

"That's better." He tucked his badge away. "Now Austin. Convince me why I shouldn't arrest you." Silas didn't have authority outside of Kansas City, but a kid wouldn't know that.

The boy jutted his chin. "I didn't steal nothin'."

Silas poked the lumps in the boy's jacket. "What's this?"

Austin twisted and fought, but Silas kept his grip tight.

"I'm telling you—I don't steal!" Austin locked eyes with Silas. "I haven't paid for what I took, but DeShawn knows I will."

"Let's go inside and see what DeShawn has to say...."

The door swung wide, and Silas's friend filled the open space.

"It's okay, Silas," DeShawn said. "Let the boy go. Austin and I have a working arrangement." A strange mixture of sadness and determination wound through the big man's words.

"Out of respect for my friend, I'm letting you go." Silas released his grip. He waited, and to the boy's credit, he didn't run."

Austin ignored the detective and focused a brooding stare on his bicycle.

"Austin, remember the story I told you about detective Silas Albert?"

The boy smirked, clearly a skeptic. Then he seemed to notice Silas's prosthetic. "You are him." Amazement altered the sullen face. "You got the punk who killed DeShawn's son."

"Austin, you can trust Silas Albert. He's a man of his word."

Silas placed a hand on Austin's shoulder. "That's the only kind of man to be. Now you better get on out of here before I change my mind."

CHAPTER THIRTY-ONE

Hadley sped toward the shelter. Janelle's call had his brain in a tailspin. Walter's body had been discovered in a bad part of the city. What were two kids doing near at old warehouse at six o'clock in the morning? Who were they? How had they found their way to The Elle?

He turned into the small lot and parked next to Janelle's red Cadillac. Another car sat near the back fence. *What was Woody Mendez doing here?* The absence of the Studebaker gave Hadley his first clue. A mischievous thought curled through his mind. Woody had his eye on Lila Girard, and whether Silas wanted it or not, his niece was doing more than smiling back.

Lila was visiting the cemetery today. He'd promised Silas to check on her when she returned, but there was no need. Woody would do a fine job. Hadley chuckled. A break in the Walter Long murder case would keep him much too busy to get in the middle of Lila's love life.

Janelle met him on the step, bringing along a whiff of bacon. The psychiatrist, usually a jolly person, didn't smile.

"How are they doing?" Hadley asked.

"Good, considering what they've seen." Janelle said grimly. "I couldn't reach Silas. I sent him a text."

"Did the kids tell you their names?"

"Elsa and Gordy. Rowland is their last name. You and Silas sent their father Wade to prison five or so years ago. The girl couldn't have been more than seven then, the boy only four. I don't think Gordy remembers much about his father. Elsa remembers too much."

A jolt of concern passed through Hadley. "He was bad news. Where's their mother?"

Janelle checked over her shoulder. "In jail for a minor crime. She'll be released in a week or two. They were in foster care, but took off. They've been living on the street. For an unknown reason, Walter looked out after them." The psychiatrist laid a hand on the detective's arm. "The system already failed these kids once. Take it easy with them, Hadley. The man they saw murdered was maybe the best family they've ever had."

Hadley nodded. "Understood." He followed the psychiatrist through the house and into the kitchen. A small TV sat on the counter. A commercial about insurance flashed across the screen. The sound muted. A boy with dark curls and a blond-headed girl sat on the floor shoveling scrambled eggs into their mouths. A cardboard box substituted as a table and held Solo cups of orange juice.

"You must be Gordy and Elsa. I'm Hadley Barker." He smiled

"Are you a cop?" Gordy spoke around a mouthful of food.

"Yes."

Elsa leaned back on her hands, gaze steady, judging.

"Hadley is my friend," Janelle said. "He's trying to find out who hurt your friend. I asked him to come." She nodded toward the counter. "I fixed you a plate. Sorry, no coffee." She waggled a carton with oranges on the front.

Hadley pecked the doctor on the cheek. "You're a goddess."

Gordy giggled. "She is not, but she's nice."

"Mind if I join you?"

Gordy exchanged a glance with his sister.

Elsa shrugged. "Help yourself."

Hadley lowered himself to the floor. Janelle handed down the plate and a red cup filled with juice to match the others.

"I cooked the bacon," Gordy said.

The detective stuffed a piece in his mouth. "Umm. Delicious. Cooked exactly right." He fist-bumped the boy. Conversation halted, replaced by the crunch of bacon and the scrape of plastic forks against cheap plastic plates.

"You can ask me questions if you want," Gordy blurted. "It won't bother me."

Hadley swallowed the last of his eggs. "First, I want you and Elsa to know I'm sorry your friend died."

"Thanks." Elsa blinked rapidly.

Gordy's fists knotted.

So much for not being bothered.

Janelle broke in, "Start at the beginning." she said softly. "Tell Hadley how you met Walter, and how you became friends."

The story came out in bits and pieces. Gordy talked for a while. Then Elsa took over. "Right before he was shot, I heard the killer mutter, *Sorry, Walter.*" Elsa's words caught in her throat. "It was just a whisper, but I know I got it right. Doesn't that mean they knew each other?"

"That makes sense," Hadley agreed.

Gordy shot a wide-eyed glance at his sister. "I forgot that part. But I remembered something else. The killer has red hair. Walter's hair is mostly white now, but he told us it was red back when he was in the Army."

Hadley's nerves tingled. Even if he included those who used dye, there weren't that many redheads in the world. The reporter, Rebecca Haze was the only one the detective could think of.

No.

There was one more. CSI found red hair on Rose Pham's clothes from the night of her abduction. The odds of a connection were one in a million. But red was a color hard to mistake. Earlier the kids had described the killer as dressed in dark clothes with a hood. Gordy identified the perp as tall, Elsa said medium. Neither remembered a skin tone.

The detective probed deeper. "How could you tell the hair color? Was the person's hood up or down?"

Gordy's mouth pinched as though he'd failed a test. "Dunno, I just remember red hair."

"That's okay, Gordy," The psychiatrist placed a hand on the boy's blonde curls. "You've given the detective a very important detail."

"The hood was up. The top was splattered with white." Elsa stated with conviction. "Pieces of hair stuck out from under. Red for sure. Another thing. The killer had on sunglasses. I think that's weird since it was real early in the morning."

Dark clothes, a hood, and sunglasses made up a disguise. Hadley's pulse picked up a beat. "Had you ever seen this person before?"

"I don't think so," Elsa said. "But everything happened so fast, and the shadows from that old building made it hard to see."

Gordy's head bobbed. "Yeah, we had to get out of there. We might've got shot too."

"That was smart," Hadley agreed. He thought back to the details of the crime scene. "Walter had a wallet. Did you ever see it?"

Elsa's face darkened. "Why are you asking us that?" She jumped to her feet hands on her hips. "You think we'd steal from a friend?"

"Hold on, Elsa." Janelle stepped in close and placed her palm on the girl's forearm. "Give Hadley a chance to explain."

Gordy hopped up to stand beside his sister. "We don't steal—that is unless we're hungry." He skewed his eyes toward Janelle. "That don't count, does it?"

The psychiatrist grinned. "Not today."

Hadley lumbered to his feet. "I never once thought you took your friend's wallet, but it is missing. The investigation leads us to believe the person who did this to your friend was searching for something specific that might have been inside. That's why I asked the question."

Elsa glared, not ashamed, and not backing down.

"He did have a billfold," Gordy piped up. "Remember, Sis. He showed us pictures of his kids. Two little girls. Wonder if they know something bad happened to their dad?"

Attempts to notify next of kin had not turned up any record of Walter Stone ever having been married or fathering any children. Hadley's investigative instincts quivered. More than one murder had been committed to hide a past infidelity. "Did he tell you their names?"

Gordy twisted his lips, thinking. "One of them had a boy's name."

A phone pinged. All heads swiveled in Janelle's direction.

"Hello," Janelle answered. "Tell me you have good news." The psychiatrist listened. Her eyes sparkled. "Yes, Ruth Anne, they're right here. Hang on. I'm putting you on speaker."

"Elsa, Gordy—it's, Momma."

The boy's mouth fell open. His sister stared at the phone, at Janelle, then back again.

"Momma," Elsa choked out. "Is it really you?"

"Yes, Baby. It's really me. I'll be able to see you in a seven or eight days. Gordy, Sweetie, are you there? I've missed you both something terrible. Are you guys okay?"

Hadley raised his eyebrows at Janelle. Was there no end to the psychiatrist's connections? The kids had been there less than two hours. She'd got them bathed, fed, tracked down their mother, and arranged the telephone call.

Over the tops of the kid's heads, Janelle sent the detective a wink then held the phone out for Gordy to talk.

"Momma. It's Gordy. We took care of each other like you said." A tear coursed down the eight-year-old's cheek. He swiped it away. "Elsa made me say a prayer every night that you would find us. I love you, Momma. But—but—why can't you come today?"

Hadley winced at the raw longing in the boy's voice. The detective had learned from Silas to build relationships within the judicial system. He knew lawyers and a judge or two. There was a way to speed up the mother's release.

"I love you too." Ruth Anne cleared her throat. "Gordy, you know I did something wrong, and I had to go to jail. But I'll be out soon. Can you be strong for one more week?"

Elsa put her arm around her brother. "Don't worry, Momma. Gordy's brave. We'll be fine until you come." She glanced at Janelle. "We're safe here. This place is called, The Elle. It's a shelter. Remember that and you can find us."

The three spoke for a minute or two, but not once did Hadley hear anyone ask about the father. They hadn't seen him in five years, and they probably didn't care if they ever saw him again.

"Time to go," A man ordered in the background.

"I love you guys more than anything. I promise I'll see you soon."

The kids murmured tearful goodbyes and the call ended.

Elsa threw her arms around Janelle. "Thank you..."

The doorbell broke the two apart. Hadley peered outside. "It's a moving van."

"The furniture," Gordy shouted. "Now we won't have to sleep on the floor."

Janelle laughed. "Well, what are you waiting for? Somebody let the movers in."

Both kids rushed for the door. The troubles of the last few minutes eased by new possibilities.

Hadley dodged the psychiatrist in her frenzy of furniture placement. The two kids danced between the table and chairs, touching, and sitting. Their enthusiasm was contagious. But what would happen to these kids and their mom now?

Ruth Anne faced an uphill battle. Affordable, safe housing was hard to find. The detective guessed family support was weak or nonexistent. Hadley's wheels began to turn. This woman needed a person in her corner. A person who wanted nothing in return.

Less than five minutes was all it took for Hadley to sweet talk a lawyer into working on Ruth Anne's early release. Then, the detective remembered he still had police work to do. He contacted the department and arranged for a police sketch artist to work with Elsa and Gordy. He didn't hope for much, but cases cracked in the strangest ways.

Hadley took a minute and sent Silas a short note about who had witnessed Walter's murder, he added a little sarcasm.

Elsa and Gordy say Walter's killer has red hair. Hmm, who do we know that fits that description. Think Rebecca Haze would interview herself if it's her? Ha Ha. Investigation continues.

Hadley smirked and hit send.

CHAPTER THIRTY-TWO

"This has got to be one for the books, my friend," Silas said, as Austin peddled across the parking lot.

DeShawn frowned. "I'll explain inside. Get your lady and go to my office." The store owner yanked the back door open and disappeared inside.

Silas located Sydney, drooling over the sweet rolls.

"Where'd you go? I thought you'd brought me to heaven and dumped me." She smiled up at him her eyes sparkling in a way that made his pulse jump.

"Sorry," Silas said. "Something has happened." He guided Sydney to a quiet corner of the store, where he described the shoplifting incident. "I don't know what DeShawn's got himself into, but we need to have a listen."

"And your gut is talking to you."

"Practically shouting." Silas took her hand. "Ada and DeShawn live in the back of the store. They're waiting for us in their apartment."

Side by side, they walked down a wide hallway to an open door where Ada waited. She wrapped Silas in her arms the way a momma bear does her cub. "She's real pretty," Ada whispered in Silas's ear.

"I know," Silas agreed.

Inside DeShawn's office, Silas made brief introductions.

"Since you're the first lady Silas has ever brought to meet us, I'd be honored if you joined me here." Ada lowered herself to a love seat covered in bright persimmon fabric and patted the cushion next to her.

The other Page settled behind a scarred wooden desk. Silas pulled a plastic kitchen chair from a corner and plopped down.

"Now Ada, leave Silas's lady alone. I need to explain about Austin."

Silas leaned forward. "What's his story?"

"The Rowlands are a troubled family. The father's half-crazy." DeShawn ran a hand over his bald skull. "He works, but never enough. Sometimes they don't even have electricity. The kids are scared to death of him. Trish tried to leave him once, but he found her and—well you can guess what happened."

Silas's stomach lurched. Another Rowland? What had he stumbled into?

"How many kids?" Sydney asked.

"Austin has a sister, Bella—six-years-old and cute as can be." DeShawn's face softened. "I don't want you to think I'm encouraging the boy to shoplift. It's not like that at all."

"You mentioned an arrangement."

"I caught Austin stealing." DeShawn's lips tightened. "He begged me not to tell his dad. He was so pitiful, I agreed. Thought that was the end of it. Then he stole again. I used a little *scared straight* talk on him. He broke down. Come to find out, his father had put the boy up to stealing. Threatened to hurt Bella if Austin failed to follow orders. I wanted to kill the bastard myself."

"I can understand," Sydney said. "I'm glad you didn't."

"I still might." DeShawn's jaw jutted, but continued. "In the city, I've seen parents pimp their own children. When we came here, Ada and I thought we'd left that kind of meanness behind. These hills have a healing power that brought us peace. We've made friends because of Homer. We've even had one of your police commissioners stop in. He introduced us to Clyde Rowland. Didn't take long for us to figure out those kids needed help."

"A commissioner—from Kansas City?" Sydney raised her eyebrows.

"Yeah. Clarence Rochester. It's been a while now. He didn't see the humor in Homer's greeting. He's the kind of guy who'd complain to the county and try to make me get rid of the store's main attraction. Struck me as one unhappy man. You know him?"

"Yeah," Silas remarked. "Let's just say, we're not exactly on the same page."

"I see you still have Homer." Sydney smiled.

A mischievous grin spread across Ada's face. "You can't imagine how a dozen of my sweet rolls takes the anger right out of a man."

Silas chuckled. "They are magical."

DeShawn's lips twitched. "Anyway, a couple of days later the commissioner came in with Clyde."

"Really?" Silas frowned. "Unusual relationship. Wonder how they met?"

"No idea, but if Rochester waved money under Clyde's nose, there's not one thing that man wouldn't agree to do. I was curious myself. Clyde loves to brag, so the next time he came in, I asked him what he was doing rubbing elbows with a Kansas City commissioner."

"What did say?" Silas asked.

DeShawn's eyes held the glint of a sly fox. "I guess Clyde thought his dealings with a big city guy would impress me. According to him, Rochester was paying the brothers to buy up abandoned or run-down properties on the quiet. Claimed the city had a big development planned and they'd make bundles of money. I almost laughed."

Inside Silas's head, puzzle pieces turned. One or two slid into place. *A new football stadium. Insider knowledge. Embezzlement and child trafficking would both be lucrative sources of income. Enough to fund the purchase of land to support hotels and restaurants.*

"Did he say where the properties were located?" Sydney spoke up as though she'd read his mind.

"Not far from The House of Audrey. And, Austin told me his dad and uncle have been spending a lot of time traveling back and forth to Kansas City."

"Interesting." Silas thought he knew the identity of the other Rowland but he wanted to be sure. "Does Clyde have a buddy with weird tattoos on his arms and neck?"

"His brother Wade. I wouldn't be surprised if you had reason to know him. He's the worst of the two."

Silas wondered if DeShawn knew how much worse. "I ran into Wade recently. The man was having a private conversation with Rochester. A commissioner and a known convict who appeared to be conspiring together didn't mesh well in my mind. Guess those instincts are still good."

"Wade lived in Kansas City for a while," DeShawn said. "Had a nice wife. I think her name was Ruth Ann. They had a couple of kids too. Don't know what happened to Wade's family after he got in all that trouble. From what I've heard, the brothers never were too smart. Clyde strutted around here that day crowing louder than Homer. I wanted to slap him upside the head."

Sydney smiled "You should be a detective. You ask the right questions." She turned serious. "Austin's father sounds like a real piece of work."

"I'm only telling you this to help those kids. They'll never be safe until Clyde's out of the picture. In jail or dead."

Silas's nerves twanged. He didn't want DeShawn involved in *dead* of any kind. "I'll help if I can, but you've been dancing with the devil. Tell me more about Austin."

"He's an innocent child." DeShawn slammed the top of his desk with his fist. Sydney and Ada jumped. A stack of notebooks toppled to the floor. For a long second, no one spoke. "Sorry, it's—just—that bum has no idea how precious a child's life is." DeShawn intertwined his sausage-sized fingers.

At that moment, Silas figured DeShawn was thinking of the loss of his own son. "You're letting Austin take groceries. Why? You could give the boy a couple of sandwiches."

"Sometimes I do. But I was afraid if I got busy and the boy had to wait, his father would get suspicious. I told him to take whatever his father said, and we'd settle-up later. If Clyde Rowland ever caught on, I don't know what the man would do."

"DeShawn wanted to call the sheriff on the man," Ada said. "I talked him out of it. Tess is a good mother. I didn't want those babies split up."

The couple didn't realize how close to the edge of a cliff they stood, or how devastating the fall would be. His friends believed they were protecting the kids. Silas sensed a pending disaster.

Sydney placed a hand on Ada's arm. "Have you seen evidence of abuse?"

Ada glanced at her husband. The man's eyes shifted.

"DeShawn," Silas interjected. "You can't protect Austin and his sister. They need outside intervention. For those kids' own safety, you have no choice but to call authorities."

Tears glistened in Ada's eyes.

"I guess we knew this was coming," DeShawn gripped the arms of his chair. "It's the right thing."

"Sheriff Rose is an old friend. If you have his number, I'll call him and let him know you want to make a report."

"We know Rufus. We voted for him for sheriff. I don't have his number in my phone, but I think it's right here." Ada dragged an old Rolodex across the top of DeShawn's desk, whirled it to the Rs, and read the number off to Silas.

"Silas, my man. What's up?" Rufus replied as soon as the detective identified himself.

It took a moment for Silas to explain.

"Trouble follows you around, doesn't it?" Rufus said. "I'm aware of domestic issues with the Rowland's. DeShawn and Ada, they're good people. Clyde Rowland's another story. Vultures wouldn't pick his bones if he lay dead on the highway."

"That's what I've gathered." Silas agreed.

"It's your lucky day. Angela, the supervisor for our county's social workers and me have been checking on an elderly abuse situation nearby. We're about three miles away. Angela is familiar with Austin and Bella's situation. We've discussed the kids and their mother multiple times. The report from the Pages' may be just what she needs to intervene on those kid's behalf."

Austin's dilemma tugged at Silas's conscience. The idea of the boy caught in the middle or Rufus facing Clyde without backup, didn't set well. "If she decides to visit the Rowland family I'd like to ride along with you if that's okay. We can talk about old times."

Sydney turned away, but not before a knowing little smile tweaked her lips. *Damn it's irritating when she sees right through me.* He had to admit there was a little adrenaline moving through his veins.

"I don't see why not," Rufus said. "Angela has her own vehicle. I tagged along today in case she needed me to cart somebody off to the hoosegow. I, for sure, don't want her going into the Rowland house alone. We'll be at the Page place in a few. It won't take long for Angela to write up the report. Then, you're my investigative advisor."

Silas's curiosity stirred. It wasn't uncommon for a social worker to have police protection, but that's what deputies were for. And Rufus had called her Angela. "I'll have DeShawn and Ada list what they've witnessed." Silas disconnected.

"Are you good with staying here?" He asked Sydney.

"Of course." Sydney nodded. "That family doesn't need an army invasion."

Ada's hand went to her throat. "I hope our information is enough."

"While we wait, write down what you remember. Dates and times are helpful if you have them. Don't sugarcoat what you've seen."

DeShawn's dark eyes smoldered. "You write it up, Ada. Best for you to do this and not me."

Silas understood the anger. He'd seen it worn by family members and officers at violent crime scenes. During those times, death hovered less than a blink away.

"We'll stop this, DeShawn."

"It's past time."

"The sheriff will be here any minute." Silas headed for the door. "I need to get something from my saddlebag."

Sydney followed him outside. He sensed her distress as he retrieved his gun.

"Hope you won't need that," she said.

"Me too. If social services agrees to act immediately, things could get dicey. I need to be ready."

Sydney stared at him for a long moment. "You think the brothers are part of the trafficking ring, don't you? This gives you an opportunity to check Clyde out."

Silas tucked the gun into his holster. "DeShawn said, Clyde would do anything for money. Wade's worse. Logic says the boss in this business would delegate the dirty work. If the brothers were already on Clarence's payroll, it would be a short step to expand their job duties. Besides, somebody needs to have the sheriff's back."

CHAPTER THIRTY-THREE

The laptop hums to life. The morning has taken a toll on me, and the amphetamine buzz from earlier is gone. My limbs weigh a hundred pounds each. My brain has turned to sludge. *What did Wade mean that we have a problem?*

The lure of another pill is strong. I can't let Leah see me in this state. But she's taking a nap across the hall. She won't know. The tablet goes down easy.

I check the time stamp on the computer screen. Wade should have completed the delivery. Outside the wind picks up. A loose shutter bangs against the house. A prickle of paranoia skitters along my spine. I pull up the offshore account. No deposit. My stomach drops.

Stop. There've been minor delays before.

I do a little calculating. There's enough money in the account to cover my plans plus Mary's expenses at Sunny Hills Care Center. At my last visit, the doctors say she has weeks, a month at the most. I've done everything I can. I never abandoned her. She would have done the same for me. The knowledge doesn't ease my pain, but life moves on.

The thought jolts me back to the current problem. I don't have another girl to fulfill the third part of the contract. I check for messages. No photos or even an excuse from, Clyde Rowland. I pace the length of the room and back. My ring tone warbles into the air behind me. The song is a favorite, but today it brings no pleasure.

"Yes."

"It's, Wade. Things have changed."

Anger spikes my pulse. "I got your message." I don't disguise my annoyance. "I'm still waiting to hear from your brother."

"You haven't talked to him?"

"No. He didn't send the pictures either."

"He will. But that's not the problem." Wade's voice is corkscrew tight. "I couldn't make the delivery to Chicago. The plane crashed right after take-off."

My guts turn cold. "What about the girl?"

"She's with me. We're about halfway to the farm. When we get there, we're gonna need help."

"Did you steal a car?"

"Not exactly. Two people helped us get out of the plane. One was a cop. I had to shoot him. The other person is, Lila Girard. We're in her car."

I am dumbfounded into silence.

"Boss, I know this sounds bad, but without a car to link to the crash site, nobody will have a reason to search for Girard. Especially not in the Ozarks. This will work out like getting the extra girl last night. Girard's a looker. We can use her to fill one of the orders. Or—I will take care of her. Whatever you want me to do."

My shock morphs into utter fury. The death of a homeless person is soon forgotten, but cops never stop hunting the killer of one of their own. I bite my tongue to keep from screaming out obscenities. The page showing my account winks from the still open computer. My brain switches gears.

"Go on to the farm," I say. "After I arrange for a rental car, I'll meet you there and take you to the agency to pick it up. There's still a delivery to make."

"You know where to go?" Wade sounds surprised.

"Wade." I let out a mirthless chuckle. "I even know what shots you've had. Guess brothers don't always tell each other everything. Me and Clyde, we've been acquainted for a while now. Been all over that little farm of his." I plant the first seed of doubt.

"I don't believe you. Clyde would have told me." The lackey's voice is edgy, carrying a note of menace. "What game are you playing?"

"No game, Wade. Just business. Your brother's not too bright, but he's never done anything as stupid as shooting a cop. Here's a warning. Don't let your grudge against Silas Albert make you do something to spoil the merchandise—any part of the merchandise. Do you understand me?"

"How do you know about Silas Alb...?"

"Wade," I cut him off. "I have access to all the police records. You shouldn't have told your brother what you did. But you needed him to hide the corpse. I know all about the death of that child, and what you did to her before she died."

Wade's sharp intake of breath is a satisfying rattle in my ear. I'm in control again.

"I didn't hurt that girl."

"According to Clyde you did, but he hid the evidence. Did he ever tell you where? He told me—just so I'd trust him." I allow a second for the unspoken meaning of my words to take hold. "But this is different, Wade. You and I know, Silas Albert. You hurt his niece, and he will hunt you to the ends of the earth."

"Okay. I got the picture." His tone is icy. "When will you be at the farm?"

"After dark." I leave him listening to dead air.

I swipe the screen, find breaking news. The plane crash pops up. The report supports Wade's story. The pilot is dead at the scene and another person is critically injured.

Critically injured. Not dead.

A cold chill crawls down my spine. If the cop lives, he can identify Wade. Serpent man will give up his brother. My teeth grind together. Clyde will point to Paul and me to save himself. Leah will turn on me. A pain shoots through my chest. I won't lose her again.

I slam the computers closed and yank the cords from the wall. Papers and books tumble to the floor.

"What's going on?" Leah calls out from across the hall.

My brain spins the perfect lie. "Paul called. There's an emergency." I rush into the other bedroom and grab the escape bag. A quick check verifies the fake passports and pre-packed clothes are in order. I toss in the drugs."

I don't bother to lock the door.

CHAPTER THIRTY-FOUR

Beneath a cheerful mid-afternoon sky, the chickens clucked, and the birds sang. A turtle trudged at a steady gate toward Ada's lily bed. The picturesque scene supported why DeShawn thought he and Ada had left the violence behind in Kansas City. Too bad, the dregs of humanity consumed space in the peaceful hills of Missouri too.

Sydney was inside helping Ada complete the report for social services. While Silas waited for Rufus, he opened a text from Hadley. Silas grinned. Hadley was always the smart ass. There was no doubting his opinion of Rebecca Haze. Silas had to admit, the reporter's ability to arrive first at a crime scene was a mystery all on its own.

Minutes later, the sheriff's cruiser pulled into the parking lot. A blue van followed close behind. A tall woman, carrying her height with grace and confidence stepped from the van. Shiny dark hair pulled up in a messy bun, she wore fitted blue jeans, a white shirt open at the throat, and square toed western boots.

As Rufus and the social worker joined Silas, she extended a dainty hand. "You must be Silas Albert," she said. "I'm glad to finally meet you. I'm Angela Pasey." Her smile was broad and genuine her grip surprisingly strong.

"My pleasure," Silas replied. Intelligent and very dark blue eyes met his. There was an air of toughness about the woman. Good thing, the harsh realities of social work required grit.

"Good to see you, Rufus." The two men shook hands.

"This shouldn't take long," Angela said. "I already have a thick file on the Rowland family. If the report matches what Rufus told me, I would be able to take action today."

Inside, Silas introduced Sydney then Angela got to work. She was right, within fifteen minutes it was time to leave for the Rowland farm.

At the door, Silas kissed Sydney on the lips.

"Be safe," she said.

"Always."

Silas joined Rufus in the sheriff's cruiser. Angela followed in the blue van.

As soon as they were on the road, Rufus hooked his thumb toward the convenience store. "Kissing in public. Must be serious." The big man side-eyed, Silas. "Do I know her? She seems familiar."

"You've met. You tried to pick her up at a training seminar last year."

"Oh yeah, the ME. I knew her name sounded familiar." Rufus chuckled. "She very tactfully rejected my offer. But my luck's improved since then. I'm trying to talk Angela into marrying me."

"You—married. No way." Silas clapped a hand to his chest. "Well, you could use a little work on your social skills. Maybe she can help." He set his mouth in a smirk. "Mrs. Angela Rose. Umm. Nice."

"That she is." Rufus beamed then his expression turned serious. "The Rowlands live on the farm where Austin's mother grew up, about two miles down this way. Hope this doesn't backfire on us. Domestic issues are crazy unpredictable."

"From what DeShawn said, Clyde's bad news."

"Scum." Rufus shook his head. "Austin's grandfather threatened to kill the bum. Then, last year during the big flood, Burl Godfrey disappeared. Tess said he went out to check the cows. We found a boot on the creek bank but no human remains. Was ruled a drowning, but one or two folks around here think Clyde murdered Burl for the farm. But the old man was too smart. He had the place set up in a trust. Clyde's made life tough for Tess and the kids ever since. I've tried to get her to file charges, but she's too proud—or too scared."

The sheriff turned off the paved road onto a narrow lane. "Their house is right behind those trees."

"Does Clyde carry a gun?"

Rufus raised his eyebrows. "Most everyone around here does. Why?"

"Need to be prepared in case I have to take it away from him."

Rufus smirked. "Remember—it's advisory—not adversary. Don't make me have to clean up after you." The sheriff parked the cruiser in front of a white house with faded green shutters. Weeds filled a yard that hadn't seen a mower this year. A smattering of gravel marked an empty parking area.

"We're lucky," Rufus said. "No vehicles. No Clyde."

The men got out and waited as Angela pulled the van in beside the cruiser.

"I'll go in first," Rufus ordered when the social worker joined them. "Don't come inside until I say. Got it?" He fixed Angela with a pointed stare.

"Yeah, I got it," Angela retorted. "I've done this before, you know."

Silas hid his grin.

The sheriff whirled, made for the porch, and clomped up the stairs. Before he could knock, the door flew open. A little girl with dark ringlets threw herself into the sheriff's arms. "Uncle Rufus," she squealed in delight. "I've been missing you."

Uncle Rufus?

Silas's didn't remember his friend having a sister, let alone a niece and nephew. Whatever the connection, the sheriff was more than a sideline supporter of the Rowland children.

A woman stepped into the doorway. Silas noted a strong family resemblance to Austin in the shape of her face and the dark hair. Yellowing bruises surrounded dark eyes and ran the length of her jaw. The sight reminded Silas of why he ran a women's shelter.

"Bella! You're going to knock the sheriff off the porch." She frowned at the little girl. "Hello, Rufus. Don't tell me Clyde's been writing those checks again."

Rufus lowered the squirming Bella to the floor. "No Tess, not this time. I don't see Clyde's truck. Is he at work?"

"I don't know." Her chin wobbled. "I haven't seen him for a couple of days."

"Can we come in?" Rufus motioned for Silas and Angela to approach.

As the social worker and Silas climbed the steps, Tess visibly stiffened. "Has something happened to Austin?"

"He's not here?" Rufus exchanged a look with Silas.

The boy should have been home by now.

"He's off on his bicycle somewhere." Tess cast her eyes downward. "I'm a worrier, that's all." She took Bella's hand. "Now I'm being rude. Please come in."

Inside the house, Rufus introduced Silas as a case observer. Colorful quilts brightened decent but worn furniture in a spacious living room. The floors gleamed. An antique harpsichord sat at the end of the room. A rare piece, and a pleasant surprise to find here in the hills of the Ozarks.

At a distance, Silas admired the polished walnut and the delicate Queen Anne legs. Where a hand carved leg should have been, a stack of bricks supported a sawed-off stub. A chill as slow as a fly crawling on ice traveled the length of the detective's spine. The damaged harpsichord gave off vibes of an act of defiance, or a flagrant threat. Either way, a time bomb was ticking inside this house.

"Tess, I'm here on official business," Angela said. "I am required to record our conversation."

"Business?" Tess's eyes narrowed. "Record? Why?"

"I have to ask you some questions about the safety of you and the children." Angela smiled at the little girl. "Bella, why don't you take Uncle Rufus in your room and show him your books?"

"Goodie." Bella danced over to, Rufus. "Come on. Momma got me a new book at the Goodwill. It's about a dog and a cat becoming best friends. Isn't that funny?" A moment later the big man was led down the hall under the spell of an enchantress.

"Tess," Angela said "We've been friends for a long time. The reason I'm here is because Austin was caught stealing food. A concern was raised for you and the children's physical safety, as well."

Tess crossed her arms. "Come on Angela, you know, Austin. He's never stolen a thing in his life. Who's telling this lie?"

"According to the report, Clyde is forcing Austin to steal."

"What? Clyde's lazy and he and Austin have their differences, but my husband wouldn't..." Tess turned and walked to the window. The ugly truth marked in the slump of her shoulders.

The scene fell straight out of the mold for domestic abuse. A woman trying to hang on for another day, week, or month, thinking her man would change—for her—for the kids.

Angela hurried to her friend and pulled her into a hug. After a moment, she held Tess at arm's length. "I see those bruises. Tess, you need protection. Clyde could come back any minute."

"No, I couldn't go. The kids would hate a shelter."

"Then you leave me no choice. The report's been filed. I'm required by law to do an assessment. I'll check for adequate food in the house, evidence of abuse to the children, and safe living conditions. I will need to speak with Austin and Bella."

"Food. We don't have much. I was about to go the grocery." Despair raked Tess's face. "Please Angela, don't take my children."

"Only if they're in harm's way." Angela walked from the room.

Cabinet doors opened and closed, measuring the progress of her investigation. A moment later the social worker's voice mingled with Bella's giggles, then her words became more subdued. Occasionally, Rufus's deeper tone found its way down the hall.

Silas joined Tess at the window. "Is the sheriff your brother?" He asked the question, knowing a close relative should not be involved in a family situation.

Tess gave him a blank stare.

"I heard your daughter call him Uncle Rufus."

"Oh that." She touched the bruise on her cheek. "Only a good friend. He's helped me out a time or two when times were hard. I didn't see any harm."

"Does your husband know Bella calls him uncle?"

"No. We don't mention the sheriff when Clyde's here." Tess's head drooped as though the admission left a visible mark of failure. "They don't exactly get along." Her glance strayed to the mutilated harpsichord.

"That is a beautiful instrument."

"A family treasure. My mother taught me to play." Sadness crept into Tess's words.

"The leg can be repaired, you know." Silas resisted the urge to give her a hug. "I could give you a contact."

"No. I don't want it repaired. I cut the leg off so Clyde couldn't sell it."

Any response froze in Silas's throat. Tess had basically spit in her abuser's face and so far lived to tell the story. Not an action Silas recommended, but the defiant chose odd ways to take a stand, and Tess did still have the harpsichord. A burning urge to find Clyde Rowland and hold him accountable rippled through Silas's brain.

"There's Austin, now." The boy was pushing a bicycle up the drive.

"Something's wrong with his bike." Tess rushed for the door. "I have to fix it, or Clyde will be mad."

One more reason the man needed to pay for his actions.

CHAPTER THIRTY-FIVE

The kitchen was silent, as excitement at The Elle had moved upstairs. The flicker of the TV caught Hadley's attention as he waited for a reply from Silas. A news bulletin was in process. The camera showed a field filled with emergency vehicles. He located the remote and turned up the volume. According to the news anchor, a plane had crashed near Liberty Cemetery. Hadley's nerves crackled. It could be nothing, or it could be everything.

He called central dispatch and asked for the supervisor. "I hate to bother you, Drew, but I've got a friend that might be close to that plane crash in Johnson County," the detective explained. "What do you know about the situation?"

"Hey Hadley. We coordinated back up support, but I don't know much else. Give me half a minute." There was the click of a keyboard. "Okay, here's what we have. The plane was en route to Chicago. It didn't explode but took a hard landing. One fatality, a male. One other male taken to St. Luke's trauma center. Sorry no names. Lila Girard called 911 at 10:46 a.m. The operator asked her to stay on the line, but she disconnected. Is she your friend?"

"Yes. She's Silas Albert's niece. Silas is out of town, but I wanted to be able to let him know Lila is safe. Will you reach out and verify if she's on the scene? She would be driving a 1953 Studebaker. She may have Woody Mendez with her."

"Oh yeah, I know Woody. Hold on."

Hadley paced the room, the cell pancaked against his ear, the thump of his pulse clicking off the seconds.

"Hadley?"

"I'm here. What've you got?"

"Nothing good. The pilot is the fatality. No one has seen Lila Girard or her car, but the patient transported to the hospital is Woody Mendez. There was no one else at the scene. The crazy thing, Hadley. Mendez wasn't hurt in the crash. He sustained a bullet wound to the chest."

The detective halted mid-step. "What?"

"The investigators believe Woody pried the door to the plane open. Then someone on board shot him. They did find a carry-on bag with tranquilizer drugs and a syringe. Sorry man. I don't know any more than that."

"Thanks for the info, Drew. I'll be at St. Luke's. Call me if you learn anything you think I should know." Hadley clutched the counter. He needed to call Silas, but not until he knew Woody's condition.

The detective strode to the foot of the stairs. "Janelle. Can you come down here, please."

The psychiatrist hurried down the steps her gray curls bouncing. "What is it?"

Hadley explained his concerns. "I'm on my way to the hospital. I hope to find Lila there. I'll call you as soon as I know more."

Janelle gave him a hug. "God help you. If something happens to Lila, it'll push Silas over the edge for sure."

"I know." Hadley ran for the cruiser. Hours had passed since Lila placed the 911 call. The siren and red lights cleared his path.

Ten minutes later Hadley stood outside the hospital waiting room. He swallowed back his fears and pulled the door open. A half-dozen people stood at the windows or occupied chairs lining the walls. Lila was nowhere to be seen. Hadley approached a middle-aged man sitting with an older woman. "I'm looking for the Mendez family."

"Right over there." The man pointed.

"Thanks."If the family was here, Woody was still alive. He introduced himself to the couple in the corner. "I know Woody from the force."

"I'm Joe, Woody's father. This is his mother Regina. Thank you for coming."

Hadley shook hands. "How's he doing?"

Joe clenched his fists. "Critical condition. He's in surgery. The ER nurse talked to us. According to him, Woody was in and out of consciousness in the helicopter."

"That's a good sign. Woody's tough and he couldn't be in a better hospital. Was he able to speak?"

"One or two words," Regina said. "Didn't make sense to us." She wiped at a tear.

"What did he say?"

"He said the name Silas. And something about snakes."

Snakes. Hadley's mind raced to make a connection. *Was it possible? Had he meant serpents?* "Did he say anything else?"

Joe ran a hand through thick black hair. "I don't think..."

"Yes he did," Regina interrupted. "He said, "Lila. The snake man has Lila."

Oxygen sucked from the room. "I may know what he meant." Hadley said. "I'm sorry to run out on you." Hadley started for the door, then turned back. "When Woody wakes up, tell him, we'll find Lila."

Hadley gunned the cruiser out of the parking lot. *Serpent tattoos equated to Wade Rowland. Wade met with Clarence Rochester. Wade had threatened Silas's life. Lila was missing.* Fear crawled up his throat. *The serpent man had Lila.*

"Call Silas," He placed the verbal request through the onboard computer. He wanted his closest friend to know he was doing everything possible to find Lila. The call went to voicemail.

"Silas, this is Hadley. We have an emergency. Call me immediately." The detective closed the call. There was not time to wait for Silas. The dispatcher said the shooter was on the plane. But there wasn't a person alive lucky enough to drive to a remote airport, arrive at the exact departure time of a flight, and overwhelm a pilot. That left a booked flight.

Seats on a private aircraft didn't come cheap. A desperate man running from the law would need help. Clarence Rochester owned the house where three missing girls had been found. The facts hit Hadley's brain with the impact of bullets. He wiped sweat from his brow. Child trafficking by air. A brazen scenario, but one that explained how Woody and Lila had become victims.

Before Silas left for Branson, he had warned Hadley to avoid the commissioner and let the FBI handle the investigation. Hadley didn't have a problem with that. The FBI did their own thing. He helped when he could.

But that was before Lila disappeared. Now every second mattered and asking permission to question Clarence wasted time. But he couldn't go roaring into City Hall threatening a city official. The detective made a second verbal request through the onboard computer, and a moment later he was speaking to the commissioner's office manager.

"I need to speak with the commissioner immediately."

"I'm sorry, he's gone home for the day. I can give you his cell number."

Hadley thanked her and wheeled the cruiser toward Columbus Park. He thought of his career. It was about to end if he was wrong about the commissioner. Silas was thinking of getting out of police work. The two of them could always start a private detective agency.

The Rochester drive was empty when Hadley pulled in. He stepped out of the Dodge Charger, walked to the front door, and rang the bell. A faint chime sounded from inside. After the third ring, he peered in the window, and then walked around the side of the house. The garage door was open.

Hadley's heart almost stopped. A black Mazda was parked inside.

CHAPTER THIRTY-SIX

T hick clouds chased the Studebaker through the hills. Lila's abductor hadn't said a word since he ended the call with his boss. The vengeance in his eyes spoke for him. He'd shot Woody without a second thought. There would be no hesitation to kill every person in sight if she made one wrong move. She was determined he wouldn't get that chance.

The Blackbird glanced at Odessa slumped against the passenger door faking sleep. The girl had to be terrified. Lila swallowed back her own fears and began to analyze.

She replayed every word of Wade's phone conversation in her head. The man never once called the Boss by name. But whoever it was had mentioned police records and knew everything about the brothers.

Any computer savvy punk could run a background check. But the details the Boss held over Wade required another level of access—and ice where blood was meant to flow.

Not hard to figure out, the Boss planned to pit the brothers against each other and cut his losses. But Wade had served five years in prison and survived. A sense of dread washed over Lila. Two opposing sides placed the women in the crossfire. With the other sister and Josie in the mix it created the elements for a massacre. Lila chewed her lip. There was a way out. Blackbirds found solutions where none existed.

Wade required money, a car, and more than anything else, revenge.

The situation came down to who killed who first. Her insides shivered. Her best estimation said she had fifteen minutes to stop this runaway train.

The Studebaker approached a tee in the road. Lila slowed the car. "Which way?"

"Left," Wade ordered.

"Are we close? I'll need gas soon."

"We're close."

They traveled in silence. Oaks, spruce, and firs reached for the sky on both sides of the road. Undergrowth grew thick. She had to make a move.

Wade motioned to a break in the trees. "Turn there." A narrow lane barely wide enough for one car disappeared into the woods. An ancient sign read, Table Rock State Park.

Lila touched Odessa's arm. If the girl was to have any chance, she had to be ready to run. Odessa jerked upright, eyes wide, but she didn't make a sound.

Above the sparsely graveled track, a thick canopy of leaves created the impression of entering a tunnel. On a different day, Lila would have loved a horseback ride here. Now the Blackbird prayed for a way to keep herself and this young girl alive.

They bumped along for what seemed like twenty miles but couldn't have been more than three. Every rut sent a reminder that Lila's rib cage hadn't healed on its own. The road made a bend, and a shanty came into view, it's lapboard gray and weathered. *Love* was spray painted across the door. It seemed a bad sign. The hint of a drive hugged the side of the house.

"Used to play here as a kid," Wade said. "Pull in behind. Nice and easy."

Lila twisted the steering wheel and drove down the faint trail. Tall grass whispered against the tires. She rounded the corner, forced to a stop by a mulberry tree blocking the way.

Was this where their lives ended?

"Give me the keys."

She turned off the ignition. "You can't drive a stick shift, remember?" She handed him her means of escape.

"I'm not driving anywhere." He tucked the keys in his shirt pocket. "Get out of the car. You first, Lila." He cocked the gun.

Would he shoot her? Lila refused to give in to the fear crawling beneath her skin. She climbed from the Studebaker, stiff. Pain sliced through her side with every movement.

Odessa wore a brave face when she joined Lila. For the first time she realized the girl was barefoot. She caught the girl's hand and squeezed. For now, encouragement was all the Blackbird had.

Ten feet separated them from their captor. Wade leered at Lila's chest, then razed Odessa's figure with demented appreciation. "Sweet," he whispered, cheeks flushed, tongue darting over narrow lips.

He'd picked the perfect place for an assault. Lila's brain scrambled for a way to break the pervert's train of thought. "Remember the Boss's orders," she said with faked strength. "Don't mess with the merchandise."

Wade's throat bobbed. His gaze shot down the drive toward the dirt road.

Lila pursed her lips. "Too bad you can't trust your own brother. Ever think, he might be playing you?"

Wade's focus returned to Lila. The heat of lust replaced by uncertainty.

"Not your problem," he said. He motioned with the gun toward the shack. "Get inside."

A spark of hope burned in Lila's brain. Confusion created opportunity. The Blackbird led the way down a broken limestone walkway spattered with green moss and rust-colored lichens. One second was all she needed. She slowed and fell in behind Odessa. The stink of Wade's sweat marked his location. Close, dangerously close.

Twenty feet to the door.

Ten.

A flash of black caught Lila's eye. There it was again.

"Snake," Lila screamed, pointed, and bet her life on the six feet of slithering distraction. Then she stopped in her tracks, twisted her body, and with all her strength rammed an elbow into soft flesh. Her injured ribs screamed in protest. Momentum carried her around for a chop to the throat, but her original blow had driven him out of range. The gun popped loose from Wade's hand and twirled through the air.

"Run, Odessa. Run!" Lila plowed into Wade. The impact sent them both to the ground. She caught a glimpse of Odessa's churning legs carrying her to freedom. Then the monster was on top of Lila, hands at her throat, pounding her head into the dirt. The world blazed into shooting stars until a black hole sucked away her vision.

CHAPTER THIRTY-SEVEN

Through the window, Silas observed the interaction between Austin and his mother. Austin studied the ground and gave the bicycle a kick. Tess hunkered and placed her hands on her son's shoulders, much the same way Silas had earlier.

Austin hung his head. He unfastened his jacket and held out the items from the convenience store. He motioned toward the house.

Tess slapped the food to the ground, pointed to Angela's car, and then to the sheriff's cruiser. She didn't scream, but if Austin's red face was any indication, there was heat in her words.

Silas was about to intervene when Tess wrapped Austin in her arms. After a moment, she broke the hug, said another word or two, and gathered up the food. She walked to a trash barrel near the corner of the garage. Even inside the house, Silas heard the thump of anger as the packages landed hard against metal.

Silas strode outside. "Got a problem with your bike chain?" The bicycle was the least of the complications here, but Austin needed a friend.

Austin shrugged.

"Maybe I can help." Silas inspected the linkage. One spot showed signs of an earlier repair. "Who fixed it last time?"

"Grandpa," Austin said.

"You still have the wrench?"

"Doubt it. Dad sold most of Grandpa's stuff."

"We'll find something that will work." Silas took a step in the direction of the garage.

Austin squinted at his mom, but she was staring at the trash barrel, fists clenched.

"I'm in bad trouble," Austin stated the obvious.

"Not really. She's mad at your dad, and she thinks she let you down. Best to do something positive, so she knows better."

Austin let that register. "Maybe I know where the wrench is."

Inside the garage, sunshine poured through the windows, striping the pegboard covered walls with shades of bright and dark. Items hung from metal hooks, but the overall emptiness was a message all its own. From all appearances, Clyde had cleaned out Burl's shop.

Austin went to a far corner and dug through a pile of junk. He handed Silas a device that resembled a miniature instrument of medieval torture. "Guess Dad didn't find this, or he would have sold it too."

"That'll do the trick. Come on. You can help me."

Silas was conscious of Tess entering the building.

"Where did this come from?" She yanked an object from the workbench, dangling it in front of Austin's nose.

Austin shrank at the fierce expression on Tess's face. "I don't know, Mom. But what difference does it make, it's only Grandpa's old holster? Dad's been wearing it. He must have left it in here."

Tess clasped the leather to her chest. "When? Austin, tell me when your dad was wearing this."

"Mrs. Rowland, what's wrong?"

Tess's lower lip trembled. "This was my father's. A gift from Mom on their fortieth wedding anniversary. She had it hand tooled for him." Tess's eyes brimmed with tears. "She passed away the next year. There's a few bears and wildcats around this area. Dad never went anywhere near the woods without his gun in this holster."

The cold meaning behind Tess's words hit Silas hard. His detective instincts surged. "This is important, Austin. When did you see your father with this holster?"

"Couple of weeks ago, I guess." Austin's expression changed, flashed understanding. "Why? Why would Dad hurt Grandpa?" A sob burst from his throat. He spun and raced from the garage.

"Hey there Austin. Slow down. What's going on?" The sheriff's voice was a welcome sound to Silas's ears. Rufus would comfort the boy.

Tess stared at the empty doorway as though her world had ended. "Dad was wearing this on the day he went missing. Never in a thousand years would he have given it to Clyde."

"There may be another explanation. Maybe your husband found the holster and didn't want to dredge up painful memories." Silas's remark fell just short of a lie, but the woman needed a second to regain her mental footing.

Waves of despair rolled from Tess. Silas waited for the defiant woman who had sawed off the harpsichord leg to dig her way to the surface.

"You're not really a case observer, are you?"

"No, Mrs. Rowland. I'm not. I'm a homicide detective from Kansas City. I'm on vacation. The sheriff and I are old friends."

She swung to face him. "There's not one chance in hell, Clyde was protecting me. My husband takes pleasure in seeing others in misery. Especially me."

The Clyde Rowland's of the world ruined women. This one was intelligent, but human, and subject to the frailties of human nature—love, trust, but hope as well. "Tess, Clyde's still a threat. I have reason to believe he's in serious trouble. Let Angela take you and the kids to a safe place. Show them your strength. I'll see how Rufus wants to proceed."

"I can help." Tess balled her fists. "I know Clyde better than anyone. My father's body is out there somewhere, and he didn't drown in a flood. He did his best to protect us, and the least I can do is make sure it wasn't for nothing."

"We'll get to that, but Austin needs a parent in his corner right now, and Bella does too. Be that person." Silas placed a hand on her arm. "Rufus will need that holster. "

Tess thrust the holster into Silas's hand. "I'll be inside. Austin and Bella need me." Tess's back was steel-fence-post-straight when she walked outside.

Rufus burst through the door. "What's going on? Austin's freaking out."

Silas held up the leather holster. "Clyde Rowland just made a big mistake."

"Shit," Rufus groaned. "I know who that belongs to. I saw Burl Godfrey wearing it the day he disappeared. No wonder Austin's upset. Poor kid." Rufus glanced toward the door. "There just wasn't any proof."

"I don't think Clyde would leave Burl's gun, but help me search." Silas checked under tables, and inside drawers.

Rufus dug through the pile of junk. "He must have it with him."

"Even if we found the gun, you can't arrest Clyde for murder, but DeShawn and Ada will testify if you bring him in for child endangerment."

"I'll put out an APB."

"He may not be in the area. Kansas City Police are hunting for his brother. My bet is they're together." Silas filled Rufus in on the incident at the Burger Nest. "The FBI is investigating Rochester for embezzlement. Child trafficking too. To be honest, that's why I'm on my way to Branson."

The sheriff's expression turned steely. "There's an epidemic of abductions in Kansas City. You work homicides, and you're out of your jurisdiction. Coming out here was no accident. I thought you were too well known to work undercover, but I'm thinking I was wrong."

Silas shrugged. "Remember Special Agent Archie Hamilton?"

"Yeah. He helped us with a drug case two or three years back. Good man."

"The abductions you mentioned, are feeding a child trafficking operation. The agency has uncovered a link between the kidnappings and the resort. Sydney and I've been planning a trip to Branson for weeks. Agent Hamilton convinced me we had the perfect cover. And now we're not relaxing, but to the casual observer we're on vacation."

Rufus frowned. "Damned sorry vacation. And Sydney, how does she fit into this little operation?"

"She's been on board from the very beginning. The stop at the Page place had nothing to do with the investigation at first. I've known DeShawn and Ada for years. I wanted Sydney to meet them. Then we ran into Austin."

Silas picked up an old tractor manual from the work bench. Through the grease smudges, he read Burl Godfrey's name scrawled across the cover. The detective's throat tightened. He swallowed and went back to his explanation.

"DeShawn gave us information that supports the FBI's theory. There is evidence the brothers work for the commissioner. No proof they're part of the kidnappings. Yet. I didn't want you going in blind without backup."

"I knew the brothers were a couple of lowlifes, but this..." Rufus rubbed a hand over his face. "If Clyde's job at the Oak Hill's Resort is the connection, what's the next move?"

The thick manual dropped from Silas's hands. "Clyde Rowland works at Oak Hills?"

"From everything you said about the brothers working for the commissioner—I—well—I guess—I assumed you knew."

"I didn't." Silas shook his head. "But I'm glad you did. The more we know the easier it is to stay undercover. Would Tess be familiar with Clyde's work associates?"

"Let's find out." Rufus headed for the house. "She'll be glad to hang his butt out to dry."

Inside, Silas found Tess making tea in the kitchen. Angela was talking to the kids in the living room. "Tess, we're going to do our best to find Clyde, but we need more information. Was your husband friendly with anyone from his work?"

Tess frowned. "Don't know if you'd call it friendly. He made fun of a guy named Paul. Said Paul's wife had passed away, and he was being a cry-baby. I was so mad. I met the wife, Leah once. Clyde's truck had broken down. She was with Paul when he gave my husband a ride home."

Was it possible?

Silas mentally replayed his partner's words.

"*Rose is getting her memory back. She said, the kidnapper talked to Leah, but it was a one-sided conversation. There was no one else in the car.*"

And, Kelsey Springer the victim Silas rescued had confirmed the name Leah in a similar story.

If Leah was a ghost, who was she haunting?

Tess continued. "She was the sweetest thing. Clyde said he would throw up if the crybaby mentioned Leah one more time. He claimed Paul wouldn't even have the job at the hotel if wasn't for his wife being related to one of the big shots there."

Silas tamed his spinning thoughts. "Did he mention anyone else?"

Tess's brows drew together. "Yeah. One of the assistant managers. He called her blue-haired Alice. He hates her because she spies on him."

Rufus spoke up, "What made him think she was spying?"

"Sorry. I didn't ask. He's been paranoid lately."

Silas swallowed. "Is Paul Vietnamese?"

CHAPTER THIRTY-SEVEN

Tess tipped her head to the side. "No. But his wife was. Why?"

"Sorry, I can't give you more details, but this is critical information. When Clyde isn't at work, where does he go?"

"Mostly to a bar. But sometimes he's gone a couple of days. He'd been to Kansas City. I found receipts for gas and a hotel in his shirt pocket. If that's important, I still have those tickets."

Rufus nodded. "A timeline and points of purchase would confirm opportunity."

"We want Clyde arrested," Silas added. "But we want the boss too."

"Austin," Tess called to her son. "Go in my bedroom and bring me the shoe box under Grandma's quilt."

Austin jumped from the couch and was off like a flash.

"Tess," Silas said. "You know it's not safe for you and the kids to stay here."

Tess squared her shoulders. "Why? Rufus will arrest Clyde then we won't have to worry."

"Until then, you need to keep your family safe." Silas held Tess's gaze. "We believe Wade and your husband are involved in a child trafficking operation."

Tess's hand went to her throat. "Wade." A spot of sunlight set sparks to a tear sliding from the corner of her eye. "Wade's out of prison."

"Yes," Silas said. "He and Clyde may be together. You know what your husband is capable of, but do you know about Wade?"

Tess's face paled. "Yes. I—I do." Her glance darted to Bella.

"Mom." Austin stood in the doorway a small box gripped in both hands. "We can't stay here. Uncle Wade is a pervert."

Silas's gut clenched.

"How do you know that, son?"

"Dad told me. He warned me if Uncle Wade ever got out of prison, to never let Bella be alone with him. Dad said Uncle Wade might hurt her."

Angela joined Austin. "Come with me, Tess," Angela pleaded. "Don't put the kids at risk."

Tess went to Austin and took the box. "We won't be safe anywhere until those two are behind bars. We'll go with you, Angela. But it's only because I don't want to commit murder myself."

Angela fist pumped. "I'll accept that reason."

"We'll wait until you're in the van then we'll follow you to the highway," Rufus ordered. "You've got ten minutes."

The social worker shooed Austin and Bella toward the back of the house.

Tess walked with Silas and Rufus outside. "I wish I could do more," she said, handing the receipts to Silas. Her jaw clenched and unclenched. "There wasn't any proof, and I didn't want to see the truth. But I knew Dad didn't drown." She swayed as though the world was more than she could bear.

Silas moved in close. He placed his right hand under her elbow. "Your situation made it hard to see there were options."

She lowered her voice. "Austin idolized his grandpa. It nearly killed him when Dad went missing. How will I ever get my boy past his own father being a murd..."

Rufus met Tess's gaze. "I'll talk to him when it's time. Angela will put you in touch with the professionals trained for these situations. Hang in there, Tess. You'll be better now." He patted Tess's back and headed for the cruiser.

"Your son is a good boy, Tess." Silas gave her arm a squeeze and followed the sheriff.

"Thanks for helping us." The front door slammed on her last word.

Ten minutes later the cruiser fell in behind the blue van. Silas glanced back at the Rowland house. "DeShawn is right. This must end."

CHAPTER THIRTY-EIGHT

L ila opened her eyes to near darkness. The smell of mouse urine burned her nose. She coughed. The fire in her throat brought the fight scene alive in her mind. Wade must have throttled her unconscious and dragged her inside the old house. Panic clawed at her chest.

What else had he done to her?

She lay on her side, arms drawn tight behind her back. Zip ties cut into her ankles and wrists, she had her clothes on, and she was alone. "Thank you, Lord," she whispered.

A second later Lila's brain caught up.

Odessa.

Lila remembered the girls bare feet flashing past. Wade had been so busy pounding Lila's head to a pulp, Odessa escaped. The girl had time on her side. But Wade knew the land. Odessa didn't.

Lila gritted her teeth. The next minutes would hurt. The Blackbird rolled to her back, brought her knees up to her chest, and rocked her protesting body into a sitting position. Dust swirled. The room spun, settled. Her eyes locked on a rusty shovel.

Time for a little butt-scootin' boogie.

She reached the bent and mangled scoop, drenched in sweat, and stinking of mouse poop. The need for a tetanus shot flitted through her mind. She giggled. Her ribs sent a sharp reminder that the situation wasn't one bit funny.

The Blackbird's shoulder sockets ached from arms locked in an unnatural position, but she didn't stop. She used her feet to knock the shovel to the floor and into a corner. A final kick lodged the handle and blade against the wood. She turned herself around and found the blade with her hands. Stroke after stroke, the zip tie raked across the ragged metal. With each passing moment, Lila imagined Odessa at the hands of the child molester.

At last, the plastic snapped. Lila rubbed her hands together, urging a return of normal blood flow to her fingers. Seconds later, she attacked the ankle restraints with the jagged edge of the scoop. Then she was free, grabbing the shovel, and rolling to her feet.

She staggered outside. Thick air thumped her in the chest. The sky darkened by towering thunderheads made her stomach twist. A zing of ozone road the wind. A storm wasn't far away.

For a second, Woody's face flashed before her eyes. *Had he made it?* She swallowed hard. Woody was where he would get help. Odessa was not. The Studebaker received a longing glance as Lila jogged past.

The Blackbird searched for sign. At the edge of the dusty lane the imprint of bare toes pointed into the timber. Lila shivered. Beside Odessa's tracks was the mark of a man's boots.

The trail of disturbed undergrowth emerged on a picturesque hillside dotted with feathery Maidenhair ferns and moss-covered stumps. A gust of wind rattled the branches of oaks too big to wrap her arms around. Her shovel clinked against a rock. Lila froze. Then she picked up a piece of granite and left the farm tool behind.

At the bottom of the hill, she found broken zip ties next to a jagged rock, blood on a clover blossom, more on a fallen log. Her side hurt, but the exercise loosened her muscles.

Bent weeds and mashed grass showed Odessa had stopped and turned back toward the road. Then the marks of her steps continued in a straight line. Lila sensed a purpose in the girl's movements as though she had a plan.

The Blackbird followed the trail across a creek. Cool water, bubbled in the stream and taunted her raw throat. She climbed the opposite bank. Stopped. There was only one set of prints, and they didn't belong to a barefoot girl. Lila backtracked. Nothing.

The unmistakable rumble of the Studebaker startled her. Taillights flashed red, and then a laser of white cut through the trees. The vehicle swung south and kept going. Rain spattered her arms and she wanted to dance in it.

"Odessa," she yelled. "Odessa. Where are you? It's okay. Come out, he's gone."

A tree branch snapped.

"I'm not gone, Lila." Wade emerged from behind a tree, a gun in his hand. Mud caked his clothes. A rip in his jeans exposed a scraped knee. His lips twisted in an evil smirk.

Lila gaped. "You—I thought." She twisted toward the road and back again. "Where's Odessa? Who took my car?" Then one and one made two.. Lila laughed.

"Shut up."

"The smartest fighter never strikes a blow." Lila poured sarcasm into her voice. "You let a girl trick you."

"That smart ass talk don't impress me." He stroked the barrel of the gun. "This is what holds a person's attention."

"Really. A child led you down this hill like a donkey. You fell." She pointed at his knee. "Guess you dropped the keys. You can't even drive a stick shift, but she can. What do you think happens next? You're done for."

Wade's face darkened. "That's where you're wrong." He took a threatening step toward her. "I've still got you."

She held her ground, rock curled tight in her fist. "If you touch me, you'll have to kill me. Poof. Bargaining chip gone."

Wade's face contorted with rage. "Bitches deserve what they get." One hand dropped to his zipper.

The click of the metal teeth drove needles of terror beneath Lila's skin. The Blackbird gathered her strength, every muscle tensed. She hurled the rock. Hard against soft. A solid thud. Wade screamed and dropped the gun. The weapon fired. Pain seared Lila's arm.

Wade staggered backward hands plastered to his eye.

Lila regained her poise, spun, and planted a high kick to the tattooed man's throat. She felt the impact in her teeth and a sense of justice when his body hit the water.

"Bastards get what they deserve," she shouted, watching the predator sink to the bottom. Red fouled the beautiful clear stream. She hoped Wade was unconscious and drowning, but she dared not hang around to see.

Lila plunged across the creek and labored up the hill to the road. Muddy, wounded, and determined, she found the middle of the lane, put one foot in front of the other, and started the kind of slow jog that ate up ground and conserved energy. The shed was a rough fifteen minutes ahead.

Lila planned to convince Wade's brother his boss intended to kill them all. How, Lila accomplished that was up in the air. She had to get to him first.

CHAPTER THIRTY-NINE

Silas half-listened to Rufus order the APB as the sheriff pulled onto the paved road behind the blue van. The power of a dead woman over the living had the detective worried. There was a reason for the quote, *insanely unpredictable.*

Rufus ended his instruction to dispatch and brought Agent Hamilton into the cruiser via a secure radio channel. Silas got down to the business of the Rowland brothers and the elusive Leah. "This will be our last conversation until Sydney and I get closer to Branson," he said, when he finished. "No phone reception in these hills."

"Understood."

Archie cleared his throat. Silas sensed the positive before the negative.

"About the kidnappings last night." The hush of silence filled the car. "We found Clyde Rowland's blood in the garage."

Silas's arms tensed. "Josie has jeopardized her life to save those girls," he snapped. "What the hell is the agency doing?"

"We're scouring the earth, Silas. We'll find them."

Silas caught himself. There was nothing to be gained by attacking the agency. "Here's a place to check. In addition to what I told you, Clyde's wife gave me receipts from trips he took to Kansas City. This is a hotel where he stayed." Silas read off the name and address.

"We'll check it out," Archie replied. "We will bring Clarence in.

Believe me, Silas, we're doing everything possible."

"I know. Sydney and I will maintain our cover. Clarence's man on the inside will know how to reach Clyde. We'll work that angle. There's been a couple of days between each of the last three abductions. This one didn't go well, so they'll be nervous. Somebody is going to make a mistake." Silas closed the radio channel.

The blue van continued on after Rufus turned into the parking lot of DeShawn and Ada's store. "A Blackbird team, a missing Eagle, and Lila works with the FBI?" Rufus whistled. "Next you're going to tell me your parents are part of a special ops. group."

Silas stared out the window.

The sheriff flat-handed the steering wheel. "Well, I'll be a cockeyed mule." Then his tone changed from incredulous to serious. "I'm surprised a Special Agent would be so candid."

Silas chuckled. "You're easy to trust, Rufus."

A tide of red crept up the sheriff's neck. "I—well—I'd better get back. Tess may have gained a second wind of stubbornness and decided to stand her ground." Rufus jerked his chin toward the Rowland farm. "Thanks for getting involved today. Austin's a good kid, and now he and his sister have a chance. The Rowland brothers will be in jail before dark. Be careful just the same."

Silas shook Rufus's hand. "Likewise." The detective crawled from the car.

Sydney rushed outside face drawn eyes anxious. Silas caught her in his arms. "Everyone's safe," he murmured, then kissed her like he hadn't seen her in a month.

A horn honked and Silas turned to see the sheriff stick his thumb in the air. Then his friend sped out of the drive and disappeared in the direction of Tess and her children.

Inside the Pages' living room, a doubled barreled shotgun rested against the sofa.

Silas exchanged a glance with Sydney.

"DeShawn got worried."

"That's damn worried."

"You had about five minutes before he came after you. He was hunting for a second box of shells."

"Not too surprised. I'd do the same for him."

In the galley kitchen, Ada offered her solution to all problems. Food. Between bites, Silas shared what he'd uncovered. He kept the Leah connection to himself.

DeShawn inserted questions but mostly stared out a window.

"The FBI is involved of course," the detective added. "The Special Agent in charge just informed me that there was another abduction last night."

"I knew it," DeShawn growled, returning to the breakfast bar. "That's why I haven't seen Clyde for days. But finding those ole boys won't be easy."

Ice cubes clinked as Ada handed her husband a glass of tea. "I'm glad Tess decided to go with Angela. Who knows where Clyde and his brother might be?"

"There's a storm brewing," DeShawn mused. "These hills hold a hundred places to hide. Hill-raised men know their backroads. I hope your FBI friend doesn't expect these boys to come driving down U.S. 65."

Silas rubbed the back of his neck. DeShawn had taken Silas up and down dozens of dirt roads around Table Rock Lake. There was no way to secure them all.

"That's why Sydney and I are going on to Branson. Part of the trafficking operation originates in the hotel at the resort. I can't tell you more than that. We have a lead on Clyde's connection at the hotel. Our job is to get that person to collaborate with us. I trust the agency.

A gust of wind scraped a tree limb against the metal roof. Sydney chased the sound with her eyes. "We'll work both ends against the middle—undercover."

Ada shot a glance out the window. "You two can't be riding a motorcycle with this storm coming on." She scooted a set of keys across the counter to her husband. "Go get my SUV."

The detective opened his mouth to argue, but the big man cut him off. "The queen hath spoken." Keys in hand, DeShawn disappeared outside.

* * *

Traffic was light on the Branson loop. The white Acadia handled well even on the wet highway. Contrary to Sydney's normal quiet introspection, she peppered him with questions and ideas. Silas wanted to insert what he'd found out about Leah's identity, but he held back. Sydney needed to unwind.

Silas was worried too. All three girls could be dead by now. He knew he had to lighten the mood, or no one would believe they were happy vacationers. "What should we do first, find blue-haired Alice and give her Pentothal, or lock Paul in the laundry room and torture him until he takes us to his leader?"

Sydney groaned. "Glad you can make fun. Answer me this, smart guy. What drew starched-shirt Clarence to a hotel designed around the image of the Ozark hills, country music, and hillbilly hoedowns? The other thing that doesn't add up, is the man on the inside. Paul. How did Clarence decide on him? This guy didn't just pop up out of thin air. Want to know what I think?"

"Is this a trick question?"

"I've got a theory that Clarence knew Paul before he ever decided to get into the child trafficking business. If we knew their history, we'd have a better chance of asking the right questions."

CHAPTER THIRTY-NINE

"Slow down, woman. I can't get a word in edgewise."

"Sorry. But I'm sure I'm right." Sydney clamped her lips tight.

"You are right. I wouldn't have let you go into the hotel without knowing what else I learned from Tess Rowland." Silas said, then explained who Leah was.

"So Clarence Rochester is a deranged maniac driven by his daughter's ghost."

"Let's not get ahead. If you have phone service, call Archie. He's confirming the relationship triangle. He'll know the brand of Paul's underwear by now."

Sydney dialed. The call went to voicemail. She left a message.

He was pulling under the hotel's canopy when Sydney's phone pinged. "Archie sent a text. Oh my God," she gasped. "Silas. Woody Mendez has been shot. Archie's been trying to reach you."

The air turned cold. "Woody? Is he—is he alive? Does Lila know?" Silas located his phone. "Great. It's dead."

"The text says Woody's alive. In surgery. There was a plane crash and someone on the plane shot Woody. Archie's team is investigating. No mention of Lila." She returned her attention to the screen. "His team did confirm Leah is Paul's wife and Clarence's daughter. Archie assigned Mason Croy to give us the full background on Paul. Isn't Croy who Lila was working with?"

"Yes." Silas drummed his fingers against his knee, registered Archie's information, but thought of Lila. "I told her I wouldn't pester her, but this is different."

Sydney dialed. "She will understand." Lila's phone rang once and went directly to voicemail. "Hey Lila, this is Sydney. We wondered if you'd heard about Woody. Silas is without a phone, so call me back when you have a sec."

"Maybe she's at the hospital," he said, ignoring the worry crawling inside his chest. "She'll call you back." He reached in the back seat for the saddlebags he'd placed there earlier. There's nothing we can do for Woody from here. The best use of our time is to work on Paul while the agency has Clarence occupied."

"Wait just a second. I want Hadley to know we heard about Woody. He can keep us updated." Sydney tapped the keypad then shoved the phone into her pocket. "Let's go."

They entered the hotel arm in arm the way happy vacationers would.

"Can I help you?" The clerk's hair was a vivid blue and spiked. She flashed a brilliant smile that didn't have a ghost of a chance competing with the statement hair. According to the red letters embroidered on her shirt, they'd found blue-haired Alice.

"Checking in," Silas said.

"Welcome." Alice bobbed her head. Not one hair so much as shivered. "Could I have your name please?"

"Silas Albert."

"For validation purposes, I'll need to see your driver's license and credit card please."

Sydney sidled closer, as Silas placed his identification on the desk.

Alice scooted the cards in front of her computer. Sassy orange nails clicked across the keyboard.

The hotel's automatic doors slid open bringing the scent of rain mixed with the acrid smell of hot asphalt. A couple approached the desk.

"I'll be right with you." Alice waved to the new arrivals, took a step back, and leaned around an aqua blue partition, separating the desk from an office area. "Paul, I could use your help now."

Sydney's fingers tightened on the detective's arm.

Alice returned and answered the phone. "Please hold," she said, cradling the receiver between her jaw and shoulder.

The man Alice called Paul hurried from behind the partition. "I can help whoever is next." Paul's focus slid across the scar where Silas's right eyebrow used to be and hung on his artificial hand one second longer than necessary. Recognition flickered in the depths of the man's eyes. This had to be Clyde Rowland's contact and Clarence's son-in-law.

The waiting couple stepped in front of Paul's computer. "Name please."

"Wyatt and Maggie Franklin. We were supposed to be here yesterday, but we had car trouble." Wyatt slid his identification and credit card across the counter. "I apologize for not calling, but I dropped my cell on the pavement and ruined it, and the battery in Maggie's phone failed. Not a clever way to start a vacation."

Paul's attention skewed in the detective's direction. Silas caught a blip of fear in the man's eyes. The couple didn't show any sign they'd met the detective or the clerk. The name they registered didn't ring any bells for Silas, but Paul was on high alert. Why?

Paul covered his initial reaction with a smile. "Hope the car repairs weren't anything serious."

"We don't know yet," Wyatt Franklin replied. "They couldn't get to it until Monday. We had to rent another vehicle."

"That's too bad. But you're here now, and Branson will make you forget all your troubles. Starting now." Paul tapped the couple's information into the computer. "We're almost full, but I'm sure we can find accommodations to take care of you."

Alice completed Silas's registration and explained to Sydney how to access the resort's various amenities. "This is your room number." She placed a diagram of the hotel layout in front of Sydney. "You are here." Alice marked an X with an ink pen. "The elevator is right over there." Alice smiled at Silas and handed Sydney the packet holding their key cards. "Enjoy your stay."

"Thank you." Sidney took the folder. "I'm can't wait to take a dip in the pool."

"Right through those doors at the end of the hallway." Alice pointed her orange tipped finger. "There's a nice assortment of towels available for your convenience, and the chairs on the deck are comfortable."

Silas followed Sydney to the elevator. Inside, he turned to find Paul staring in their direction. The doors slid shut.

"That was weird," Sydney said. "I know you have an electrifying effect on women, but unless you had a gun in your hand, that's the first time I've seen you make a man breathe fast." She edged close to Silas and slipped her arm around his waist. "Should I be jealous?" Her lips formed a luscious pout as she glanced up at him. "Is this undercover enough?"

Silas kissed the top of her head. "Perfect," he said. "And Paul's got plenty to be edgy about."

"Seriously. He recognized you."

The elevator door swished open on the tenth floor. "The costs of being a celebrity." Silas guided Sydney into the corridor. "Remember, I'm just a cop on vacation."

Inside the hotel suite, Silas bent over the small desk while Sydney took a shower. He tried to take pictures of the receipts Tess had given him, but the images were fuzzy.

He couldn't help but think about Lila. It wasn't normal for a young person to turn off their phone. She hadn't answered Janelle's call, and now she hadn't answered Sydney's either. He hated this sense of being on a remote island, isolated, and forced to speculate on reality. Was Woody's life slipping away? Where was Lila? And why was his stomach throwing such a fit?

Silas wanted answers. For a boy who loved his grandpa the same way Silas had loved his own, and for all those girls passing through a child trafficking ring. There was only one thing to do. Get to work.

The shower stopped. Silas tucked the receipts into his pocket, approached the bathroom door, and knocked. "I'm going down to the lobby for a private talk with blue-haired, Alice."

"Okay."

The door opened. Sydney stood there, engulfed in a thick terry cloth robe three sizes too big. A white towel covered her hair. Her dark eyes danced with mischief or was it promise—maybe the two were the same. Heat rushed through his lower belly. She stepped in close.

Silas slid his fingers down the lapels of the robe and tugged her to his chest. He breathed in the scent of citrus and lowered his head. She met him half-way. Their lips molded, tongues intertwining. The towel tumbled loose and fell to the floor. Temptation burned strong, but a picture of Austin's face slid into the detective's mind. He pulled away.

Two tiny lines formed between Sydney's brows. "You've got an idea. I can see it in your eyes."

"Clyde Rowland is a murderer and a kidnapper. If Paul is working with Clyde, Alice will know. To hell with undercover.

Sydney stroked his cheek. "I'm glad to see you back in true Silas Albert mode. I wondered what it would take to drag you out of the darkness you'd dropped into. Who would have thought the sniff of a crime deep in the Missouri hills was all you needed?" She picked up the towel and rewrapped her hair.

"It's not all I need. You helped me see that, but I can't waste another minute. There's too much at stake." He kissed Sydney lightly on the lips and made his way to the elevator. As the doors slid shut, he heard the neighboring elevator open.

CHAPTER FORTY

J osie woke to rain on her cheeks and a dull throb inside her skull. Her fingers searched, explored a lump, and found a laceration longer than her index finger. A strange weakness clung to every muscle.

She struggled to a sitting position. A green tarp lay where her head had rested. The same tarp the Blackbird had hidden beneath in the bed of the kidnapper's truck. Macy must have dragged it out for her to lay on. A gloom deep as early dusk clung to the hillside. Her throat tightened. Could it be evening already?

She spotted a six-pack of bottled water and a flashlight.

God bless you Macy, but where are you?

There beside the water was a note held in place by the Glock. A cold knot formed in Josie's stomach. She squinted to read the words.

Went to get help. Sorry for taking your boots, Macy.

The last sentence was slow to register. Then Josie's mouth tipped at the corners. She wiggled her toes.

"Macy girl, you're a superstar."

Most kids wouldn't have thought to take the boots off a live person. Macy was only twelve and if courage made a difference, she was safe.

But Josie was exposed.

Clyde had been dead for over twelve hours. Long past the time for brother Wade or the Boss to have conducted a wellness check. Josie sipped the water. If she didn't throw up, she'd stand up. Evil would come. She had to be ready. A piece of lose tin banged a tune of urgency. Strength ebbed into her arms and legs. She'd been in worse situations.

She thought of the Vietnamese girl she'd tried to get off the street and all the others who had disappeared. They deserved to be rescued. She didn't want to think about it being too late, but if it was, justice would be served. She eyed the Glock. Blackbirds trained to capture and not kill—unless they had too.

Gun cold against her palm, she checked the safety, and then the magazine. The first was on and the second fully loaded. She tucked the weapon inside her waistband.

Thunder rolled and raindrops grew to the size of a quarter. Josie grabbed the rake, pressed it into the dirt, and climbed to her feet, weaving a little. The shed wasn't that far. A Blackbird would make it.

"Come on woman," Lila would have said. "Don't be a wuss."

Up the hill Josie hobbled, heels and toes punished by rocks and sticks.

The smell of death met her at the door. She fought back the urge to vomit and switched on the light. The sight of Clyde didn't help. For a big man, he had small feet, and sturdy boots. She averted her eyes. Her feet didn't hurt—that bad.

Josie stepped deeper into the shed. She propped the rake against a shelf, hefted a hammer, and studied an old fence charger. The hazard label highlighted by a lightning bolt brought back another grandpa-on-the-farm memory. The glimmer of a plan unfolded.

On a nearby table, she came across a coil of electric fence wire. Her brain hummed. She found wire cutters and pliers, hoisted them like trophies, and placed them with the wire.

"I do believe curly hair is back in style," she said to no one.

She spied a pair of hip waders, turned them upside down, and hoped the spiders fell out. The frog togs came up above her knees, but the fit wasn't important. Hunger gnawed at her insides. Her body begged to lay down in the dirt and rest. Instead, she drank half the water and went to work.

The bridge was barely visible through the rain when she finished. She found a snug spot and settled in to wait. Wind slapped the power line against the building. God help her if the electricity failed. Her eyelids grew heavy.

The rattle of loose boards and metal girders startled Josie awake. She clutched the fence charger and twisted the knob. The voltage meter lit. She glanced toward the bridge, surprised by the erratic flash of brake lights. She half expected the car to go over the railing. The red orbs disappeared into the storm. Had she missed a rescue or been granted a reprieve?

"You have to stay awake," she muttered. "That driver could have been Wade, and you would have never heard him approach."

Josie drank the rest of the water and set the bottle to catch runoff from the roof. She waited for it to fill, sipped, paced, and sipped again. She avoided Clyde and studied the implements parked nearby. A mysterious rustle led her to half a box of protein bars.

Bits of shredded paper and other mouse sign littered the packages. Three had the corners gnawed. The Blackbird's mouth watered. She ripped the wrappers away, snapped off the chewed edges and stuffed the remainder in her mouth.

A sugar buzz was just what she needed. Strength renewed. Josie dragged an old piece of canvas from the spot where the old Johnny Pop had been parked. "Yuck." She slapped a hand over her mouth. A rat must have crawled under there and died.

The Blackbird turned her face away and covered Clyde. She returned to the shed The odor was stronger than ever. A piece of cloth caught her eye. The rat must be there. She grabbed the rake and stepped into the space left by the tractor. The stink had to go.

Wood creaked beneath her feet. She sensed the dirt crumble and backed away. A piece of plywood tilted, and one corner dropped. An unmistakable stench rolled out of the hole. Josie clenched her fists. There was no choice. She inched closer.

The light was dim, but it was enough. Two bodies—one an adult, the other smaller, lay in the bottom of the pit.

Josie dropped to the ground and began to wail.

CHAPTER FORTY-ONE

When Silas reached the lobby, Alice stood behind the counter. Silas knew where to find the tech booth, but sometimes, a detective's best tool was feigned ignorance. He stopped. "Hi Alice, I need to fax a couple of documents. Would you be so kind as to point me in the right direction?"

"Sure thing, Mr. Albert." The clerk showed him the sign that identified what he'd asked for.

"You put in long hours," he said.

She smiled. "Part of the job."

"How long have you worked here?"

"Going on ten years. Started right after the hotel opened."

"That's a long time. I'll bet you've met a character or two along the way."

"For sure. But not as interesting as those you've met. My associate, Paul, says you're a homicide detective." She studied his reaction. "Dangerous work."

"Yeah. As you said, goes with the job. Where is Paul?"

"His shift is over. He's gone home.

"I'm curious about another employee. Do you know Clyde Rowland?"

Alice's friendly smile faded. "He works here. Why?"

"Do you know much about him?"

"Not really." She twirled a ring around her pinkie finger. "He does

232

maintenance work."

"Is he around? I wanted to ask him a question."

Alice's face hardened. "I haven't seen him for a couple of days. Didn't call in either. But aren't you working out of your jurisdiction?"

"Our department and the Sheriff operate in tandem."

"Oh? I didn't know you could do that."

"We have a special arrangement. Are Clyde and Paul friends?"

"Paul Winston?" Alice found a speck of dirt to rub off the counter. "I wouldn't know. I don't get involved in employee's personal lives."

Silas caught the change. Alice was willing to discuss Clyde, but she was protecting Paul. Why?

"I don't mean to be rude, but I have work to do." Alice clicked the keys of her computer.

"I apologize. I didn't mean to take so much of your time." Silas took three steps toward the tech center then stopped. "Alice, sometimes a friend can be in trouble and not know where to turn. I'm here. There's a good chance I can help."

Silas strode off down the hall. He was counting on Alice to appear in the doorway before he finished sending the receipts to Archie.

The last document fed through the copy machine. He gathered the sheets of paper, tapped the edges into perfect alignment, and fed them one by one into the fax machine. The detective sighed. She wasn't coming.

"Paul is my friend." Alice's voice trembled. "He's in trouble."

Silas wheeled to face her. "I figured as much."

"I'm scared he's in over his head. He might even get himself killed."

"What makes you think that?"

"Paul is a good man and a good father but troubled with bad luck. He owes thousands of dollars from when his wife was sick. Leah died and left him with the sweetest little girl, but she has Down Syndrome. Her special school is expensive."

Silas figured he knew the rest of the story, but he let Alice talk. Alice twirled the pinkie ring. The fluorescent lights brought a rainbow of colors to the surface of the opal setting.

"Paul's been paying his bills as best he can. He got behind on his rent. That's when he started gambling. Now he's doing something else bad. I think loan sharks are after him." Alice twirled the pinkie ring. The fluorescent lights brought a rainbow of colors to the surface of the opal setting. "Can you help him?"

Silas studied the blue-haired woman for a moment, letting the weight of silence take its toll. "Alice, you've given me plenty to think about, but you've left something important out."

Alice blinked. She chewed her lip and frowned. "No. No—I—I don't think I have."

"You haven't told me about Paul's connection to Clyde Rowland. Why don't you take a seat and tell me what you're afraid of?" He pulled a chair away from the tech booth and patted the seat.

The sound of a ringing telephone traveled down the hall. "I need to answer that." Alice took a step toward the front desk.

"The phone can wait." There was steel in Silas's voice.

The clerk stopped in her tracks.

Silas guided Alice to the empty chair. "I'm here to help. I can't if you don't tell me the whole story."

"I don't know the whole story."

"Clyde and Paul are working together, and that work has you worried. What have you seen? What have you heard? Tell me. It's the only way to help your friend."

Alice pressed her fingers to her temples. Silas expected tears but she only bit her lip.

"I don't like Clyde. Never trusted a man who bragged about slapping his wife around. The housekeepers are afraid of him. He's always talking on a flip phone instead of doing his job. Then, Paul got one, too. Paul has a regular cell phone, I couldn't understand why he needed another one, especially when he's strapped for money. I'm sure I overheard him talking to Clyde once or twice. That's when Paul started acting different, nervous, jumping at shadows. You know what I mean?"

"I think I do."

"He used the hotel computer more than usual. I don't know what he was doing. I can't tell you how surprised I was the day I saw the two of them together in the parking lot. I'm telling you right now, those two are total opposites. When Paul handed Clyde a packet, you could have knocked me over with a dandelion tuft. I knew then Paul was in trouble."

"A packet? Drugs?"

"No. No. Paul would never get involved in drugs."

Silas grimaced on the inside. What person didn't think they knew their friends and family members, until a grenade of reality exploded in their midst? Silas was familiar with the shock.

The spiked blue hair trembled when Alice shook her head. "I was one car over when the wind caught the folder and flipped it open. There were pictures inside. But I couldn't tell of what, or who. I'm worried, Detective."

Silas placed his palm on Alice's arm "If Paul was my friend, I'd be worried, too."

"Are you going to arrest him?"

"Serious crimes have been committed. I can't make promises, but it's in Paul's best interests to come forward. I need his help to find Clyde Rowland."

"I told Paul I knew he was doing something wrong, but I didn't want to know what. I told him to talk to you, but I don't know if he will.

Again, the phone rang in the lobby. "I need to get back to the desk." Alice stood.

Silas dug a business card from his pocket and wrote Sydney's number on the back. "Call this number if you think of anything new."

"I—I will."

"You did good, Alice." He waved her toward the ringing phone.

Alice wasted no time in making a move for the lobby.

Deep in thought, Silas rode the elevator to the tenth floor. He checked left and right before he stepped through the open doors. Not a soul moved along the hallway. The lush carpet suffocated the scuff of his shoes.

He paused in front of the hotel suite, searching for the key card. A sound slid under the door—a high pitched squeal or—a cut-off scream? Silas grabbed for his gun.

Damn.

He'd left the Glock in the drawer of the bedside table, and Sydney was in trouble.

He hated limited options. This time, there were only two.

Go in.

Or—go in.

CHAPTER FORTY-TWO

I guide the BMW through the streets of Branson. A traffic jam in Springfield has delayed our arrival, and I'm nervous Paul will reach the apartment building first. A light rain dampens the streets. I step on the gas, pass slower cars, and cut in front of others. The vehicle skids as I narrowly avoid rear-ending a Volkswagen at a red light.

Leah twists in the seat. "That old lady gave you the finger."

I stick mine up in response. Leah giggles. I laugh with her.

We reach the complex, but I miss the first parking slot and circle the building. A moving van blocks the drive. I scratch at my scalp fighting the impulse to honk.

At last, the driver moves the truck, and I round the corner to find the spot filled. My nerves jump. Paul Winston exits the car and jogs up the sidewalk, shoulders hunched, fists knotted at his side.

Panic flutters in my chest. I made up the emergency. Didn't I?

Paul disappears inside.

"I want to see, Kia." Leah grumbles.

"I know, baby. That's why we're here." I swallow hard. I haven't called Leah baby since I found out she was sick years ago. I push the thought away. There is too much pain in the memory. Five minutes pass before I locate another space where Paul's car and the building's exit are visible. My thoughts are a jumble. Leah will never forgive me if I take her daughter by force.

Then Paul bursts through the door. He has Kia by one hand and a suitcase swings from the other. He hurries her inside the car and jumps behind the wheel.

"Where's he going," Leah's voice rings shrill—or is it my own I hear?

Rain spatters against the top of the BMW. The sky feels close. I peer through the fan of wiper blades, following every turn of Paul's Ford Focus. "He must have forgotten something at work," I say, when he turns into the resort.

"He always was forgetful," Leah mutters.

Paul avoids the front door. Suspicion knocks loud inside my brain. I can see Alice at the desk. I don't dare go inside. Alice will recognize me. A gust of wind rocks the BMW. Minutes pass.

Leah wipes fog from the window.

I turn on the radio. The southern blues music eases my jitters. I keep an eye on the lobby and the Ford Focus visible. A man approaches the desk. The night he loaded Rose and her howling cat on the back of the motorcycle flashes through my mind. I struggle to process what his presence means.

"That's Silas Albert," Leah says. "Why is he here?"

"Cops take vacations too." I try to put Leah and myself at ease.

What if the wimp, Paul, has turned into a snitch?

I glance at the escape bag. It would be easy to drive on to St. Louis, book a flight, and disappear. But I'm not willing to destroy my little corner of commerce quite yet. A person needs to keep their options open.

The clock blinks off five minutes, then ten. My anxiety grows with each click of time. Clyde could do something stupid and get caught. And Wade knows too much about the delivery depots. The exposure of those addresses would be disaster. The quicker I end my business arrangement with the lackeys the better. The remaining merchandise creates a minor problem, but I'll figure out a solution. I always do.

I pretend to read a text. "Paul says false alarm. Problem solved. Meet back at the apartment at nine o'clock." The made-up story gives me time to tie up loose ends.

"Okay—I guess." Leah is hesitant. She doesn't quite believe me.

The tires splash through puddles as I turn the BMW around.

Leah peers through the rain. "Where are we going?"

"I have a meeting with Clyde."

"Why do you do business with him? He's a maggot. He called Kia an idiot."

"Criticize. Criticize. That's all you do." I resist the urge to slap her. "Why can't you sit there and be quiet? I'm taking care of Clyde."

"Stop the car. I want out." She reaches for the handle.

I click the child safety locks. "You're not going anywhere, until I say you can," I raise my hand, somehow pull it back, and slam it down on the console. "You hear me?"

My vision blurs.

Is she cowering? I can't believe I almost struck her.

"I'm sorry. I'm so sorry. You don't understand what's at stake. Clyde won't ever bother Kia again, I promise." She turns her face to the door. The sound of sobs tears at my heart. My own cheeks are wet. I swipe them dry and ignore her as best I can.

The wipers fail to keep the windshield clear, and I click their speed up a notch. The weather worries me. When the water rises, the bridge becomes impassable. I jam the accelerator—hard.

Miles fly by. I think of Mary. In the days that remain for her, she will be lost. I wish for an opportunity to read her a story one more time. At least I'll have Leah. Later I'll have Kia too. Without me Mary has no one.

Lost in thought, I miss the exit. The next turn off is miles down the road. Fifteen minutes pass as I make the loop. I clench my hands around the steering wheel.

Wade may already be at the shed.

CHAPTER FORTY-THREE

Silas dragged the key card over the magnetic reader. The light glowed green. He twisted the handle, shoved the door open, and plastered himself against the wall. A man jumped to his feet—a bat held ready to swing.

Silas charged, rammed his shoulder into the man's chest, and rode the body to the floor. A table flipped. The lamp shattered. Shards of glass shot across the room. Air whooshed from his target's lungs, brushing warm and damp against Silas's face. The bat thudded to the floor and rolled under the sofa. He drew back his fist.

His arm froze mid-air. Paul Winston lay on the floor, desperately trying to shield his head with his arms.

"What are you doing in here? What have you done to Sydney?"

"Nothing. I—I came to see you."

"Bull. I heard a scream."

Hands gripped Silas's shoulders. "Stop. Silas. Stop. I'm okay. I let Paul in. He needs your help."

Silas stared at Sydney. "You didn't scream?"

"Oh that. You heard my new little friend here." Sydney reached behind her and tugged a child into view.

Silas recognized the distinct facial features of a Down Syndrome child.

"This is Kia." Sydney squeezed the girl's hand. "I was helping her in the bathroom. She got a little scared when she slipped in a puddle of water. Kia, this is my friend Silas Albert."

Kia squinted up at the detective. "Why are you sitting on my Daddy?"

"Honey, my friend Silas, and your daddy had a misunderstanding." Sydney put her arm around Kia.

Silas scrambled to his feet. "Guess I'm the village idiot."

"You're my knight in shining armor, but no doubt Paul has a different opinion. He does have an interesting story to share. You better have a listen." Sydney closed the door to the hotel hallway.

"I thought I was dead." Paul dragged himself to a chair and collapsed, his face ashen. "Thank God you didn't have a gun."

Silas imagined his own mug to be a flaming red.

Kia marched over to stand between her father and Silas. One hand on her hip, she shook her finger at him. "No hitting. Say sorry." She pivoted toward her father. "You, too."

Despite the seriousness of the situation, a chuckle rolled from Silas's throat. "Out of the mouths of babes."

"Her teacher says she's the peacekeeper." Paul rubbed his arm. "That prosthetic can do some damage."

"Sometimes I regret my protective tendencies. This is one of those times." Silas set the table on its legs and picked up pieces of glass.

"Sydney?" Kia squinted up at the medical examiner. "Does regret mean sorry?"

"Yes, honey." Sydney's eyes sparkled with humor.

Silas tossed the broken glass in a trash can and set the remainder of the lamp in a corner. "Paul, you came to see me. You brought a baseball bat and your daughter. A stranger visit doesn't come to mind. Let's hear what you have to say."

Sydney held out her hand to Kia. "I think I can find a good show on TV. Want to watch with me?"

Kia placed her palm in Sydney's and followed her into the bedroom.

"It's a long story." Paul's blue eyes tracked his daughter. "I hardly know where to begin. I know I'm going to jail for what I've done, but I want out of this hell."

"What hell?" Silas dropped into a chair opposite Paul.

"Clarence Rochester is my father-in-law. I know you and the commissioner have history. He got me this job at the hotel right after Leah and I got married. Alice told you how I lost my wife."

"Alice said your wife's treatment left you buried in debt, and you're tangled up in something illegal."

"Dealing with Leah's cancer is really where my world went crazy. That's when her mother, Jane, exposed her deepest secret."

"What do you mean?"

"Leah needed a bone marrow transplant. I wasn't a match. Her parents failed the test too. I don't know if you've ever been in such a situation, but desperate is an understatement."

Lila's face at eight years old pale above a hospital gown flashed through Silas's mind. He would never forget learning of the events that had led to a criminal becoming Lila's organ donor.

"I have," he said.

Paul wound his fingers into a knot. "Jane was no different from most mothers. She sacrificed everything to save her daughter. Turned out Leah has a half-sister. Jane revealed the secret thinking a sibling could be a donor. If that didn't work, she had planned to find Leah's father."

Blood rushed to Silas's head. "Clarence is not your wife's biological father?"

"That's right. Soldier on leave. Whirlwind romance—well you know the rest. Clarence didn't know Jane was pregnant when he married her. Clarence viewed himself as the sucker. Leah felt betrayed too. Not that Clarence hadn't been a good father—he was, but she thought her mother had been selfish and dishonest. The girl next door was more than Leah's best friend."

Silas felt like he'd been punched in the nose. He pictured the motorcycle ride past Clarence Rochester's house with Jay explaining Rebecca Haze lived right next door. The besties whose friendship dissolved, and Jay's mom didn't want to talk about why.

"Rebecca Haze is Leah's sister?"

"Half-sister. Mary had raised her daughter alone. Rebecca thought her father died in Vietnam. He didn't. When Rebecca found out, she flipped. Turned on her mother and accused her aunt of everything under the sun. I don't know if they ever made up. After all that hurt Jane unleashed, Rebecca's cells didn't match, either. Jane and her sister never revealed the soldier's identity. By that time, it was too late anyway."

Silas narrowed his eyes. "I'm sorry. That's all very interesting, but how does that place you as a partner in Clarence's crimes?"

"Clarence was a good guy once. He felt sorry for Mary. Before he found about Jane's deceit he'd helped her sister buy the house next door. When she had to go to a care facility, he paid the bill. A pricey place, Sunny Hills Care Center.

"I know of it." Silas had considered using the facility to care for his sister when she was fighting the last stages of cancer."

"He offered to pay Leah's bills too, but I refused." Paul shook his head as though he couldn't believe his own story. "I was suspicious, but I wasn't that desperate yet." Paul flushed, then composed himself, and continued. "After Jane exposed her secret, Clarence went crazy. He shut himself off from his family. Never spoke to me again, never came to Leah's funeral, and wouldn't allow Jane to come either. The poor woman had a mental breakdown."

Silas could clearly see Clarence with blinders on. "If he never spoke to you again, how did he convince you to take part in his crimes?"

"I'm ashamed of what I did. I was lost in my own mess. I owed everyone." Paul's lips twisted. "One day, I found a letter in my car offering a solution. It had to be Clarence. No one else knew everything about me and the hotel. In a crazy sort of way, Clarence wanted to make amends."

Silas thought of his meeting with the commissioner at the Burger Nest. The out of character job offer. He remembered his own harsh words. *What happened to you? You used to be a decent guy.*

Paul wiped sweat from his forehead. "I'm not making excuses, but I wasn't thinking straight. I accessed the hotel's files. A week later I was handing off arrival and check out dates, addresses, and pictures to Clyde Rowland. I guess that's how they identified their target. Now I'm going to jail, and Kia will suffer because of my stupidity."

The hotel clerk's wild story gelled with Alice's version. A desperate man lured by easy money. "That's why the Franklin's made you nervous? They were targets?"

Paul head bobbed. "They're from Kansas City. They have two daughters. Odessa and Macy. Will you make sure the girls are okay?"

The similarities between the latest abduction and Paul's admission worried Silas. "Are all the families from Kansas City?"

"Yes."

"Didn't you ever wonder why you were asked for pictures of young girls?"

"What?" Paul's eyebrows shot up. "I wasn't asked for pictures like that. I gave Clyde photos of houses and the people who lived there, their cars, everything about them."

"So you had no idea what Clyde was doing?"

"Burglary made sense."

"Do you remember the names of other families you set Clyde up with?"

"Butler, Lawson, and Springer..."

Acid swirled in Silas's stomach. Kelsey Springer was the girl he'd carried from the vacant house owned by Clarence Rochester. "Springer.

Are you sure?"

"I spent hours on their Facebook pages. I'm sure. Have all those people been robbed?"

"No." Silas dropped the bomb shell. "Their daughters have been abducted."

"Abducted?" Paul's face transformed into a wide-eyed, white-faced, picture of shock. "Oh my God. What have I done?"

In Silas's opinion, the response was genuine. But the world was filled with great actors.

"Does anyone know you and Kia are here?"

"No. Alice figured out I was in trouble and wanted me to talk to you, but she doesn't know I'm here. The other girls, you've found them—right? They're safe?"

Silas read Paul's expression. The detective had seen it a hundred times on the faces of frightened parents, husbands, wives, and children—hope. "Three have been rescued. But I'm afraid time doesn't work in favor of the others."

"Can't you arrest Clyde and Clarence?

"We haven't been able to locate Clyde. Clarence is being brought in. But we can't wait."

Paul's face fell. Then his eyes narrowed. "Where have you searched?"

Silas jumped to his feet. He took a menacing step in Paul's direction. "If you know where Clyde is, you'd best be telling me—right now."

"I don't know—exactly." Paul's throat bobbed. "But he did tell me he and his brother stored merchandise in a shed on his farm. When a buyer was ready, they would make the delivery. My God, I had no idea he was talking about human beings."

Silas's mouth went dry. Rats and snakes always returned to their holes. "We need to find that building. Did Clyde mention a landmark—trees, creeks? Was it one mile or five miles from the house—anything? Lives are at stake here."

The clerk's face filled with horror. "Clyde has the Franklin girls, doesn't he? The parents are here. I checked them in. They don't even know." Paul buried his face in his hands.

"Come on man, think. Give me a place to start."

Paul stood and paced to the window. He mumbled words Silas couldn't quite hear. It sounded a little like a prayer.

The clerk pulled back his shoulders and spun around. "There's an old bridge. It must be close to Clyde's house. He said he thought it would fall in every time he drove across."

"Let's hope you're right." At last they had something to go on. DeShawn would know the bridge's location.

Silas hurried to the bedroom, considering what to do with Paul and his daughter. Seconds counted, and the detective didn't have many choices. Sydney was curled up beside a sleeping Kia. He patted his empty holster and motioned for her to come. She was a fully trained Blackbird and he needed her to help him now.

The detective waited while Sydney eased away from Kia and retrieved his weapon from the drawer. Together they returned to the living room. Silas outlined his plans.

"Paul. I'm going to trust you to stay here with Kia while I go to the farm." He tucked the gun into its holster. "Sydney, I need you to locate the Franklin's. They need to know what's happened."

He turned to Paul. "Do you have a cell with you? I'll have to use Sydney's."

"Sure, right here." Paul dug in his pocket and withdrew a phone. "Here's the number."

Silas added it to Sydney's contacts. "Paul, while Sydney is with the Franklin's, do not open the door for any reason. We don't know for sure where all the players are. You are an important witness. Don't put yourself or your daughter at risk."

Paul nodded.

Sydney kissed Silas. "Be safe."

Silas ran for the Acadia.

CHAPTER FORTY-FOUR

Hadley's mind reeled. The Mazda parked inside Rochester's garage matched Rose's description of the kidnapper's vehicle. There was no mistaking the similarities of age and color.

The detective pulled his gun and stepped beneath the overhead door. He scanned the shadows, noted the entrance to the house was open. He was too late. He'd bet money that Clarence was gone. His guts knotted.

God Almighty, how am I going to tell Silas?

Hadley edged close to the car and peered inside. An empty vial lay alongside a syringe on the rear floor mat. The detective circled the Mazda. The driver's side was empty, a pair of sunglasses abandoned on the console, a black hoodie slung across the passenger seat. If the hood bore spots of white, the kidnapper, or his redheaded partner had crossed the line to murder.

The detective entered the house, found the kitchen empty, the living room dark and vacant. A messy office caught his attention, but he moved on. A small bedroom smelled stuffy and unused. Bed undisturbed. Dust streaked the curtains. Closet doors in the last room stood ajar, one piece of luggage absent from a set.

Satisfied the house was unoccupied, Hadley returned to the office. Papers littered the desk. A bouquet of crumbling flowers stuck out of a dry vase. Two bare spots marked where laptops would have sat.

Even the cords were missing. He found a router plugged into the wall. Broken glass littered the carpet. The person who used this office, left in a hurry.

Hadley crouched. No other signs of violence, but a half-dozen blue pills lay scattered about beneath the desk. *Amphetamines.* Then the wallet caught his eye, the crusty relic out of place in the commissioner's house. He leaned in for a better view. Despite the worn leather, the detective made out the stamped initials, W.Y.

A shiver spiraled down Hadley's spine as he drew a line on the murder board in his mind between Clarence Rochester and Walter Stone. The detective was tempted to pick up Walter Stone's wallet, open it, and discover what made it important to a killer. He resisted. The evidence was too critical to risk contaminating a speck of DNA.

The detective used his phone and snapped a dozen pictures. He stood, took a final glance around the room, and hurried back to the garage. He called the dispatcher, ordered a forensics unit, and requested uniformed support.

Hadley would work the scene as part of a homicide investigation, but Silas had taught him to respect department overlap. Out of courtesy, he notified the Crimes Against Persons Division. As he disconnected, a figure appeared in the open door. The detective's muscles tightened. How could this day get any worse?

"Stop right there," Hadley barked.

Rebecca Haze froze. "Hadley Barker, what are you doing here, and why are you pointing a gun at me?"

"Are you stalking me, Haze? How can you know this is a crime scene?"

The reporter's eyes widened. "I live next door, but what are you talking about—crime scene." She took a step forward.

"Don't move another inch." Hadley cut her off. "Have you seen or talked to Clarence Rochester today?"

"No. Why would I? Hadley, what's going on?"

"Lila Girard was abducted this morning. The commissioner has critical information that will help us find her." The detective pinned the reporter with a stony glare. "Haze, if you know where Rochester is, tell me—now."

Rebecca's slapped both hands over her mouth. "I—I don't know where he is. Can I come in out of the sun?"

Hadley motioned to the redhead and then pointed to an area inside the garage. "Do not move from that spot, or I'll cuff you."

Annoyance darkened the reporter's blue eyes. She stomped to the designated place and folded her arms.

Hadley weighed his options. He couldn't abandon a crime scene before CSI arrived, and other officers would find Clarence faster than Hadley could. The detective was convinced the commissioner was the answer to Lila's whereabouts. He placed the call and ordered Clarence brought in for questioning.

Moments later, the forensics team and uniforms rolled up. He posted one officer at the front door and had the second secure the scene with crime tape.

"I cleared the house, except for the basement," Hadley explained to the CSI in charge. "There's no corpse on site, but this is a homicide investigation. On top of that, the Mazda was used in a series of abductions." He added instructions regarding the car's contents.

Rebecca gasped, but the detective ignored her, addressing the CSI unit. "Folks, you know who we're investigating. Treat the scene as though a crime was committed in every room. Your crew always does excellent work. Make this one death-penalty perfect."

"Understood."

"One more thing. First room down the hall off the kitchen, you'll find a man's wallet under the desk. It belongs to a murder victim. I'd need to make a closer inspection."

"No problem, detective." The CSI coordinator directed three team members inside. The fourth set her crime kit next to the car and snapped it open. Her name tag read Violet.

Hadley found himself staring at Rebecca Haze. Her red hair was wound into a tight braid exposing a natural beauty more striking without the camera-ready makeup. For a second, Hadley wished she wasn't the police's number one pain in the butt.

The CSI officer backed out of the Mazda. "Detective, you wanted to see this." The black hoodie dangled from her gloved hand.

White spots dotted the dark material. The detective's nerves bounced. He stepped closer, nodded at darker stains. "Blood?"

The investigator plucked a can from her tool kit. A generous shot of spray later, the jacket glowed its message. "That would be a yes," the woman replied. "Strands of red hair too."

"Thanks." Hadley backed up.

The investigator returned to her work.

Hadley pivoted to the reporter. "Haze. That stalking remark was—well—inappropriate. But why are you here?"

"This is my aunt Jane's house. I came to tell her my mother is dying."

"That's tough. Sorry, to add this to your burdens. Any idea where she might be?"

"Most anywhere. She's not stable. Clarence may have dragged her back to the hospital. I've been estranged from my family since last year. Death tore us apart and now wants to throw us back together again."

For a moment, Hadley thought she might cry. The strangest urge to put his arm around the woman and let her know she wasn't alone came over him. Then he remembered what a great actor the reporter was and shoved the ridiculous impulse away.

"I've got to call Silas. He doesn't know Lila is missing." Hadley hesitated. "Haze. You've seen evidence only the police and the killer are privy to. Can I count on you to not tell the world? At least until we have the commissioner in custody."

"I'm not here as a reporter."

Hadley squeezed her arm. "Thanks." He stepped outside and dialed Sydney's number. She was the next best thing to talking to Silas. The detective braced himself to deliver a devastating message.

CHAPTER FORTY-FIVE

S ilas routed Sydney's phone through the Acadia's automated
system as he guided the car toward DeShawn and Ada's place.
He was about to contact Agent Croy when an incoming call
popped up on the screen.

"Hello. Silas here."

"Boss. Why are you answering Sydney's phone? Didn't you get my
message?"

"No. My phones dead. What's wrong?"

"There's no easy way to say this. Lila's in trouble."

Silas's temples pounded. "Is it her heart?"

"No. Silas, Lila's missing."

Silas's world crashed. "Missing? That's impossible." His mind flew
to the lack of security at The Elle. Lila leaving the door unlocked. The
strange message from Janelle. Silas had dozens of enemies, and the
best way to get to him was through his family. "What happened?"

"Lila went to the cemetery." Hadley said. "We know that because she
placed a 911 call from there. At that time, she was fine. She had reported
a small plane with an engine on fire. When emergency responders
arrived, they found the pilot dead and Woody Mendez shot."

"Dead? Is Mendez dead?"

"No. But Silas, there's no sign of Lila, or the Studebaker."

Disbelief rocked Silas's brain. He recalled his last conversation with his niece. She'd been at the cemetery then. It wasn't hard to figure out how Woody ended up at the crash site.

"No one at the scene even knew to search for her." Hadley paused. "I was at The Elle. Lila's Studebaker was gone, but Woody's car was there. I knew she was going to Liberty Cemetery today. When I saw the crash report on TV, I called dispatch for the details. Woody's in critical condition, Silas." Hadley choked, cleared his throat, and continued. "The doctors are not sure he's going make it."

Silas found it difficult to think. The Mendez family, a big robust group full of love, laughter, and life, would be struck a severe blow if Woody died. Not to mention what it would do to Lila.

"Lila wouldn't leave Woody," Silas's brain squeezed a logical thought into a sentence. "Whoever shot Mendez took her."

"It's Wade Rowland, Silas. Before Woody lost consciousness, he said, 'Tell Silas, serpent man has Lila.'"

Silas's mouth went dry. "Rowland had no reason to be in that area. He had to be on the plane when it went down. Woody took a bullet to protect Lila."

"That's how I see it," Hadley agreed.

The interior of the car closed in. All Silas could see was Lila at the hands of a rapist. He forced his mind to sort the facts. "Hadley, Wade, and his brother are deeply involved in a child trafficking operation. Wade must have been transporting a victim. Now he's in the Studebaker with two hostages."

"Where would he go? That car's easy to spot."

Silas tightened his grip on the steering wheel. "The men have been using a building on Clyde Rowland's property as a holding station. That's where he's headed. I'm on my way there now." He updated his partner on Paul Winston's story.

Hadley grunted a choice word "If you asked me, the whole damn bunch drank the nut juice. I ordered an APB on the Studebaker as soon as I figured out Lila was missing. Then I raced over here to Clarence's house to make him tell me where Wade would hide. When I cleared the house, I found Walter Stone's wallet. I'm waiting for CSI to finish processing it now."

"Good. That should be the last nail in Clarence's coffin. From the time I heard about Walter's murder... Silas mused. I've had one of those feelings I can't shake. Somehow, he ties the crimes together. Prod those CSI people. We need answers."

"Okay, Boss. I'll call you right back."

Silas disconnected. It took about a minute to call DeShawn and explain Josie's situation.

"I know the bridge," DeShawn said. "I'll be ready."

An eerie green tint maligned the sky. Could be a sign of hail or worse. Muddy water boiled down the ditches on both sides of the highway. Silas focused on driving, but a new question swirled in his thoughts.

If Clarence cut himself off from his family, who was paying Mary Haze's bill at Sunny Hills Care Center?

The image of a Sebring orange Corvette flashed through Silas's mind. The cost of the car was not impossible to manage on a reporter's salary in Kansas City but paying the bill at the elite Sunny Hills was a different matter. Silas didn't like the implications, and yet, the connections were there and couldn't be ignored.

But Rebecca had admitted to a broken relationship with Mary. That left one person. A suspect with the motive hardest to understand—love.

Silas anxiously awaited Hadley's return call.

* * *

Hadley returned to the garage where the CSI tech. was packing up her tool kit. "I've done everything I can do here," she said. "We'll have the car hauled downtown." She tipped her head to Rebecca and disappeared inside the house.

Rebecca searched his face. "It's not easy to deliver bad news. Especially to a friend. What will Silas do?"

"He'll find Lila."

"I hope he does. Silas cares a great deal for his niece."

Hadley swallowed hard. "I do too."

The CSI coordinator stepped into the garage. "Detective, we just finished processing the wallet." He carried a cardboard evidence box to a small table, set it down, and then used pincers to open the billfold. "Not much inside, but we got good prints off the leather."

Hadley joined the investigator and bent his head to examine the age yellowed photo holder. The faces of two little girls smiled up at him. One had flaming red hair and wide blue eyes, the other child's hair was black, her eyes dark and almond shaped. The detective's pulse quickened. Behind the children stood two ladies. Hadley gaped. Both women exhibited facial characteristics indicative of Asian heritage.

"Turn it over," he instructed.

The investigator tweezed the edges of the plastic and exposed the other side of the photo.

The detective squinted and silently read the faded words. *Walter. This is Rebecca and Leah, your beautiful daughters. We both loved you. Jane and Mary.* The detective stiffened. Silas was right. Walter Stone was the connection.

Hadley whirled to face the reporter. "Why did you lie about knowing Walter Stone?"

Rebecca gawked. "Have you lost your mind? I didn't lie. Why are you asking me about Walter Stone?"

"How convenient that it was you who discovered his corpse? And there you were again when Silas found those girls in Clarence's house. Walter witnessed you and the commissioner drag the unconscious girls into that stinking room, didn't he? He was a liability. You killed him, didn't you you, Rebecca?"

Rebecca flushed a bright red. "Hadley, you're talking crazy. I'm not part of any scheme with Clarence Rochester." She glanced at the box then took a step. "What did you find that points to me as a murderer?"

Hadley gripped her forearm and guided her—none too gently—to the table. "Show her the picture." He motioned to the CSI coordinator.

Rebecca stiffened. "That's me. That's me and, Leah." She reached out trembling fingers. "Where did this come from?"

"Don't," Hadley ordered.

She let her arm fall to her side.

"This wallet belonged to Walter Stone." Hadley didn't bother to soften his tone.

Rebecca continued to stare as though she hadn't heard. "Mom and Aunt Jane bought those matching dresses for our...sixth birthday." Her voice cracked. "Clarence took the picture."

"Turn it over." Hadley motioned to the investigator.

The reporter leaned in, her red braid slipping over her shoulder. A sob burst from her throat. "Walter Stone is my father?" Her gaze found Hadley's, pain in her eyes. "Mom never told me his name." Tears rolled down Rebecca's cheeks. "I stood over his body and never knew." Her confession came out raspy and raw.

"If that's all you need?" The CSI picked up the box.

"Yes. Thanks." The detective hesitated. Even the color of Rebecca's hair was evidence against her. He raked a hand across his face. He'd never read a woman who looked like this one Miranda Rights.

Hadley turned to the uniformed officer. "Cuff her and read her rights."

"Yes Sir."

Afterward, Hadley addressed Rebecca. "Rebecca Haze, you are under arrest for suspicion of murder in the death of Walter Stone and as a possible accessory to kidnapping."

Rebecca glanced up at Hadley, eyes unfocused. Gone was the feisty, no-holds-barred, journalist. Her full lip quivered, but she didn't speak.

"Haul her downtown. I'll be there in twenty minutes to handle the formal questioning."

"Yes sir."

A moment later, the officer escorted Rebecca to the cruiser. The hunch in the reporter's shoulders spoke of defeat. Hadley wheeled away from the disconcerting sight, but a nagging thought forced its way into the forefront of his mind.

Rebecca was in custody, but Clarence was still out there. Would he run for the hills and the protection of Wade and Clyde Rowland or take off for parts unknown? Three men desperate for their lives didn't seem like good odds, even for Silas.

Hadley dialed his partner. The call went to voicemail. Hadley cursed.

CHAPTER FORTY-SIX

The sky opened. Dirt became mud. Lila's shoes turned into anchors. She could barely see her hand in front of her face. A ruthless wind snapped tree limbs and tossed them to the ground. Once she thought she heard Wade call her name. She plodded on.

Lightening flashed. Lila froze. A building sat less than ten feet ahead. She could have walked right by. A sliver of light sifted through cracks in the wall.

Then a high-pitched wail rose above the wind.

Josie. It had to be Josie.

Lila tore through the mud. A mass of vines caught her toe and she crashed into the metal siding.

The wailing stopped. Had Josie quieted on her own, or been shut up?

Lila pulled herself to her feet. No time for caution. Whoever was on the other side of the wall knew she was here. She rushed around the corner.

"Stop right there or I will shoot you."

Relief flooded over Lila. "Josie, it's me, Lila. Don't shoot. Are you alright?"

The beam of a flashlight settled on Lila's face.

"Lila. Is it really you?"

"It's really me." Lila took a step.

"Wait." A moment later, Josie stepped out of the gloom and motioned Lila inside. "Glad I heard you. I built a trap." She held up two strands of wire. "One hundred and twenty volts would knock you down. If the connection isn't broken, it could kill a person."

Lila threw her arms around her fellow Blackbird. "Thank God you're alive." The two women clung to each other.

Then Lila pushed back and clamped a hand over her nose. "What's that smell?"

Josie pointed to the hole. "There's two bodies in there." She gulped. "I don't know who they are." The Blackbird's chest rose and fell. "One is a child."

Lila pulled Josie close as sobs wracked the older woman. "I'm here, Josie. You're not alone. We'll get through this."

After a moment Josie composed herself. She reconnected the wires of her trap and turned the switch on a small box. "Clyde Rowland's under that tarp." She waved to a lump on the floor of the next room. "He's dead too."

"What about Macy?"

"Clyde and I had an argument. He lost. But I took a nasty blow to the head. I passed out and Macy went for help."

"You're bleeding."

"So are you." Josie inspected Lila's arm. "I'll patch you up." The Blackbird walked to the workbench, grabbed a rusty first-aid box, and snapped it open. "How did you get here?"

"Clyde and his brother Wade are part of a child trafficking ring." Lila glanced toward the tarped body. "At least Clyde *was* involved. The two brothers abducted Macy and Odessa. Wade had Odessa. He shot my friend Woody and took me hostage. He forced me to drive. He was supposed to meet up with Clyde and the manager of their operation here."

"Where is Odessa?"

261

"She escaped. Wade went after her. I went after him. While I was tracking Wade, Odessa circled back and took my car. She'll be with Macy by now. I'm not sure about Wade. Hopefully he's lying dead in a creek. I kissed him with a rock." Lila touched her shoulder. "He sent me a parting gift."

Josie poured brown liquid on a wad of cotton and swabbed Lila's wound. "Odessa must have been in the car that crossed over the bridge earlier. Those two girls are something. Thanks to them, help should be here soon." She wrapped gauze around Lila's arm and secured it with duct tape.

"I hope so, because Wade's boss is on the way." Lila explained the conversation she'd overheard.

"We'll be ready." Jose handed Lila a protein bar and the bottle of water.

Lila devoured the food and slugged back the water. "You dressed for the party." She made a face. "Love the frog togs." She scooted the first-aid box closer. "Let me check out that gash."

The ghost of a smile slid across Josie's face. "I'll shoot you if you put duct tape in my hair."

Lila winced at the split in Josie's scalp. No wonder the woman had passed out. There wasn't much she could do but try to disinfect the wound. She picked up the bottle and silently read the label. Veterinary iodine. Not for use on humans. Lila filled the cap and poured it straight on the wound.

CHAPTER FORTY-SEVEN

Mother Nature's drummer pounded a mad tune against the metal roof as Silas parked the Acadia beneath the convenience store canopy. The sound chewed at his frayed nerves. He needed DeShawn's knowledge to find Lila and the others, but his mind pictured a rising creek.

DeShawn pushed through the door a chiseled set to his jaw. A revolver hung from his hip. He carried a sawed-off shotgun. A few days earlier, Silas would have chastised his friend for owning an arsenal. Today he was glad.

Silas lowered his window. "What's going on?"

"Macy Franklin's inside," DeShawn shouted.

The detective peeled himself from the car and hurried after DeShawn. Inside the Pages' living quarters, he found Ada on the couch, cuddling a young girl wrapped in a blanket. A pair of muddy black boots sat on the floor. Silas recognized the style as being identical to those worn by Blackbirds during a mission.

"Macy," Ada said. "This is Detective Albert. Tell him about Josie."

Silas steeled himself for the worst.

"Please find her—fast." Macy started to cry. "She killed Clyde, but she's hurt."

Ada pulled the girl close. "It's alright, sweetie."

"No." Macy pushed away from Ada's comfort. "Nothing's right.

That awful man knew where my sister was. Now he's dead, and no one will be able to find her."

Silas hunkered. "Macy. We know who has Odessa, and we know where they're headed. Believe me when I say, we will find them."

The girl choked back her tears. "Maybe Josie will kill him first."

A blast of wind rattled the windows. Silas's stomach clenched. "When you last saw Josie, was she conscious?"

Macy shook her head. "She'd been talking crazy. I helped her get in the shade, and then she fainted. I knew she needed help, but I didn't have shoes." Her pale face flushed. "I took her boots."

"Girl, that was a smart move." DeShawn handed Macy a cup of hot liquid. "Drink this, it'll warm you up."

A whiff of bourbon, lemon, and cloves tickled Silas's nose. Hot toddy. The detective struggled to his feet.

"Make a jug of that to take with us." He nodded at Macy's cup.

"Done." DeShawn disappeared in the direction of the kitchen.

Macy sipped. "It started to rain," she said, running her tongue across cracked lips. "I covered Josie with a tarp, left some bottled water, and Clyde's gun," Her chin quivered. "I didn't want to leave her. Did I do the right thing?"

Silas could have been talking to another Blackbird, yet this girl was only twelve. "I wouldn't have done one thing different."

The detective wanted to tell Macy she'd saved Josie's life, but that detail wasn't proven, and false hope wouldn't help her. "She had a head injury, then?"

"A big knot and a gash where she head-butted Clyde." Macy shuddered.

Pride, fear, and anger collided in Silas's brain as Macy recounted the fight, the hours she sat with Josie waiting for her to wake up, and the grizzly detail of how Clyde died.

"Macy. You don't know Lila. She's older, brave, and tough. I have reason to believe she is with Odessa."

Macy's eyes widened. She searched Silas's face as though seeking a hidden lie. "Does Lila do work like Josie?"

Silas sensed Macy was fully aware that Josie hadn't discovered her at the mercy of Clyde Rowland by accident. The detective tilted his head ever so slightly. "She does."

The girl's lips spread in a sly smile. "Then she will protect my sister the way Josie did me."

Silas shivered on the inside. Killing another human was never a good thing. The act stayed with a person for life, even if it was justified. A bolt of lightning followed by a tremendous clap of thunder propelled Silas into action. God was telling him to hurry.

He motioned to DeShawn. "The storms getting worse. Let's go. We'll find them," Silas promised. Then he followed his friend outside.

"Get in the Jeep. I've got blankets and the jug you requested."

Silas shook his head. "I'll drive in as close as I can get. At least three victims are out there. We'll need two vehicles to transport them. How things turn out for brother Wade is not too clear. Yet."

DeShawn's eyes narrowed. "Okay." He nodded. "I get your drift." He looked up at the sky. "This weather is going to get worse before it gets better. It's almost dark now. Wait just a minute." He opened the back of the Jeep and handed out a slicker and a coon hunter's lamp. "Remember how to use this?"

Silas settled the helmet. If his memory served him correctly, the lamp was waterproof. "Time to go hunting." He shrugged on the slicker and climbed into the Acadia.

CHAPTER FORTY-EIGHT

This time I take the exit a bit too fast. The car skids, but I bring it back under control. I pass the convenience store. Leah hasn't uttered a sound for miles.

"It won't be long now." I break the silence. "You can stay in the car while I finish this business with Clyde. Then we'll get Kia and find a new home close to the beach with lemon trees and orchids. We'll get Kia a dog."

"You're crazy." Leah's voice is filled with sarcasm. "Paul will never let you have Kia. He'll have you arrested."

I grit my teeth. I will not let her get to me again. "Then we'll let Paul come too. Now help me count the hills. I don't want to miss the turn."

"There are three hills before the turn." Leah says in a sullen tone. "Here's the first one." Moments later. "Two."

The BMW plunges into fast moving runoff. A wave of water heaves over the hood. Leah screams. The car begins to tip. I gun the engine and the vehicle responds, climbing the opposite hill.

Headlights slice through the deluge. I swerve. The BMW fishtails but clears the oncoming car. I cling to the steering wheel and glance over my shoulder. The car has disappeared.

"It's okay, Baby. We're almost there."

A flash of lightening illuminates the lane leading to Clyde's farm. The house is dark. I follow the trail to the bridge. My muscles knot as the wheels bump onto the plank floor. The sound of rushing water conjures images of uprooted trees and spinning debris. The gentle flowing creek is an angry protester rising against the control of steel and wood.

A beacon of light winks through the rain. I smile.

"Look, Leah. I see the shed, and Clyde's left a light on for us."

The hulk of a truck is visible beneath the trees. There's a tractor too.

"Clyde must be asleep. I'll have to wake him up. You'll hear a pop but don't worry. He won't be mad." A cold resolve possesses me. This job will be easier than I thought.

CHAPTER FORTY-NINE

DeShawn led the way, and Silas focused on dots of red, barely visible through the sheets of rain. Tension knotted his neck. The whine of the Acadia's engine measured incline and descent. At the crest of a hill, the Jeep's brake lights snapped on.

Silas let off the gas and brought the SUV alongside the Jeep. Tire tracks rutted the edge of the road then disappeared through smashed weeds and broken tree branches. A dim glow rose from the ditch.

His eyes strained. Not many travelers would be out on this stormy night. He twisted a lever, dimmed the lights, and jumped from the Acadia. The door as a barrier, he glanced to his right. DeShawn had done the same.

"Cover me," Silas shouted. He zig-zagged along the edge of light, coming to a stop in waist-high Goldenrod. He switched on the hunting lamp and froze. Another step and he would have fallen fifteen feet.

The stink of anti-freeze, steaming metal, and scorched oil rose in a fog. Wind slapped the yellow slicker against Silas's thighs. He peered at the wreck. Then his knees went weak. Lila's Studebaker rested half in and half out of the drainage ditch below. The windshield was missing, but a miracle had landed the car wheels down.

"Lila. Hold on," Silas shouted. "I'm coming."

He clasped his prosthesis with his good hand, sat, brought his knees to his chest, and scooted off the edge. Rocks and sprouts pummeled his back as he flew down the embankment. The ground met him with a butt-tenderizing thump. He mentally shook it off and climbed to his feet.

Fogged glass blocked a clear view of the inside of the car. "Lila, can you hear me?"

"Help. Please. The door won't open. I can't get out."

The frightened voice didn't sound like Lila. It wasn't a man either. That left Odessa. Silas's nerves tightened. Was Lila unconscious? Or worse?

"This is Silas Albert. Stay calm. I'm here to help." The detective gripped the handle and yanked. The door gave an inch. He yanked again. Another inch. He set his jaw and tugged with all his strength. The door popped free.

Odessa Franklin, looking just enough like her sister to confirm her identity squinted against the bright light. Silas scanned the interior for Lila. He refused to consider the ominous message of an empty car. "Are you bleeding?"

"I—I don't think so, but I can't use my right arm."

The detective leaned through the opening. "I'm going to release the seat belt and lift you. Don't struggle. Okay?" The safety latch clicked. Odessa screamed. "Shush. I know it hurts. Relax if you can." He clasped her trembling body to his chest.

After a moment, the girl calmed.

"This is Lila Girard's car," Silas said, as he inched Odessa free from the Studebaker. "I know Wade Rowland kidnapped you. Is Lila alive?"

"Yes. At least I think so. Oh my God. You're her uncle," she babbled, teeth chattering. "Wade was going to rape us. Lila fought. She yelled at me to run. I got away."

A different storm than the one ripping at the world above, raged in Silas's mind. "Easy now," he soothed, forcing strength into words where his fear threatened to leak through. "Where was Lila then?"

"There's an old shack on the other side of the bridge." Odessa sounded a bit more in control. "He dragged her inside. I ran, but he came after me."

Silas scanned the bank. Water covered all but a narrow strip barely wide enough for one person. He waded in close and set Odessa's feet on solid ground. Small tree limbs and trash nipped at his knees. They had to get out of this ditch.

Odessa clung to his arm. "I think she got away too. I found the cut zip ties in the old house. Lila was gone."

Silas dared to hope. He removed his slicker and wrapped it around Odessa. Above the sounds of the storm, he heard DeShawn yell. The detective shielded his eyes from the pouring rain and glanced up.

A stretcher slid down the bank on the end of a rope. "Time to get you out of here." Silas snapped the gurney flat. "You'll be with your sister in a few minutes." He told Macy's story, keeping Odessa calm while he secured her to the stretcher. "She'll be proud of you."

Odessa groaned when he tightened the last strap. "I was so scared I'd never see her again," she said. "Thank you."

He yanked on the rope, signaling to DeShawn to haul her to safety. "Macy's waiting. Up you go." The rushing current consumed the last sliver of solid ground as the stretcher bumped and jerked its way to the top.

Then a low roar advanced down the ditch. The hair on the back of Silas's neck quivered. One foot slipped. He fought for traction, but his mud-slimed shoes skated out of control. Swept against the Studebaker, he dragged himself inside and clung to the steering wheel.

The branches of a tree smacked the roof and tore off the door. An unbelievable force lifted the car. Next to the Studebaker, a lawn mower, old tires, and a chicken coop bobbed along nonchalantly as ducks in a pond.

Water poured in. Silas kicked off his shoes. A moment later the raging torrent dumped the vehicle over a steep incline. Wind whipped through the opening where the windshield once was. Silas's grip broke. Time slowed. Then, he was flying through space alongside the Studebaker.

The drop couldn't have lasted more than a New York second, but for Silas it spanned a slow Missouri hour. Images of Sydney, Lila, and his parents flashed through his mind. Would he ever see them again?

Silas sank deep, thrust his legs hard and brought his head above the surface. If he avoided becoming trapped in debris, he had a slim chance. An invisible object rammed into his ribs. He gasped, sucking in a mouth full of foul-tasting muck.

By some miracle, the hunter's lamp stayed on Silas's head. He had no idea where he was, but the creek was wide and less turbulent. The Studebaker had disappeared. Ahead a light flickered, sputtered, and went out. Silas fought his way to the bank, caught a low hanging limb, and pulled himself to solid ground.

"Thank you, God," he gasped.

Lightening lit up the sky and outlined the girders of a metal bridge. He drew a mental line between where he lay and his last glimpse of the flickering light, dug deep, and found the strength to climb.

CHAPTER FIFTY

Lila and Josie covered the pit with metal siding and boards, then added an old rug to seal off the smell of decaying bodies.

Lila wiped her face with her shirt. "At least we can breathe without throwing up." She shared the bottle of water they'd captured from roof run-off and helped the other Blackbird finish the remainder of the protein bars. Neither mentioned the raggedy paper or the broken corners.

Josie peered outside. "The rain's letting up. I can see the bridge cables. The wind's died down too." She leaned forward. "I hear an engine."

The bridge girders rattled. Lila ran to Josie's side. "Strange, they would send a car."

"I don't care if it's a hay wagon. I want out of this place."

"Turn off the light."

Josie squinted. "Why?"

"That's a BMW. No one would drive one of those here for fun. Especially in this storm."

Josie handed Lila the gun. A moment later near darkness filled the shed. The two women flattened themselves against the wall.

"Remember the plan," Josie whispered. She held the fence charger close to her chest.

"Let the trap do the work."

The driver dimmed the head lamps. A door opened and clicked shut. Lila eyed the voltage meter. It was pegged out. Seconds passed. Josie was a statue beside her.

Three more steps.

Two.

One.

Sparks flew. A scream cut the air.

Josie switched on the light.

The prisoner flayed left and right, caught in the wire.

A gun landed at Lila's feet. She kicked the stray pistol out of reach and put a foot on the prisoner's back. "Stop fighting. You can't get away." The body went still.

A cool draft of air brushed Lila's skin.

"Hello Lila."

Lila spun. A mud-spattered Wade filled an opening along the back wall of the shed. One eye was swollen shut or missing. Lila couldn't be sure.

"You should have killed me when you had the chance. For a person who thinks she's so smart, you did something dumb. You forgot to pick up my gun." He aimed the revolver at her chest. "Where's Clyde?"

"He's taking a permanent nap," Lila snapped. "You were right. He was stupid."

Wade turned his one good eye on Josie. "Did you kill him?"

"I did." Josie's lips twisted into a cold sneer. "You're next."

Wade stepped closer. He picked up a box knife from the work bench. "I should shoot you, but a bullet is too quick. I'm going to make you both suffer." He slashed the blade through the air.

"I don't think so." A familiar voice, cold and threatening, rolled from behind Wade.

"Get down," Josie shouted.

Wade spun.

Silas charged through the door wielding a fence post. One blow brought Wade to his knees. A second rammed him into a concrete block. He dropped his weapons. The one eye rolled back, and he fell to the ground limp as a rag.

Josie scraped up the gun and the knife.

Lila grabbed the duct tape, and tossed it to Silas. He secured the man's wrists, ankles, and mouth. She'd never been so glad to see her uncle.

"How did you get here? Are Macy and Odessa safe? What about Woody? Is he alive?" Lila peppered Silas with questions.

Her uncle finished his task. "Long story." He rose to his feet. "The girls are okay. Woody was in surgery the last I heard. Not in good shape, but alive."

Lila threw herself into Silas's arms. "Worrying about him helped me to keep fighting."

Silas hugged her tight. "Are either of you hurt—bad?"

The women shook their heads. Both Blackbirds interpreted the question behind the question. *Had they been raped?*

A woman's screams interrupted the reunion. "Leah. Where are you? Momma's coming. Everything will be alright. Leah. Answer me."

Silas rushed to the front of the shed. He knelt by the person trapped in the wire. "Help me get her out of this."

Lila and Josie flew to his side. "Do you know who it is?" Lila asked.

"I think so." He bent down and rolled the figure over.

As Lila removed the wires, she recognized the face from photos of police banquets Silas had attended. "Jane Rochester," she gasped. "She must be Wade and Clyde's boss?"

"The commissioner's wife?" Josie leaned forward. "But why?"

"The most basic reason of all—love of a child." Silas removed the remaining wire, lifted the woman, and carried her inside.

"What do you mean?" Josie spread an old blanket on the ground and

Silas laid the woman down.

"Jane had a mental breakdown after her daughter died last year. She never accepted Leah's death, and lived in a fantasy where Leah was alive. I believe she was behind the abductions and probably killed Walter Stone."

"I think we should restrain her," Lila said. "She may hurt herself."

"No." Josie settled on the blanket and pulled the woman close. "I'll watch over her."

CHAPTER FIFTY-ONE

F amily and friends gathered near the shed where Burl Godfrey's body was found. Silas and Sydney stood arm in arm as DeShawn and Ada Page sang, Amazing Grace. The scent of fried chicken drifted from picnic tables set beneath trees, turning gold in the autumn sun.

Tess Rowland opened the rosewood urn tucked under her arm and walked to the center of a recently cleared spot of land. "Rest in peace, Dad," she said. "We are safe now. I pray you can witness our hope. May a small part of Burl Godfrey's goodness and strength enter this ground and help guide those who come to us in need." Tess tipped the urn and let the ashes float free to settle where they would.

A breeze lifted a smattering of gray flecks, spreading them to the creek, the woods, and the hayfield. One landed on Silas's arm. He didn't brush it away. Who was he to say he didn't need a dose of goodness and strength?

Tess returned to the group, head high, eyes shining. She handed the container to Paul Winston and gathered Austin and Bella into her arms. "My dad was never a big talker, but he believed in helping others and second chances. He would agree with using this land for a children's shelter." She smiled at the hotel clerk standing next to her. "Paul has to be away for a while, but when he returns, there's a job for him here."

"I'll be here too," Piped up Kia, squeezing in next to her father.

"Yes, Baby, you'll be here too." Paul tugged her pigtail.

Everyone in the crowd knew Paul's story. He would be on trial in November for the role he played in Jane Rochester's child trafficking scheme. Kia would stay with Tess until he completed his sentence.

A strange twist of events had come in the form of Walter Stone's will. Before PTSD drove the veteran to the street, his savvy stock management amassed a broad portfolio of investments. Rebecca and Leah inherited two million dollars each. The reporter donated a sizable amount to the new shelter. Paul received Leah's share. Silas helped him hire the best attorney in the country.

"Most of you have met my sister in-law, Ruth Anne," Tess continued. "Please welcome her, and her two children Gordy, and Elsa. They are building a new house here on the farm. I'm counting on Ruth Anne to help me get the shelter up and running."

There was a smattering of applause.

"Please, everyone, fill your plates." Tess waved her hand toward the tables loaded with food. "Let's give my dad a proper send off."

A cheer rose from the onlookers.

Silas smiled as he watched Gordy and Elsa pile food on their plates. Walter's lawyer had conveyed what a special place in Walter's heart those two had gained. His will set aside one million dollars for their care. From the looks of their appetites, Silas wasn't sure it would be enough. Silas filled his own plate.

"I think your partner is smitten." Sydney tilted her head toward a table where Hadley seemed oblivious to everything but Rebecca Haze. "I didn't expect Rebecca to be so forgiving."

Silas nodded. "That took some doing on Hadley's part. She needs a person like him. Once he's on your side, he'll be there forever."

"Will she still do the documentary?"

"We'll see. She has some healing to do first."

"Let's sit with Josie." Sydney carried her plate and settled on the bench next to the Vietnamese woman.

Silas joined Sydney and dug into a mound of potato salad. He had something planned to go with dessert, and he needed his strength.

"The Franklin's won't be here," Josie said. "They asked Lila and me to come with them when there's not a crowd."

Sydney gave Josie a hug. "That will be good for Odessa and Macy."

Silas's gaze roved the crowd, finding Lila behind Woody's wheelchair one hand on his shoulder. Temporarily paralyzed on one side, Woody was expected to make a full recovery. Silas's parents stood nearby. Janelle was there too, whispering in his mother's ear.

Lila blew Silas a kiss. His throat tightened but he managed a wave. The best way he'd found to repay Woody for saving Lila's life was to accept him into the Blackbird's inner circle.

Two months had passed since Wade Rowland shot Woody and abducted Lila. Wade was back in prison awaiting trial for a dozen crimes, including the assault and murder of the girl found in the pit with Burl Godfrey. The parents of the victim had received closure at last.

Silas finished his fried chicken, used a couple of napkins to wipe his hands. Took a third napkin and scrubbed again. His thoughts turned to Jane Rochester. She would spend the rest of her life in a hospital for the criminally insane. The information discovered on Jane's computers led to the destruction of the human trafficking ring, hundreds of arrests, and the rescue of almost fifty girls. Jane never stopped talking to her dead daughter, Leah.

As it turned out, Clarence Rochester was innocent of everything except embezzlement and being a total jerk. That was enough to send him to prison for fifteen years.

Silas made eye contact with Tess and gave her a thumbs up signal. He climbed to his feet. He was ready.

Tess clapped her hands. "If I could have your attention, please. Silas

CHAPTER FIFTY-ONE

Albert has a special announcement. Come on Silas. Let's lighten the mood."

A dozen steps brought him to the front of the group. "Sydney if you would join me, please" Palms damp, Silas waited until she was by his side. He dug a small case from his pocket and dropped to one knee.

"Sydney. You asked for a proper proposal. I'm a simple man who doesn't deserve you. But I love you with all my heart. I will do everything in my power to honor and cherish you forever." He opened the case and removed his grandmother's ring. "Will you marry me?"

A shaft of sunlight broke through the trees, setting fire to the diamond and the tear that slid from the corner of Sydney's eye.

"Yes. Silas." Her voice came out husky. "I will marry you."

The crowd clapped and cheered.

Silas slid the ring on Sydney's finger, lifted her off her feet and kissed her long and hard. Where life took him next waited to be seen, but he'd turned the first page of a new and exciting chapter. In his heart, he knew wherever he went the Blackbirds would be with him to support those who chose to be—*the defiant.*

Made in the USA
Middletown, DE
02 February 2024

48979141R00170